M000013040

"*Road to Deer Run...* is a sweet and tender love story that will warm readers' hearts. Don't miss this delightful tale! You'll not only learn a good deal about the history of our country, but also about the deepest longings of the human heart."

—J. M. HOCHSTETLER, author of the American Patriot Series

"Within the pages of this historical novel, Cooper manages to weave the passion of the early Americans with the ardent love of the main characters. From beginning to end, this story promises tension, conflict and resolution — all bound together by the desire of the characters to follow God's will, especially when the history-makers must choose between what seems acceptable and what is ultimately right."

— RJ THESMAN, author of *The Unraveling of Reverend G*

"*Road to Deer Run* by Elaine Cooper is a beautiful story of forgiveness, grace, and mercy. Based on the true historical account of a British soldier who fell in love with an American woman, *Road to Deer Run* is certain to leave you cheering for the couple whose love is threatened at every turn."

-LINDSEY BELL, author of *Searching for Sanity* and *Unbeaten*

Road to Deer Run

BREWSTER, KANSAS USA

ROAD TO DEER RUN
Copyright © 2010, 2015 Elaine Marie Cooper

ISBN: 978-1-936501-29-8

All rights reserved. No part of this publication may be reproduced or transmitted in any form or by any means, electronic, mechanical, photocopying, recording or otherwise, without written permission of the publisher. Published by CrossRiver Media Group, P.O. Box 187, Brewster, Kansas 67732. www.crossrivermedia.com

Scripture quotations are from the Holy Bible, King James Version (Public Domain)

Certain characters in this work are historical figures, and certain events portrayed did take place. However, this is a work of fiction. All of the other characters, names, and events as well as all places, incidents, organizations, and dialogue in this novel are either the products of the author's imagination or are used fictitiously.

For more information on Elaine Marie Cooper please visit — www.ElaineMarieCooper.com

Editor: Debra L. Butterfield
Cover Artwork: © Andiz275 | Dreamstime.com - Winter Forest Photo. © Jackie Dix - Cover Model Photo.
Cover model: Tanner Weishaar
Model Costume: Special thanks to Janet Alexander, costumer for Robidoux Resident Theatre, St. Joseph, Missouri, for help with costumes.
Printed in the United States of America.

This book is dedicated to the memory of my daughter,
BETHANY JEANNE COOPER
December 12, 1978 – October 20, 2003

In a family of writers, her creative star shone the brightest.

Acknowledgments

There are so many who have contributed advice, technical expertise, and enthusiasm for this novel. I could not have accomplished this lengthy effort without you.

First and foremost, I acknowledge the support and patient efforts of my editor-husband and soul mate, **Steve**. Your understanding of the written word and your tireless efforts to help this undertaking have been so appreciated, and your humor has been a welcome relief from the strain of editing. Thank you for believing that this work could really be accomplished.

To my wonderful editor, **Debra L. Butterfield** and my publisher, **CrossRiver Media**, thank you for your help to bring new life to this novel. I am so grateful to you!

To **Elaine Germano**, Certified Nurse Midwife, DrPH, FACNM, of the American College of Nurse-Midwives, I say a hearty "thank you." Your expertise in midwifery gave credibility to an eighteenth-century scenario. Bravo to you, brave midwives!

To my treasured **readers** through the years, thank you for your encouragement and faithfulness. I am so grateful to all of you.

No acknowledgment would be complete without thanking the two very special grandparents of mine from the eighteenth century, **Daniel Prince** and **Mary "Polly" Packard**. They are the inspiration for this story. Their love overcame the difficulties brought on by being on opposing sides during a time of war. Theirs was the ultimate example of a courageous and romantic love story.

Elaine Marie Cooper

I also owe a debt of gratitude to **Karen Kingsbury**. Although we are not directly acquainted, her wonderful fiction has inspired me and shown me the impact a novel can have in one's Christian walk.

And special thanks as always to my Lord and Savior **Jesus Christ**, from Whom all blessings flow.

Prelude

Ode to a Soldier

Soldier boy, so far from home,
Walking paths that are unknown.
"Will I live or will I die?"
The soldier boy's lonely cry.

I trained to fire my musket gun,
To shoot so straight at someone's son.
But when I saw his face turn gray,
I longed to be so far away.

This path is full of fear and strife,
My next turn may just end my life.
So let's be cautious in our zeal,
'Cause death's dark door is very real.

Soldier boy, so far from home,
Walking paths that are unknown.
"Will I live or will I die?"
Only God can hear his cry.

From the diary of Mary Thomsen

Daniel

he road never ended.

Nor did the thoughts that haunted the young British lieutenant Daniel Lowe night and day.

How did I ever get to this place?

Although just twenty-two years of age, Daniel felt as ancient as the granite stones lining the dirt highway. This war had long ceased being an adventure. He had seen enough bloodshed, starvation, and disease to last his entire lifetime. Only last night he held one of the regimental soldiers as he gasped his last breath, one more victim of the food shortage. The lad was only seventeen, the same age as Daniel's brother had been. He would never forget the young man's bones poking through his clothing.

"Lieutenant, sir." Another soldier's greeting interrupted his thoughts.

"Yes, Smythe." Daniel glanced sideways at the thin-faced recruit.

"How much longer, sir… 'til we get to Boston, that is?" Smythe's eyes widened with anxiety.

Daniel tried to appear encouraging, but he didn't know what to say. After all, they were prisoners of war. Although the Continental Army had stated the prisoners would be put on ships to return to England, as long as they never took up arms against the colonies again, he knew better. There was no way the Colonial rebels would allow them so easy an escape. The "Lobsters," as the King's soldiers were called by the colonial rabble, would be confined to a putrid camp where disease would rage and death would soon follow.

But this poor soldier looked for any hope he could hang onto, no matter how slim. Without hope, Daniel knew the young man would not survive.

"I do not know the distance, Smythe. It is a long way to the boats... and it's a long way home. But you are still strong, and you'll make it."

"Thank you, sir." The younger man fell behind his lieutenant once again in the ragged line of prisoners.

Daniel breathed in a shallow breath of frigid air and tried desperately to ignore the mounting pain in his left leg. He held little hope for his own survival. While attempting to save his regiment, he gave away enough of his allotted food to jeopardize his own health. Not that the weevil-infested sea biscuits were sufficient for even one man. His muscular frame shrank from weeks of deprivation and miles of forced marching. His filthy and tattered uniform hung loosely on him. And then there was that wound.

That last battle near Saratoga brought his first encounter with rebel lead. The ball found its home, shearing a large hole in his thigh muscle. He treated the injury as best he could without clean water and bandages.

As Daniel glanced down at his leg now, he sickened at the sight of green pus draining through the old bandage. As each step became more excruciating, he knew his limb was in serious trouble.

"Move along you wretches," a Colonial guard yelled at the slow-moving prisoners. "No time to coddle the lot of you." The remnants of the army of British General John Burgoyne were being marched by the Continentals to Boston, still a rebel stronghold. It was late October, and Daniel knew the chill in the air promised an early winter.

Snow flurries dusted a thin layer on the bare oak and hickory trees along the dirt road. The stark outlines of gnarled branches and the dead leaves surrounding every tree trunk only added to the grim and lifeless scene as hundreds of men dragged their legs forward one step at a time.

The freezing wind whistled through the creaking tree limbs, eliciting painful groans from the poorly clad soldiers.

Daniel's long hair came undone from the ties that usually held it in place. Each gust of wintry air whipped the strands into his eyes, stinging each time. Weariness had drained his strength and any inclination to retie his hair.

Enticing aromas from nearby hearths beckoned at Daniel's nostrils.

The intense hunger of the men played vividly on each face as the scents of unobtainable bread and roast venison only heightened their sense of hopelessness. Daniel glanced at the eyes of his fellow soldiers. Most of them were filled with tears from the cold wind as well as from despair. He waged the same battle of disheartenment.

This is a death march to be sure.

The excruciating pain in his limb grew overwhelming. Nausea welled in Daniel's stomach as he forced himself to put one foot in front of the other. But he knew he couldn't keep up much longer. He devised a plan. At some point, he would slip away into the thick woods along the highway.

Better to crawl under a tree to die than fall on the road and be shot by some impatient guard.

When the exhausted army of prisoners trudged through a local town, Daniel saw a chance for escape. Several youngsters from the village threw rocks at the British soldiers while shouting, "Dirty Lobsters!"

As the bellowing voices of the angry colonists distracted the guards, Daniel sprang for the woods, the pain in his leg overshadowed by the fear of being caught. His heart raced. His lungs sucked in deep pockets of cold air that fairly choked him. In his frantic escape, he lost all sense of time.

"Prisoner escaping!" shouted the guards, but he kept running. He threw off his red uniform — it would only be a target for a Continental marksman. Without his coat, the cold air gripped his torso. But he didn't stop. The sound of musket fire and the whistling of lead forced his legs to move faster than he thought possible. But he wasn't thinking about his actions. He responded to a visceral desire to survive.

His race ended in an abrupt and anguished halt as his leg gave way. Falling on the ground, he dragged himself behind some thick berry bushes that were long since void of fruit. The thorns dug into his chapped hands, but he hardly noticed the pain because his leg screamed for attention.

For a brief moment, he sensed something had changed. He forced himself to lie still. All was quiet.

The musket fire has ceased. They've stopped their pursuit.

Despite Daniel's relief, the throbbing pain in his limb reached a crescendo. Nausea thrust him in to spasms of heaving, but there was nothing in his stomach to expel.

As the retching ceased, he lay on his back in complete surrender. He stared at the cold gray sky through the trees overhead and hoped for one last glimpse of life, but even the forest birds had hidden themselves from his sight.

It didn't matter. After all, he deserved all of this. And nothing could change all that had occurred in these last months of war. Nothing could erase his many transgressions.

Now, all he had to do was close his eyes and let the inevitable shadow of death completely darken his already blackened soul. All was lost anyway. His war, his troops, his health, and, worst of all, those he loved.

Believing his life was ebbing away, Daniel held little hope of reaching heaven. But he couldn't take this hell on earth. He closed his eyes and waited for the reckoning of his Maker.

Mary

M ary Thomsen stared into the fire for what seemed like hours. In fact, it had only been a few moments.

That's how time had become for her. As a young farmwoman barely nineteen, she should have been contemplating a hope-filled future. Instead, she struggled with despair. Standing in front of the long fireplace did little to comfort her body or spirit.

Ever since her brother Asa was killed in battle, Mary faced the reality of war in a sickening and personal way. She wrestled with thoughts of what her younger brother probably endured in those last moments of his life. Had his death come in an instant so that he did not suffer? Or had he lain there for minutes or even hours in pain, knowing the end was near?

Tears brimmed her eyes.

Dear, sweet Asa. Only sixteen, he loved music as much as he loved life. It was his gift on the fife that awakened his patriotic fervor and drew him to join the cause of liberty. He wanted to lead Continental soldiers to victory through his melodies.

"No one will aim their musket at a fifer," said Asa the day he signed on. "They have better targets to attend to."

He was always the optimist.

But in the midst of an explosive battlefield, no amount of hope could keep the barrage of lead balls from finding their mark on Asa's body. Even his fife, which their older brother James returned home after that last battle, was scarred from musket fire. It was a bittersweet reminder of his short life. It now rested on a brick above the fireplace. Mary touched the instrument lovingly with her fingers, imagining the sweet sounds Asa's lips could bring from the whittled wood.

"Mary." Her mother's voice caught her attention away from the hearth.

"Yes, Mother." Her voice had taken on a monotone timber in these last few weeks.

"Why don't you and Sarah go aleafing while there's still enough light of day? We want to have a good supply for the bread-making this winter."

Mary knew her mother wanted to rally the spirits of her older daughter. Mary and Asa had been best of friends, sharing a love of music that seemed to stir from within them both. It seemed now as if the melodies had left Mary's heart forever, much as Asa's breath had left his body.

Sarah's childish voice spoke up in protest to their mother's request.

"Please, Mother. I do not wish to go out in the cold. I'm so tired of winter already." Six-year-old Sarah huddled by the fire.

Mary stared at her younger sister. Born eight months after their father's sudden death, the blond-haired girl was a gift from heaven. She brought life and laughter, and spread her loving smile to friend and stranger alike.

Mary wished she could capture into her soul some of the warmth emanating from Sarah. But Mary was empty, alone, and as cold as the winter ice on their pond.

She stared at her mother in wonderment. Despite so much heartache in her life, Widow Thomsen was as steadfast in her faith as the stalwart cliffs not far from their farm — never changing through any raging storm.

Mary often heard her mother quote the verse, "The LORD gave, and the LORD hath taken away; blessed be the name of the LORD." She knew her mother grieved greatly over this most recent loss. Although her parent cried easily at the mention of Asa, Mary also saw that her mother's belief in a loving God never wavered.

Mary was far less sure of God's concern for their welfare. Her faith in a caring Creator was shaken to the core. How could a God who truly loved them have allowed so unfair a death?

Why did He take Asa away?

She forced her thoughts back to the moment at hand, and her sibling's concern.

"Let Sarah stay indoors near the fire, Mother. I can gather enough oak leaves and sticks myself. There is no sense in both of us facing the wind and cold."

Sarah raced to her big sister and hugged her heartily.

"Thank you, Mary."

A small smile spread across Mary's lips.

"You are most welcome, Sarah." She kissed her little sister on top of her mobcap and hugged her as she fought back the tears that flooded her emotions so frequently these days. Her head often ached from crying.

The outdoor air might be refreshing, she told herself as she put on her gray cape.

"Here is a blanket to gather the leaves in, Mary." Her mother tucked the woolen piece under Mary's arms. "Do not be gone too long. The storm may become severe."

"I shall hurry."

The frozen air hit her bare face as she left the farmhouse. She gathered her hooded cape closer around her neck. Although the painful cold numbed her skin, Mary knew that the real dullness she sensed was in her wounded soul.

She forced her legs to plow through the frenzied wind. The swirling movement of the wintry air reflected the agitation in her mind.

As she headed deep into the woods on their farmland, Mary's thoughts wandered from Asa and then to her father, now long gone from a drowning accident. Just as quickly, her mind turned to her older brother James, still fighting in the war of revolution. They hadn't heard from James since he'd brought Asa's body home some three months ago. What if he, too, was dead? It could be months or years before they knew. Or would they ever hear word of him again?

The only thing Mary was certain of was that she hated this war and she hated death. Would she ever know joy again? Would she ever feel safe? Would she ever feel alive?

As she walked farther amongst the thick trees, Mary searched for the dry oak leaves that would cushion the bread dough in the Thomsen's oven.

She was so engrossed in her task that the sudden sound of musket fire in the distance made her heart skip a beat. Instinctively, she dropped to the ground to take cover.

Unhurt but frightened, she huddled close to the earth. Mary clung to the blanket and tried not to give way to panic.

I must keep my senses about me.

Her whole body shook with fear. Soon the woods were quiet once again and the only sound she heard was her own breathing, which came in rapid spurts.

Mary waited until her breath slowed before she dared look up.

Standing gingerly, she hugged the blanket tightly. Her whole body stiffened from the cold and from sheer terror.

Should I run home? Should I keep going?

As she tried to decide her next move, she sensed something different in the woods.

There was a presence.

3

Samaritan

Mary smelled him before she saw him.

She knew someone was nearby but she could not see a soul. The wind carried the scent to her person, as if beckoning her to follow her senses. The odor was unmistakably that of infection. Perhaps even death.

Frightened but curious, Mary pursued the source. She went several yards before the smell became stronger, leading her to a thick grove of berry patch. As she peeked through the twisted branches, what she saw made her gasp in fear. There lay the body of a man.

He wasn't moving. His clothing, face, and hands were smeared with dirt and old leaves, while a scraggly beard and unkempt long hair added to the unsettling sight. His breeches were torn over his left thigh, exposing a large bandage soaked with brown and green stains.

Was he dead? She could not tell if the man's chest was rising. Dare she run away and leave the poor soul? What if there was any breath left in his body? What if someone had found her brother Asa like that, and did not at least sit with him 'til he died? Even a stranger can bring some comfort to a dying human.

Can I abandon this poor wretched person? She knew she could not.

Using the blanket to protect her hands, she spread the prickly branches aside and drew closer to the body. The stench of illness permeated the small clearing where the man lay and Mary fought the nausea that gripped her.

Then an alarming realization hit her as she surveyed the man's attire more carefully. He was a King's soldier. Even without his scarlet uniform, his finely woven breeches and waistcoat gave away who he was. And to Mary, he was the enemy. She'd heard the remnants of Burgoyne's troops were coming through town. But seeing one face to face elicited shivers down her back.

Dear Lord, what shall I do?

Her mind went to the story of the Good Samaritan. In that tale, the only person who would help a beaten stranger was a Samaritan, the victim's sworn enemy. She never imagined she would be faced with a similar scenario. And she had never understood before now how difficult a choice the rescuer had made. But although the Samaritan may have wrestled with the decision, he had chosen the right course.

Can I make the same choice?

She knew she must, for her heart would not let her abandon this man. But was he still alive? With trepidation, she placed her hand on the man's chest.

Mary's touch awakened him. The dazed soldier's eyes opened wide in alarm, and he grabbed her arms and cried out.

Fear seized Mary and the pressure on her arms was almost unbearable. "Please, sir," she begged. "Let me go. I mean you no harm." Her words choked in her throat. Mary had heard frightening accounts of the King's soldiers attacking colonial women. The thought beset her with horror.

Despite his apparent confusion, the man released his firm grip. He rubbed his eyes as if to clear his thoughts.

"What is your name, sir?"

He stared at her. "Such kindness, miss — I've not heard that in so long." He paused a moment before answering. "My name is Lieu… Lowe. Daniel Lowe."

Mary's fears calmed as his expression softened, and she realized the man was just confused. She remembered her mother telling her to look into a person's eyes and you could read his soul. And Daniel Lowe's eyes reflected many things — fear and pain for certain, but another quality also. Gentleness. It seemed ironic to her, considering his occupation. "I am Mary Thomsen. I live not far from here."

Daniel stared at her.

"Where am I?" His words seemed to come with difficulty.

"You are near the village of Deer Run in Massachusetts colony, sir."

The British soldier tried to lift his leg but the effort elicited a wince.

Mary noted the discolored bandage. It was soaked in a putrid liquid, undoubtedly the source of the smell. She was certain the dressing had not been changed in some time. The thought of such neglect — even toward the enemy — outraged Mary.

"Sir, did they not attend to your wound?"

"Once," he said. "Many days ago."

He shook his head. "Why do I hear compassion in your voice, miss? Surely you must know who I am… I must be dreaming…" His eyes widened. "Good heavens, miss! Did I hurt you? I was having a nightmare — I thought you were someone else. Please tell me I did not injure you."

"I am unharmed, sir." She looked at the bedraggled man. By all appearances, he was weak, probably starving and in terrible pain. "I think 'tis you who needs assistance."

The snow fell in large flakes and the wind increased in intensity. Mary knew she needed to move this man to shelter or he would not survive the night. But where?

Bringing him home was impossible. Her mother would never help a soldier of the Crown. As Christian a woman as her mother was, she still reeled from Asa's death. She would consider any King's soldier to be responsible for his murder.

Then Mary remembered the English wigwam. The remnants of an earlier settler's home, the wigwam had been patterned after the structures built by Native Americans. Although she hadn't been to the shelter made from bark and branches in several years, she hoped it would provide enough protection for this soldier. When she and Asa played there as children, Mary never imagined it would ever serve as more than a playhouse in the woods. It would now be transformed into an infirmary.

"Mr. Lowe, we need to find suitable protection for you or you will die from this cold. I know a shelter not more than fifty rods from here.

I shall help you get there."

"Why are you helping me, miss? Do you not know who I am?"

"I know that you are a person in dire straits, sir. I am not here to decide who lives or dies, but to help a wounded person who will surely die without my assistance. Do you think you can get to your feet?"

"I shall try, miss."

The weakened soldier crawled out from under the thick shrubs while Mary used the blanket to hold back the thorny branches. He cried out in pain when he bore weight on his left leg. Mary encouraged him with her words to keep him upright and moving.

"Sir, we can do this together. Lean on my shoulder."

Walking brought a gasp from Daniel Lowe with every step. Mary held her arm around his left side to support his efforts. She was appalled to discover his bony ribs protruding from underneath his waistcoat.

Did the Continental guards treat their prisoners with such cruelty?

Mary's lean shoulders strained beneath his right arm.

"Miss," he gasped, "I fear your strength will give out."

"Do not fear, sir. These shoulders have borne many a burden. And you are not the heaviest I have carried."

They were both quiet for a long time as they concentrated on the effort at hand. She breathed as hard as he did, and the cold air made the struggle even greater.

The crude structure appeared in the distance.

"We're nearly there." Mary gasped between breaths.

Although the wigwam was in sound condition for its age, some of the bark strips attached to the branches were askew. But this shelter would have to do. Mary didn't have the strength to go on.

They both struggled through the open door and fell upon the earthen floor. When she was able to catch her breath, she looked at the weary man staring at her. His dark hair and his face were covered with sweat and his deep-set eyes glistened.

Despite his apparent agony, he managed to say, "Thank you, miss."

She looked down at the woolen blanket still grasped under one arm. "Let me put this over you to keep you warm."

Before she laid the cover over his thigh, she took a good look at his bandage. The sight made her ill and frightened all at the same time.

Mary was thankful she and Asa had brought several armfuls of straw to the wigwam from their barn many years ago. The siblings would sit for hours on the comfortable piles and make up songs. She now used the old stalks to help insulate Daniel Lowe from the cold.

"Mr. Lowe, I must get some medicinals and change this bandage for you." She looked at the putrid cloth and tried not to imagine what lay beneath. "I cannot tell my mother that you are here, but I shall manage to bring the supplies that you need. Before I depart, I shall bring you some snow to quench your thirst."

Mary stepped outside of the wigwam and scooped up a handful of the powdery substance. She hurried back inside and helped support his head. The bristly edges of his beard scraped against her hand as he devoured the snow from her cupped fingers.

"Do not swallow too much, sir, or it will chill you," she cautioned. "I shall bring you some warmer liquid when I return."

He grabbed her arm once again. This time it was with gentleness. "Miss, I do not know what to say, I…"

He started to say more but she placed her hand over his and whispered. "Hush, sir. Please save your strength." She felt his rough hands and noticed they were covered with dried blood. "I shall bring some slippery elm for these wounds, sir. I shall sally forth lest the darkness set in."

When she stood up, Mary realized her long brown curls were coming undone from her linen cap, loosened from the effort of helping Daniel Lowe to the shelter. She grabbed at the wayward locks and tucked them back inside her cap, suddenly self-conscious in front of this stranger. Her face burned a little as her eyes met his.

"I shall not tarry at home for long, sir."

She could feel Daniel Lowe stare at her as she slipped out the doorway.

Lies

*M*ary's heart raced as she ran back to the Thomsen farm, her mind whirling with conflict.

What shall I tell Mother? She'll be suspicious.

How could Mary explain the medicines, rum, and bandages she would need to help Daniel Lowe? More worrisome, how would she explain she was helping a King's soldier? She was still mired in these thoughts when she arrived at the farmhouse door.

Breathless, Mary thrust the door open. She stood there and gasped for air, her face reddened from cold and exertion.

Widow Thomsen's eyes opened wide.

"Good heavens, child, what has happened to you? I should never have sent you out into the woods by yourself. These are troubled times."

"Nothing has happened to me, Mother." Mary inhaled a deep breath. "I… I found a dog. But he's wounded and I need some supplies. I think he may have been shot and the wound is festering and horrible."

Mary hated herself for lying, but she went on. "I think he may die without help." At least this last part was true.

"A dog? Mary, he may carry contagion to you. Hydrophobia is rampant in the woods and dogs can bite if they're in pain."

"Mother, he's as gentle as can be, but suffering. Please allow me to dress his wound." She ignored the guilt that pricked her conscience.

Her mother scrutinized her.

"All right, Mary. I see this mission has given you renewed purpose.

But let me go with you to assist."

"No, Mother." She shouted with far too much energy and bit her lower lip. "I'm sorry. It's just that… I do not wish you to have to take Sarah into the cold. Just show me how to tend the wound and I can manage."

She hoped she'd not given herself away. Her mother stared at her again. At last she said, with pride in her voice, "You're becoming quite the young woman, Mary. 'Twas not that long ago that looking at a small bleed would send you into a faint. You've come a long way, have you not?"

"Yes, Mother." Her cheeks burned with shame from this blatant lie to the woman she loved the most in the world.

Mary gathered the supplies while her mother explained how to treat the infection. Mary prayed in her heart that someday her mother would understand — and forgive her.

Mary faced the outdoors once again and ignored the biting wind as best she could. She hurried along the familiar, well-trodden path.

The extra blanket her mother had used to hold the supplies would provide another layer of warmth for the British soldier. But even with two woolen blankets and the old straw, keeping her patient from freezing was going to be difficult. It was certainly not safe to make a fire in the wigwam. Any passerby would discover this makeshift infirmary in an instant from the smoke billowing out the stone chimney.

But as she trudged through the new-fallen snow, there was an even more pressing concern. Was Daniel Lowe still alive?

Mary startled out of her troubled thoughts when she saw a rider approach on horseback.

"Good heavens," she whispered under her breath. It had not occurred to her that Continental soldiers might be looking for an escaped prisoner.

What was I thinking? What will I say?

"Good day, miss." The young soldier greeted her as he tipped his tricorne hat.

"Good day, sir." She smiled despite her racing heart. Could he see the fear in her eyes?

"You wouldn't have perhaps seen anyone in these woods hereabout, would you?" the soldier asked. "Specifically in a red coat, miss."

"A red coat?" She feigned a shocked expression. "Why no, sir. Should I be concerned?"

Her heart pounded with anxiety as she piled one lie upon another. *Am I the same Mary Thomsen who believes lying is a sin? What is happening to me?*

Still, she could not forget the desperation of Daniel Lowe. She realized her compassion took precedence over her conviction that hiding the truth was wrong.

"I should say so, miss." The corporal sat up straight in his saddle. "Several of Burgoyne's men have disappeared between New York and Boston — on their way to prisoner-of-war camp, I hear. I wouldn't mess with any of them if I were you, miss. They don't treat our ladies like ladies, if you know what I mean."

Mary swallowed with difficulty.

"I shall remember that, sir. I shall just finish taking these supplies to our neighbors and then hasten home."

"Let me accompany you for your safety, miss." The soldier's expression reflected his concern.

She imagined the blood draining from her face. Before she could reply, they both heard a shout in the distance.

The corporal looked toward the voice.

"I'm sorry, miss, but one of my men is calling. He may have found one of them Lobsters." As he rode away, he turned and warned, "You need to get yourself home as soon as possible." She breathed a sigh of relief when she saw he rode away from the hideout.

Light of head now, Mary sat on a large rock for a moment to collect her thoughts.

What am I doing?

Could she be guilty of treason? Lying to a soldier in wartime — a soldier on her own side? And hiding the enemy? What would her brother James say? All these thoughts and more raced through her troubled mind.

She suddenly felt completely alone.

Mary wept. Then she whispered a desperate prayer for wisdom.

And that's when she felt the comforting presence of her God, not condoning her lies but encouraging her to go on. Emboldening her to go forward and bring comfort and help to a wounded man.

With new resolve, she wiped away her tears with the back of her hands. Then she stood up from the rock and pressed on toward the wigwam.

Wounds

aniel was sure the woman would not return, and he did not blame her. He knew she would put herself at great risk to help the enemy. Once she thought it through, his angel of mercy would change her mind, he reasoned.

Or perhaps her mother would find out the truth. A parent would never allow her daughter to come back. In fact, the mother might report him to the rebels.

Daniel sighed in despair as hopelessness returned. He closed his eyes, nausea and pain his only companions.

No sooner had he withdrawn into his dark thoughts than he heard the hinges of the fragile door rattle. When he dared open his eyes, Mary was leaning over him.

"You're alive?" She seemed relieved. "I was not certain you would still be breathing."

"You came back."

"I told you I would, sir. And I brought you some rum to ease your pain."

Mary adopted an air of self-assurance, as if she had nursed many a wounded man. In fact, she'd never before tended a patient on her own.

Why did I not pay more attention to my mother's nursing care?

With the village doctor needed on the battlefield, Widow Thomsen often assisted the local townsfolk with their injuries and illnesses. Many midwives, such as the widow, provided nursing care. She had an assortment of medicines that were purchased a few years ago at the apothecary in Boston.

Mary recalled her mother saying, "'Tis only wise to be prepared, in case a war begins." The midwife's voice was filled with sadness and resignation.

Mary sometimes assisted her mother in cleaning wounds. But as soon as the blood flowed, her face would blanch. The widow would then excuse her daughter from further duress by sending her on an errand. Widow Thomsen would smile at the patient at such times.

"My Mary's not got the strongest constitution when it comes to nursing."

Because Mary missed out on so many learning opportunities, she was now ill prepared for the task at hand. She berated herself for not fighting fear and nausea while her mother was trying to train her.

Now the only hope for this man is an inexperienced and weak farm girl. Dear God, give me the skills and strength that I need to help him.

Mary held Daniel's head up and brought the flask of rum to his lips. He took several gulps and then gasped and grabbed at his stomach. "That burns." He coughed a few times and fell back down onto the pillow of hay.

Daniel stared at Mary and seemed to misunderstand the fear in her eyes.

"You needn't worry, miss. I'll not let on that you've helped me."

"I am not concerned about that, sir. I only fear that I will not be of sufficient help to you. Your wound looks quite poorly, but I shall do the best I can." She attempted to sound brave. She wrapped a cloth around a sturdy stick so he could bite down when the pain became unbearable.

"Let's allow the rum to settle in before I start." Mary wanted the alcohol to achieve its peak effect before she started removing that horrid bandage. Anger surged through her again as she questioned the justice of the guards who ignored so obvious an infection.

Mary sensed Daniel's gaze.

"What did you tell your mother, miss?"

She looked down at her hands and bit down on her lip, a nervous habit she'd had since childhood.

"I… I told her I'd found a dog with a wound," Mary confessed.

"A dog." Daniel snickered. "I see what you must think of me and the other Lobsters."

He turned away and stared at the straw-lined ceiling.

Mary furrowed her eyebrows and frowned.

"Sir, 'twas not meant as an affront. I did not know what to tell her. That was the only explanation I could think of to convince her I needed these supplies. I told her the rum was to clean the dog's wound."

Daniel studied her and his eyes softened.

"I am sorry, miss. After all you've done for me already, I've no right to question you."

There was silence for a few moments, then Daniel spoke.

"You've never mentioned your father, miss. Is he away at war?"

Mary looked at her hands again.

"No, sir. He died when I was but twelve. We had a terrible flood that year and he drowned in the river."

"I'm truly sorry, miss."

Mary continued on.

"My brothers went to war. But Asa…" She struggled to complete her thoughts. "Asa was killed in battle. He was only the fifer…" She could not go on. Tears flowed down her cheeks and she sobbed. "He was my best friend in the world."

Daniel's eyes moistened. "What idiot would shoot at a fifer?"

Mary looked up at him with cold eyes and said in a terse tone, "An idiot King's soldier, sir."

Daniel's countenance fell, and she immediately regretted her harsh words.

"Sir, I am sorry. My words are born of a depth of sadness that I've never encountered before. Please forgive me." She wiped tears from her cheeks.

The young soldier placed a gentle hand on her arm.

"There is nothing to forgive, miss. Please do not distress yourself further."

Mary noticed Daniel's words began to slur. It was time to put aside her sadness and concentrate on dressing his wound.

She set up her supplies next to his leg and laid them out on the blanket. They included the rum, a cloth napkin filled with lint, dried balsam apple leaves soaked in vinegar, and strips of clean linen.

"Dear Lord, please help me," she prayed under her breath.

Daniel's eyes had closed but he opened them up wide at the sound of her voice.

"What, miss?" Confusion filled his voice.

"I need you to help me by staying as still as possible." Mary spoke close to his ear. "I'll lift the blanket now and remove the old bandage."

The overpowering odor of infection assaulted Mary once again. The green pus soaked the bandage, which must have been applied a week or more ago. The edges of the cloth that covered his entire thigh were dried out.

Removing this bandage was going to be difficult for her and painful for him. Mary shivered at the thought but pushed away her fears. Bracing herself she resolved to handle this like the nurse she needed to be.

"Mr. Lowe, bite down on this stick when you feel the need."

His eyes told her he trusted her. She hoped his trust was not misplaced.

With all the confidence she could muster, she untied the outer wrap encircling the bandage around his upper leg. She tore away at the edges of his tattered breeches. To reach the entire wound, Mary widened the hole in his clothing. Hiding her alarm at the extent of infection, she poured rum onto her patient's thigh to loosen the cloth. Daniel winced when the strong alcohol soaked through the pus-covered material and reached the raw, inflamed wound underneath.

As she removed part of the old dressing, Mary noted with horror that the blood and infectious matter had become one with the cloth. The sickening bandage stuck hard. She poured more rum onto the wound and gingerly tugged at the edges of the linen. Still, it did not budge.

Daniel pushed himself onto his elbows and stared at his leg. His face turned white.

"Miss, you must pull with all your might to tear the dressing off."

She shivered. "Mr. Lowe, the bandage is fastened to the wound. If I tear it away, you may bleed a great deal. And the pain…" She swallowed past the lump in her throat. "The pain could be unbearable."

Fear crept into his eyes and she heard his breathing quicken.

"I know this, Miss Thomsen. But it is the only way." He lay back and put the stick in his mouth. He squeezed his eyes shut and pressed his hands against the earthen floor, gripping the edges of the blanket.

For a moment her muscles seized with tension, then Mary grasped the edges of the bandage with both hands.

Give me strength, dear God.

With all her power, she tore away the wretched cloth from the bed of inflammation.

An anguished cry broke forth from Daniel's clenched mouth. Mary had never heard such a dreadful sound in her life.

She struggled to control her tears while pressing a clean cloth over the wound to stop the bleeding. The gaping injury with a cavernous center covered half of Daniel's upper thigh.

"I am so sorry." Her mouth trembled.

Daniel's whole body shuddered. Mary looked at his pale face where rivulets of tears rolled down his cheeks, leaving trails on his dirty skin. He clenched the stick in his mouth with such force she feared he would bite through the thin branch.

Once the bleeding had slowed down, Mary prepared the packing of lint soaked in the solution of vinegar and balsam apple leaves. His blood covered her hands but she hardly noticed, so consumed was she with finishing her task.

She packed the deep wound with the pledget of soaked lint. It took more than she thought so she prepared more packing and filled the bloody crater. Once that was done, she applied clean linen. A thin strip wrapped around his thigh kept the dressing in place.

With the task complete, Mary wiped the sweat and tears from her face, then picked up the old bandage. She was horrified to see small pieces of duck cloth from his breeches. The heavy canvas-like remnants had embedded into his leg when struck by the lead ball.

No wonder it would not heal.

"Mr. Lowe, I know why…" She stopped. "Mr. Lowe?" He lay without moving on the earthen floor. His face was so pale, and in the dim light of the wigwam, she could not tell if he breathed.

Her tears came again.

"Dear God," she cried. "Has there not been enough death? Please have mercy on this poor man. Please, Lord, let him live."

She stayed on her knees next to Daniel, closed her eyes, and put her hands on the back of her head. Heartache and sadness wracked her spirit. Then someone touched her.

Her head sprang up and she saw Daniel's eyes upon her.

"Were you praying for me?" His voice was weak and his hand squeezed her arm.

Mary was too relieved to be self-conscious about her entreaties to her Maker. "Yes."

"Why?" The young soldier stared at her, then wiped at her face. "You're wearing my blood." His words slurred as he spoke.

Mary placed his hand back on his chest and remembered how those wounds from the thorny bushes had prompted her to bring the slippery elm to soothe his abrasions. She made a paste out of the crushed bark and water and then spread it over his hands. He smiled.

"You have a soft touch, miss."

"'Tis the slippery elm that is soft, sir. 'Tis an old Indian medicinal."

"No, miss. It is your heart that is soft." He spoke slowly, the rum taking its full effect. He stared up at her as she covered him with the blankets.

"You have a lovely neck, miss." He reached up to touch her skin.

Mary rolled her eyes and placed his hand back under the blankets.

"And you, sir, are speaking from the spirits you imbibed." She smiled at his ridiculous but handsome grin.

As he fell into a deep slumber, Mary whispered close to his ear, "I shall return in the morning."

She used the rum and what was left of the flask of water to clean Daniel's blood from her face and hands. The numerous red streaks bore testimony to her mission of mercy, a mission that many might consider an act of betrayal in this heated war.

Mary started to leave the wigwam, then turned and looked once more at her slumbering patient. She whispered a prayer of gratitude as she closed the door behind her.

Fever

Fatigue came upon Mary as she trudged the long path home. While she cared for Daniel, her anxiety had energized her. Now however, exhaustion threatened to overcome her.

Mary was grateful for the wind that followed the snowfall — it would hide the tracks that might lead searchers to Daniel — but it's powerful force made her return home even more tiring. By the time she arrived home, dizziness prompted her to clutch the door for support. She tripped over the threshold, before slamming the portal closed.

"What took so long, Mary?" Her mother hurried toward her. "I thought you'd been hurt."

"The wound was very bad, Mother." She yawned as she answered. "It took longer than I thought, but it has been tended to."

"Where did you leave the dog?"

"In the old wigwam. I'm going to bed, Mother."

"But Mary, you need some supper after being out in the cold."

Mary was too tired to answer. After stumbling into her bedroom, she removed her gown and linen petticoats. Crawling into bed wearing her nightshift, she curled up on her feather mattress. She was too weary to pull the quilts over herself and shivered before closing her eyes.

Mary awoke with a start before dawn the next day.

Daniel!

Slipping into her knitted stockings, she put numerous layers of petticoats over her nightshift to keep out the cold. She then donned her blue wool gown.

She made as little noise as possible as she stepped into the main room, where her mother and Sarah shared the big bed.

Mary made every effort not to awaken them as she gathered a flask of water and more slippery elm.

I'm so relieved mother taught me how to use this tonic.

She knew this bark could soothe digestion — and coax a starving stomach back to normal eating. She wished, however, she'd paid better attention to all of her mother's nursing lessons.

Exiting the farmhouse, the powerful wind besieged her. But the cold air was not the only sensation Mary felt on this late October morning. There was a surge of emotions that she had heretofore never experienced. There was excitement and fear — and something else. It was an unfamiliar stirring in her very core at the thought of seeing her patient again. Even as she sorted through these feelings, the situation caused her concern.

How long can I keep the truth from Mother? How long can I keep Daniel hidden? And with winter nearly upon us, how will he survive out here in the woods?

Although the abandoned wigwam still had a fireplace, burning logs would signal Daniel's whereabouts to any passerby.

Mary's head throbbed.

Perhaps I should have eaten.

When she arrived at the wigwam door and stepped inside, she stopped and gasped. Daniel was still alive, but he was shivering and covered with sweat. Mary placed her hand on his forehead. His body blazed with the heat of fever.

"Mr. Lowe." She endeavored to hide her panic. "How long have you suffered from fever?"

Daniel struggled to push the words out between the shudders from his body. "I do not know, miss," he gasped. "Awhile, I think."

"Can you sip some water?"

"I can try."

Mary helped him get his head and shoulders up as she held the flask for him. He was too weak to consume more than just a few sips. His head fell back onto the bed of hay. His dark eyes looked more sunken than before and his gaunt cheeks were fiery red. His breathing came with obvious struggle.

He needs more than water.

This sickness was beyond her knowledge of care. A fearful realization crept into her thoughts. The time had come to reveal the truth to her mother. Only she would know which medicine to use.

But what would her grieving mother say about helping an enemy soldier?

Mary struggled not to panic. Somehow, she had to convince her mother that helping Daniel Lowe was the right thing to do — the Christian thing.

Dear Lord, please convince my mother, even if I cannot.

She took in a deep breath. "Mr. Lowe, I need to get you some help. You are quite ill."

"Miss Thomsen… who will you tell?" Daniel spoke in short bursts, his eyes permeated with fear.

Mary placed her hand on his.

"I shall only tell someone I trust. Please do not fear. I must get you more help than I have to offer. But do be assured, sir, I shall not desert you."

The look in Daniel's eyes elicited tears in her own. "Please come back."

"I shall." She turned to leave, then looked back at him once more before leaving the wigwam. "I promise I shall come back."

Daniel closed his eyes. He was grateful for Mary's help, yet terrified of another rebel knowing his whereabouts. He knew now he could trust this woman with compassion in her eyes. But who else would help the enemy? The wounded soldier wanted to run, but his body was too ill to move. All he could do was moan in pain and fight the fearful thoughts that assaulted his mind.

Sleep came, but with nightmares worse than ever. He envisioned pained cries from his troops as they were gunned down by fervent rebel soldiers.

Then there were the terrifying shrieks of wounded comrades still very much alive but too weak to crawl off the battlefield. Wolves tore at their flesh in the night, and anyone who tried to rescue them from this horrible death was himself struck down by enemy marksmen.

But the worst dream — the one that recurred every night — was of his younger brother Oliver taking his last breath. This nightly apparition drove the fevered soldier to wake up screaming his brother's name. It would only take a moment for Daniel to realize that the nightmare had been real. Oliver was truly gone and Daniel was responsible.

If only I had not shouted his name.

Exhausted and frail, he closed his eyes once again.

Will this unending saga of pain ever end?

Mary ran the entire way home. When she flung the farmhouse door open, Widow Thomsen stared at her with wide eyes.

"I thought you were still in bed."

"Mother, I have something to tell you." Mary spoke between gasping for air.

She now had her mother's full attention. Mary looked over to be sure that Sarah was in a sound sleep. She whispered just in case the girl should awaken.

"I have lied to you, Mother, and I beg you to forgive me." Her lips trembled with remorse.

"Lied to me?" Her mother plopped into a chair.

"Yes, Mother." Tears streamed from Mary's eyes. "I am so sorry. 'Tis not a dog I'm caring for in the wigwam. 'Tis an injured man."

Widow Thomsen's mouth dropped open in astonishment.

"Why would you lie about a man needing help, my dear? And why did you not let me tend to his wound? I do not understand."

"I did not think you would want to help him, Mother." Mary's tears turned into sobs now. She took a fitful breath but kept her voice low.

"He is... a King's soldier."

There it was. She had spoken the truth of the matter that might change their relationship forever.

The look on her mother's face turned stone cold.

"Come with me, Mary." She grabbed her shawl from the hook on the cabin wall and walked with brisk steps out to the barn. Mary followed at a short distance, dreading the unpleasant encounter she knew was inevitable.

Once inside, her mother whipped around to face her. Mary shivered at the look of fury on her mother's face.

"Mary, have you gone mad?" Her mother's voice seethed with rage. "What are you thinking? Helping the enemy, putting all our lives at risk?"

"Mother, 'tis not like that."

"Not like what, Mary? Not like we are at war? Not like the King's army haven't already killed one of your brothers? Not like you are helping the very enemy that shot him?"

Mary had never seen her mother so angry. Mary tried to regain her composure so she could respond, but the angry words were like arrows shooting at her from every side.

"Mother, please listen to me," she begged.

"Listen to what? Listen to how you are comforting the enemy, the very person who may be responsible for your brother's demise? How could you?" Her mother wept.

"Mother, how could you encourage me to help a dog but object to me helping a sick and injured human being?" The passion in Mary's voice surprised even herself. Her stinging words seemed to hit their mark.

"Mother, this soldier could be dying. He is in terrible pain. He was on his way to prison camp, where you know he would not have survived. I have tried to help him, tending his wound and bringing him water. But now he has a terrible fever and needs help beyond what I can give him. I need your help, Mother. He needs your help."

She seemed unconvinced.

"What would you have wanted someone to do for Asa if they had found him after he had been wounded?" Mary continued. "Would you not have wanted a Samaritan to see to his wounds? To bring him comfort?"

There was silence for a long moment. The only sound in the chilly barn was Susannah the cow bellowing her displeasure at not yet being milked.

Several moments passed before her mother finally replied.

"All right, Mary. I shall bring him some medicine and water." Her mother's voice sounded flat and cold.

"Thank you, Mother." Mary squeezed her parent's shoulder in gratitude. "I was not expecting this terrible dilemma either. But once I came upon him in the woods faring so poorly, I could not turn my back on him. You will see what I mean."

Her mother appeared doubtful.

"I will do my part, Mary. Please do not expect my heart to be in it. Stay at the farm with Sarah, while I take some Peruvian bark to the man. Do you know his name?"

"Lowe. Daniel Lowe," Mary replied. "Thank you, Mother."

Her mother turned to go back to the farmhouse.

"I shall be back forthwith."

With both hope and trepidation, Mary watched her mother gather the supplies and leave for the wigwam.

"Please God," she whispered, "let her see him through Your eyes."

Ruth Thomsen forced herself to walk toward the aged structure, which she had not visited in many years. The last time she'd come to the wigwam was to seek solace after her husband drowned in the river. She fought back tears at the memory of her husband's death.

"Lord," she prayed as she walked, "I miss my husband so, especially at such times of uncertainty. He would have known what to do." She wiped the tears from her face. "Lord, please show me what to do."

When she reached the wigwam, she stopped and took a deep breath, then opened the fragile door.

She gazed at the soldier lying under the blankets. He was emaciated and feverish and appeared too weak to respond. And he certainly appeared to be dying. She took in a deep breath and spoke to her enemy.

"Mr. Lowe, my daughter Mary has told me about your illness and I have come to bring you some medicine." She took out the flask of medicinal and offered him a drink.

"What is it?" His words stuttered.

"'Tis called Peruvian bark, Mr. Lowe. It has been blended with wine to make it easier to ingest." She looked at his eyes fraught with suspicion.

"You think I mean to harm you, do you not? That is not the case, sir. But I will confess that I am only here because my daughter has seen fit to take you under her wing. I do not profess to share her great concern for you. But because Mary has convinced me of your need — which is obvious, sir — I shall do what I can to help you."

"Thank you, madam." His voice trembled with fever. She helped him lift his head and instructed him to swallow several gulps.

"There, Mr. Lowe. That should help with your fever. That is all I can do."

She did not bother to check his wound, since Mary had already changed the dressing less than a day before.

"I shall come back later with more medicine and water. You seem to have enough blankets for now." She turned and left the wigwam without looking back.

He will be dead by morning.

She did not feel a tinge of regret.

Mary and Sarah prepared the evening meal that would simmer over the fire all day. But Mary's thoughts were not on the vegetables she was washing. Her mother's coldness toward Daniel elicited a shiver of trepidation down her spine. Mary had never observed such bitterness in her parent before and it frightened her.

What would her mother say to him? What would she do? Her mother had always been the epitome of compassion as long as Mary could remember. But where had her mother's heart of mercy gone?

"Why is Mother taking so long, Mary?" Sarah asked. "I thought she would be here by now. She promised to show me how to cut out the pumpkin."

"She will be here soon, I'm certain. I can show you how to do the pumpkin if you like."

Just then the door opened and Mary looked up with anticipation. "The task is done." Her mother removed her cape and hung it on a hook on the wall. She blew on her hands to warm them and said nothing more.

Mary stared at her in confusion, wanting more details. "That is all? No further news of the situation?" She cast a glance at Sarah. She could not divulge too much in front of her sister.

Her mother looked at her again but gave no hint of compassion. "I doubt the dog will survive the night."

Mary stared at her in disbelief, fighting back anger that welled in her heart toward her mother.

"Then I shall stay with him to bring comfort whilst he lives." Rage roiled in her heart. She tossed aside the vegetables for dinner and gathered more medicines, water, and another blanket for Daniel.

"Mary, this endeavor is futile," her mother protested.

Mary glared at her for a moment. "'Tis never futile to show compassion, Mother." She threw on her cape and left.

As she returned to the makeshift infirmary, she stifled back tears. She cried not only for Daniel's sake but for the deep outrage that stirred in her heart toward her mother.

How can she be so merciless? Will I ever feel close to her again?

When she opened the door to the wigwam, Mary's eyes sought Daniel's. He stared at her in relief and swallowed.

"You've come back." His whole body shuddered beneath the blankets.

"I told you I would, Mr. Lowe. I always keep my promises."

She brought out a piece of linen cloth left over from an old shirt. She poured water on it and began to dab the coolness on his face and forehead.

"That should help your fever lessen. I have brought more of the Peruvian bark for you as well."

Daniel appeared relieved.

"Thank you for all your help, miss," he said. "I do not deserve all your provision." He stopped to catch his breath. "I do not take your kindness for granted. And I know how ill I am... this may be my last chance to tell you... how grateful I am for your tenderness..."

Saying so many words caused him to speak in fit and starts.

"You do not need to speak, Mr. Lowe. Save your strength for healing."

Although she usually would be offended by a man's intense stares, Daniel's admiring eyes filled her with warmth.

"Your voice, miss. It's like listening to a sweet melody. You... have mesmerized me."

Blood rushed to Mary's cheeks. "I believe your fever confuses you, sir."

She tried to concentrate on tending to his illness. If her mother was right and he would not survive the night, then Mary determined to stay with him to the end. She prayed under her breath that her mother was wrong.

The minutes passed slowly. Several times an hour, Mary encouraged Daniel to drink sips of water. She gave him a few gulps of the medicinal wine and brought the extra blanket up around his shivering shoulders.

But she spent most of her time praying. Without God's help, she knew there really was no hope for Daniel Lowe.

As the sun sank lower on the horizon, cold enveloped the thin wig-wam walls. Her patient was in and out of delirium, and she tried not to despair. Daniel shook so from fever his teeth chattered. Soon Mary began shivering uncontrollably from the frigid air.

She drew closer to Daniel. She cradled his head in her lap, the blankets surrounding them both. The chill in her hands was a soothing comfort for his fever, while the heat raging in his body provided the warmth she needed.

In any other time or place, their closeness would have been considered improper. But at this moment, their survival depended upon ignoring convention.

7

Repentance

he day drew to a frigid close as Ruth Thomsen and Sarah finished eating their stew.

"Where is Mary, Mother?" Sarah seemed bewildered "I miss her. Are you not worried?"

"She'll be back in due time," Ruth replied. "Her patient needs her, apparently."

"Do you suppose the dog will recover? I'd so love to have a dog." Hope beamed from Sarah's eyes.

"I do not think so, dear. He is badly injured. Not everyone can survive their injuries."

Sarah looked down at her wooden bowl. "I know that, Mother."

Ruth observed a tear roll down Sarah's face.

Of course she thinks of Asa. Ruth regretted her careless words.

"Sarah, let us clean off the table and read from the Bible for awhile," she said, trying to change the subject. Asa's death still lingered in their every waking moment. It was a struggle for them all to keep their spirits from being cast into gloom.

Sarah wiped at her eyes and said with quivering lips, "All right."

The two made quick work of the cleanup. While Ruth sat in the large chair by the fire, Sarah climbed into her lap. This was the wooden seat her husband had wrought with his own hands years before. It brought a smile to her face to envision the many stories that were read to the children on this treasured piece of furniture. She opened up to her favorite book of Proverbs.

"Let us see what God's word has to say to us in the Good Book, Sarah. We can always glean much wisdom from these pages, can we not?" Her eyebrows furrowed.

I could certainly use some discernment now.

She began to read from Proverbs 25. She liked to read the chapter that coincided with that day of the month. The familiar phrases comforted her — until she reached the twenty-first verse. "If thine enemy be hungry, give him bread to eat; and if he be thirsty, give him water to drink." The words made her stop short.

"Go on, Mother," Sarah encouraged.

"I think perhaps I missed yesterday's reading. Let us go back to chapter 24." She flipped back a few pages. "There now, let us begin again." Sarah appeared satisfied with her explanation.

The reading proceeded once again until she reached verse ten.

"If thou faint in the day of adversity, thy strength is small." Ruth paused for a few seconds, then went on. "If thou forbear to deliver them that are drawn unto death, and those that are ready to be slain; If thou sayest, Behold, we knew it not; doth not he that pondereth the heart consider it? and he that keepeth thy soul, doth not he know it? and shall not he render to every man according to his works?"

Ruth lowered her Bible down onto her lap and placed one hand over her mouth as her lips trembled.

"Those being drawn to death." She repeated the words, then looked at her younger daughter. "Sarah, please sit in the chair a moment whilst I pray in the other room."

Sarah slipped off her lap.

Ruth walked into Mary's room and closed the door. She stared for several moments at the fire in the hearth. And then she prayed.

"Lord, I know well this man has been injured and is starving. He was certainly on the road toward death in the prison camp. He could even have died along the way. And there is no manner in which I can come before you to claim that I knew it not. Mary has clearly brought the matter to my attention." Tears welled in her eyes. "I know this bitterness in my heart towards the King's troops has obscured my obligation to forgive." She paused a moment as her mouth quivered. "I am so ashamed of the hardness in my heart towards someone in such desperate need." She wiped the tears from her cheeks. "Please, Lord, forgive me."

She stood a moment longer and then turned with resolve. When she came back into the main room, Sarah's eyes widened.

"Mother, why do you cry? What is wrong?"

"Nothing that I cannot make right. Sarah, come with me. Mary and I need your help."

⟋⟍

Mary fought the drowsiness that could overtake her as she and Daniel struggled to stay alive in the wigwam.

She knew of many unfortunate victims that had succumbed to the effects of a freezing night without a fire. Shivering, she had glanced several times throughout the evening at the cold and empty fireplace. She longed to set some logs ablaze for warmth, but it would not be safe. Soon, however, all she wanted to do was close her eyes.

"Your hands are getting cold, miss." Daniel's voice surprised her. It somehow seemed stronger than she remembered it.

If I could just go to sleep, I'd be warmer.

"Miss, I can feel the chill in your hands. You must go back to your home." There was urgency in his voice as she struggled to keep her eyes open.

"I just need to close my eyes for a moment." She thought perhaps she dreamt as she leaned against the bark wall of the wigwam.

"Miss Thomsen." He spoke louder as he squeezed her fingers with his. "Please do not tarry any longer."

Mary did not answer him, and he grabbed her face.

Her eyes opened against her will. "What… what are you doing?

Why is he so irritating? I'm feeling light and calm. Perhaps if I just close my eyes, the disturbance will cease…

"I am trying to keep you awake, miss." Daniel's voice grew louder and resonated with alarm. "You must go home where you can be warm."

Mary's eyes opened wider. She looked down at Daniel and became more aware of her surroundings. "Was I falling asleep?"

"Yes, Miss Thomsen. Please — you must hasten to where it's warm."

Warmth. It sounds like heaven.

As she considered what to do, she remembered her mother's lack of concern for Daniel's well being and resolved, once again, to be there for this suffering man.

"I shall not leave you as long as you need help," she said.

He left his hand on her cheek and spoke with gentleness.

"I cannot have my nurse die for my sake. Please go."

While Daniel attempted to lift his head from her lap so she could leave, they both heard a sound outside. Footsteps approached. Mary instinctively held her patient closer, as though her actions could prevent someone from abducting him. Her heart skipped a beat. She feared the worst.

Have we been discovered by soldiers looking for escaped prisoners?

Mary's throat dried and her breathing quickened. She trembled as she stared at the door, but her terror turned to astonishment as her mother and little sister came through the doorway. Renewed energy and relief replaced Mary's sleepiness. Yet many questions remained hanging in the freezing wigwam air.

"Mother, why are you here with Sarah?"

Why would she involve my sister in this dangerous secret? Why are they both here now? Darkness has already fallen. What is Mother thinking?

"I shall explain it all later, Mary. I told Sarah that we found a young soldier who is hurt and we need to rescue him. Right now we need to get you both back to the warm fire at home."

Daniel and Mary looked at each other. Mary was unable to comprehend the change in her mother's attitude.

Sarah stared at the freezing couple.

"Mary, why do you embrace that man?" Her voice sounded shocked.

"To keep him warm, silly child," their mother answered. Then she looked straight at Mary. "That is why you are holding him, is it not?"

"Yes, Mother, it should be obvious we are both freezing." Mary shivered even more as she struggled to her feet. Her stiff limbs ached with each movement. She tried to hide her own discomfort as she and her mother helped the soldier sit upright.

⁓

Daniel needed the strength of both women to get to the farmhouse. He moaned with each step and, more than once, begged to stop so he could find relief from the incessant throbbing.

"Mr. Lowe, I know this is painful for you, but we must hurry," said the widow. "There may still be troops about. We will be at our home soon."

The thought of a warm fire was enough to give Daniel strength to go on. He still had no idea what had changed the mind of Widow Thomsen.

"I'm so grateful much of the snow has melted during the day. I fear our footprints might give us away." Mary's voice sounded weak, as if her stamina was fading.

The warmth from the fire as they entered the farmhouse was a healing balm to Daniel. The women assisted him into a side room, which held a narrow bed. As he plopped onto the soft mattress he could feel his boots being tugged off. He looked down at his feet to see Mary and the younger girl struggling to remove them.

"I have never seen boots like this before." The young girl seemed bewildered.

I suppose she's not familiar with army boots.

"Sarah, please put them by the fire and make no mention of the boots," Widow Thomsen said sharply.

"Yes, Mother."

The nausea that had recently plagued Daniel returned. The dizzying sensation overwhelmed him as his stomach churned.

"Mr. Lowe..." Widow Thomsen started to speak but his retching interrupted.

The widow grabbed a basin and held it under his chin while Mary held his head. When the vomiting ceased, Mary helped him lay his head back on the pillow.

"I am sorry." Weakness made his limbs limp.

"There is nothing to be sorry about, Mr. Lowe." Mary's soft voice soothed his embarrassment.

"Mary, your face is white as bleached linen." He could hear concern in Widow Thomsen's voice. "Why do you not get some food? You must be starving. I shall tend to Mr. Lowe."

Mary didn't argue but stood up. "I shall see you in the morning, Mr. Lowe."

Their eyes met as she left the room. Daniel wished he could say something that would reflect his deep admiration for this young woman. He wanted to tell this angel with the green eyes he would never forget she had not deserted him in his desperation. But while the words were silent, his eyes expressed his gratitude to her.

The younger girl stared at Daniel from the doorway, a look of friendly curiosity about her. While her mother took the basin out of the room, the girl approached his bedside.

"I am sorry you are ill, Mr. Lowe. I hate it when I feel poorly like that." She reached out with her small hand and placed it upon his. "I shall pray you feel better soon."

Daniel looked at her closely for the first time. The child was a miniature version of Mary, although her hair was lighter in color and her eyes a rich brown.

"Thank you, little miss," Daniel said to her with a weak smile. "What is your name?"

"My name is Sarah Thomsen," she stated matter-of-factly. "I am six years old and I can help my mother and Mary cook now."

"It is pleasant to meet you, Miss Sarah Thomsen," Daniel said, amused by the child's boldness and charm.

"Do you have any sisters?" Sarah asked.

Sadness pricked at Daniel's heart. "I used to."

"Used to? What happened?"

"She died of smallpox when she was but seven." Daniel's voice caught. He'd not thought of his little sister in some time.

Before Sarah could speak further, her mother returned with the clean basin. He wondered if she'd heard their conversation.

"Sarah, please let Mr. Lowe rest now. Your talking will wear him out." Widow Thomsen escorted the girl toward the other room.

Sarah gave one last glance at the patient before giving him a smile. "Good night, sir."

"Good night, little miss."

"Forgive my talkative child. I fear the lack of men in our home at the moment has her curiosity aroused when she sees one."

"There is nothing to forgive, ma'am. Both your daughters are charming and kind."

"They are a gift to me, Mr. Lowe, of that I am sure. Now, let me look at that wound of yours."

Trying to stay awake long enough to eat some stew, Mary watched Sarah approach the table near the main hearth.

"Mary," Sarah said with a grin on her face. "The man called me 'little miss.'" She giggled and ran off to play with her doll.

Mary smiled as she took a few bites of sweet potatoes and carrots. She knew she would not be awake for long. She pulled herself up from her chair and went to lie down on the bed she would now be sharing with her mother and sister. She did not even bother to remove her gown or petticoats. She pulled the layers of handmade quilts up around her chin and sighed with exhaustion.

As she drifted off to sleep, her thoughts dwelt on two things from this day. First, the remarkable change of heart in her mother — it could only be explained by divine intervention.

Even more extraordinary, and puzzling, was the memory of Daniel Lowe's hand touching her face.

Coat

The scent of lavender infused Daniel's senses.

He was standing in a field of the purple flowers in England. The countryside breeze caressed his face and the bright sunshine warmed his body. He stretched his arms out, taking in the sensations that brought healing to his mind and soul. A smile crossed his face as he realized he was home.

"How are you this morning, Mr. Lowe?" The voice startled him out of his dream.

He felt the quilted covers on the rustic bed and remembered where he was. His eyes popped open, then flitted from one corner of the room to the next, taking in his surroundings. Mary Thomsen was stoking the flames in the small, glowing hearth. Daniel stared at the tall chimney that towered upwards past the ceiling and had been built large enough to accommodate two fireplaces, one in each room.

Certainly helps in this frigid climate.

Mary leaned in toward the fire. Her long fingers wrapped around each log that she added to the growing blaze. She deftly turned the hot coals with an iron stoker, coaxing more warmth with each move of her arm. Whenever a scorching ash escaped from the hearth, she used the iron tool to push the spark back in the stone enclosure.

Daniel studied her face in the glow of the fire. The burning embers illuminated the room in this early morning dawn, highlighting her high cheekbones and full lips. Her cheeks, which had been so pale the night before, glowed brightly from the warmth. Her gray wool gown narrowed at her slender waist and gathered in flowing folds to the floor. The wounded soldier found it difficult to pull his eyes away from her.

And that heady scent of lavender — why could he still smell those springtime petals that filled him with memories of home? He realized then the scent came from the bedding.

Mary finished stirring the logs and turned his way. "How are you, sir?"

She looked at him with a studied gaze. Her hair — at least the locks that were not hidden beneath a linen cap — glowed a chestnut brown in the light of the fire.

"I think I am better, miss." He swallowed with difficulty.

"You are still quite pale and I'm certain you must be famished. Let me get you something that will settle well in your stomach." When Mary smiled a dimple appeared on one side of her face.

Daniel did not feel hungry. Lack of nourishment and the illness had conspired against him, taking away all desire for food.

"I'm not craving any victuals, miss."

"Well then, sir, we have the right medicinal to help. I shall bring it to you promptly." She left the room in a swirl of woolen folds.

In a few moments, Mary returned, carrying a tankard of a sweetly scented drink. "I've made you a brew of slippery elm and cinnamon, Mr. Lowe. It will settle well in your stomach when nothing else will."

Daniel hesitated when she brought it to his bedside. The thought of being ill again — in front of this charming angel — took away any enthusiasm. Mary seemed to understand his hesitation.

"Do not fear, Mr. Lowe. Please try it." The earnest warmth in her voice and eyes would have won over the most stubborn of soldiers. She certainly was winning this skirmish.

She set the pewter tankard on the small log table next to the bed and helped Daniel to an upright position with feather pillows. The comfort of these soft surroundings was healing in and of itself. He took the tankard from Mary and gingerly sipped the drink.

"It has a sweet flavor to it," he said with surprise.

"I think it tastes like maple and 'tis quite soothing. You'll feel much improved soon."

As he drank, some of the liquid escaped onto his cheek. Pulling the cup away from his face, he wiped the escaped brew from his skin only to be horrified by the abundance of beard growth that he felt. His cheeks burned with embarrassment.

I must look like a wild animal.

He took a few more sips, and returned the drinking vessel to Mary.

"I think that is all I can manage for now. Thank you, miss. You and your family have been far kinder to me than I deserve. I do not know how to reimburse you."

"Mr. Lowe, there will be no talk of repayment." She gave him a shy smile, which he returned.

"That is only the second time I've seen you smile." Mary's cheeks turned pink.

Daniel struggled to recall the last two days. "Second time? When was the first?"

"It was when you were quite out of your head from the spirits I gave you." She straightened out the quilts on his bed as she spoke.

Daniel felt the blood rush to his face. "I… um… I hope I did not speak in an unsuitable manner," he stammered. "I really do not remember…"

"Mr. Lowe," Mary said reassuringly, "you were always a gentleman in both your words and actions. You've no cause to be concerned. Although… you did seem to be fascinated with my neck."

Daniel shifted on the bed and looked away.

"I'm sorry, Mr. Lowe. I've embarrassed you and I did not mean to. As I said, you were always a gentleman." Her smile took his breath away.

His shoulders relaxed and he breathed out slowly. "I very much appreciated the spirits, miss. And I very much appreciated you dressing my wound. I am sure I would not still be here without your kindness."

"It was difficult," she said, more serious now. "I've never seen such a wound. It gave me no pleasure to put you through such horrible pain. I thought I'd killed you." She looked down at the quilts.

"If I had died, miss, it would not have been your doing. Without your help, I've no doubt that I'd be with my Maker. You were remarkably brave."

"I am not so brave, Mr. Lowe. I am truly frightened most of the time these days. If it were not for my trust in God, I would just want to hide under the quilts all day and night — not that blankets would protect me from the evil that surrounds us." She stared out the window. The sun was rising behind the bare branches of distant trees.

Daniel shook his head in wonderment. "Your demeanor is so assured, miss. I never would have imagined that you were frightened all the time."

"And I never imagined that I would be having a friendly conversation with a soldier who wears a red coat."

Hearing those words, Daniel's eyes grew wide.

"My coat!" He sat bolt upright in bed. The movement caused him to wince with excruciating pain.

"Your coat? Please lay back down, Mr. Lowe. You will cause your wound to bleed." She gently pushed his tense shoulders back onto the pillows. "Now then, tell me about your coat." The warmth of her fingers on his arm nearly distracted him.

He stammered over his words as he tried to convey the story.

"I threw it down," he said. "When I escaped from the guards, I ran into the woods and threw it on the ground. I knew the bright red would make a fine target for some rebel fellow intent on firing ball at me, so I tore it off and let it go… I know not where."

Daniel stared wide-eyed at Mary, who did not seem to understand the implication. "Do you not see, miss? If they find the coat on your land, it will lead the rebels here. They will know you have helped me." He grabbed at her arm to emphasize the enormity of the danger.

Mary's eyes now widened as she seemed to grasp the great peril she and her family were in if someone found his scarlet garment.

"I shall go and find it," she said with determination. "How far from the dense thicket were you when you tore it off?"

"I know not. It may have been several hundred rods closer to the road. I'm not certain."

"I will find your coat, Mr. Lowe. I know our land well and I shall find it."

Daniel grabbed her hand, his dark eyes full of concern.

"Please, miss, if anyone sees you with it, do not admit to knowing who

I am. Tell them anything, but do not endanger yourself or your family."

"I shall be safe in God's hands. And He will give me the words to say, should I need to speak at all. Please rest now. I shall return in due time."

He released her hand and watched her go toward the door. She turned to look at him. Courage and fortitude emanated from her youthful countenance. She gave him a reassuring smile before she slipped out the door.

Daniel lay back down, drew in a deep breath, and exhaled slowly. He had never met anyone like this colonial woman before. He usually kept his emotions well guarded. But Mary Thomsen's simple beauty and kindness completely disarmed him.

Mary tip-toed toward her mother's side of the bed in the main room. She whispered so as not to disturb Sarah.

"Mother, please wake up. I must speak with you."

Widow Thomsen opened her eyes. "What is it? Is Mr. Lowe ill again?"

"No, Mother. I have given him some elm tea and it seems to be helping. I must go and find something in the woods. He dropped it and… 'tis urgent I locate this piece of clothing."

She did not want to be too specific, as Sarah might be listening to their conversation.

Her mother nodded. "I understand. And Mary… look sharp for strangers."

Mary fastened her hooded cloak and went out into the chilly morning air. It was early dawn and many stars were still visible in the sky. While the light increased with each moment, Mary's anxiety grew as well.

How will I ever locate Daniel's coat in such a huge expanse of land?

She quietly prayed an earnest plea for guidance as she forged ahead into the thick woods once more.

Ruth rose wearily from the comfort of the warm quilts. She wished that today of all days she could stay beneath the soft coverlets that were a refuge from the cold. The previous day had been exhausting. She struggled to put on her woolen gown and petticoat over her shift. No time for sleeping in today. She headed toward the fireplace.

As she stirred the corn gruel that had been simmering over the fire all night, the warmth of the flames reached out to her with a soothing touch that both energized and comforted her. With her repentance, she knew her task today was to begin making amends to Daniel Lowe.

She poured warm water into a fresh basin and gathered some bayberry soap. From a chest of drawers not far from the large bed, she took out something that had long lain untouched—some of her late husband's clothing.

As she approached the door to the small bedroom, Ruth prayed the young soldier would find it in his heart to forgive her. Daniel was already awake.

"Mr. Lowe, I hope you slept well." She placed the basin of steaming water, the linens, and the hard soap on the table and laid the clothing on the bed. "I've brought you some new attire, sir. If anyone sees you wearing your uniform breeches and waistcoat, they'll surely know who you are. You must dress like a colonist if you are to remain undetected."

Daniel stared at her in surprise.

"Widow Thomsen, why have you decided to help me? I am very grateful to you but… I do not understand…"

Speaking deliberately, she said, "Mister Lowe, please forgive my sordid demeanor yesterday. It was completely heartless of me and I am very ashamed of my attitude. It was cruel and completely unchristian."

The young soldier stared at her with a puzzled expression.

"I do not know what to say," he stammered. "I did not blame you for hating me. I know about your son, and I am terribly sorry."

Ruth averted her eyes for a moment and then returned her gaze to meet his. "Even if you had been the one who killed my son, it would still be my Christian duty to forgive you. And yesterday, the Lord gave me some words from the Good Book to set my soul on the straight path. I repented of my sin and I ask you to forgive me for my hatred."

Unbidden tears rimmed her eyes.

"I feel I have no cause to find fault with you, Widow Thomsen. I am indebted to you."

"We shall say no more about it, then. You are a guest in our home until you are fully recovered. Then you can decide what you will do about your future."

"My future? Now there is a mystery." He turned toward the window and frowned. "When I escaped from the line of prisoners on that long dirt road, I never imagined I would survive. I didn't wish to survive. Now, not only is my destiny uncertain, but I've involved innocent women in my folly — providing haven to an enemy soldier. This was not what I'd planned at all." He combed his hand nervously through his unkempt long hair.

"God brought you to us for a reason, Mr. Lowe. I do not pretend to understand what His plans are for you, but I trust that He will reveal as much to you in due time."

"God?" Anger darkened his countenance. "What would God have to do with me being here? I've completely interrupted your lives with my problems, causing all of you discomfort and endangering you. Why would you think all this has anything to do with God?" His eyes blazed with emotion.

"God has His doing in every part of our lives, Mr. Lowe, whether we realize it or not." She looked at the disillusioned soldier with understanding. She did not press the discussion any further. "Let me help you get cleaned up, sir. I can wash your back for you if you can manage the rest."

Daniel unbuttoned his waistcoat and shirt and rolled onto his side. She carefully stroked the wet, soap-covered cloth over his back.

"I can't remember the last time my back was cleaned."

She watched him close his eyes as his limbs relaxed.

Ruth smothered a gasp at the sight of the man's ribs. They stood out from his shrunken flesh, evidence he had starved for weeks. She also noted several deep marks in the skin on his back. They were scars she recognized well.

"You've had the smallpox, Mr. Lowe."

Daniel's eyes snapped open. "Yes. Many years ago."

She did not ask, but assumed it was the same outbreak during which his young sister had died. She had inadvertently heard the conversation he had with Sarah the night before.

"Well, I'm glad you survived."

Daniel rolled onto his back after she had dried him off. Ruth handed him the cloth with soap on it.

"You can refresh yourself with a washing as best you are able, Mr. Lowe. When you're done, please change into this clean clothing. We will have to hide your current attire."

"Thank you, madam." Daniel cleared his throat. "I hesitate to make any further requests." He rubbed his beard. "I hate to impose upon you further, but... is there a razor available that I might use?"

She looked at the beard and smiled. "I suppose we can find a suitable instrument to smooth out that face for you."

He looked at her with gratitude. "Thank you."

Finding the shaving instrument in the chest of drawers, she stroked it a moment before carrying it to the wounded soldier.

"It belonged to my husband." She handed him the wooden sheath that contained the folded blade inside.

"I am grateful for this valuable tool. I shall treat it with great care," Daniel said.

Ruth nodded and put her head down as she exited the room. "Let me know if you have need of anything else."

⌒⌒

Mary searched for the scarlet garment for what seemed like an hour. Everywhere she looked, she found only piles of old leaves and branches. Every glimmer of possibility turned futile, time and time again.

Until now.

At first she thought it was one more false hope. Then the light glistening off one of the coat's silver buttons proved this was the treasure she was searching for — the coat that could betray her family.

She picked it up. Her fingers touched the fine wool that had been sewn into the uniform of the British enemy. She shivered as her hands smoothed over the shiny braiding that decorated the lieutenant's attire. Such beautiful decoration for such an inglorious occupation.

When she was a small child, she had watched the troops in Boston in just such apparel. She had observed them in awe, admiring their finely made uniforms, feeling somehow protected by their presence in Massachusetts.

How things had sadly changed. These same defenders of her freedom had turned against her and her fellow citizens. Innocent women and children had experienced the frightening wrath of the King's soldiers. The fight for independence from the tyrant King George had turned into a nightmare.

Mary's tears fell onto the coat, which was blackened by gunpowder. She held it close to her face. At first she smelled only the scent of war, but then another scent emerged. It was the fragrance of her friend, the scent of Daniel.

She put aside her troubled thoughts. She had committed herself to recovering this coat, and this she had done. But it occurred to her that she had a new problem. How would she hide this bulky piece of clothing during her walk home? It was too large to tuck beneath her cloak. It would be far too visible, and the bright scarlet color would give away her secret to any passerby. Almost instantly, she came up with the only solution that made sense.

The coat will be my unborn child.

Mary folded the military garment inside out so that the freezing buttons would not touch her skin. She was wearing several petticoats to protect her from the cold, so she took the one closest to her skin and wrapped it around the jacket, scooping it into a bundle. She tied the thin linen material around her waist to support her "baby."

It was not perfect, but most passersby would not look so closely at a pregnant woman's belly. It would not be deemed proper. Mary remembered the waddling walk of many of her mother's patients. She began to imitate the awkward motion, retracing her steps back home. She gripped Daniel's coat to keep it from moving.

She had gone several hundred yards when the moment she dreaded occurred. A Continental soldier on the lookout for wandering prisoners was perusing the outskirts of the Thomsen property on horseback. Mary exhaled in relief when she realized it was not the same fellow from two days before. Otherwise, she could only imagine his suspicion at her impending birth.

"Good day, madam." The soldier tipped his hat. "Rather a long way from home for a lady in your condition, eh?"

"Hello, sir," she replied with a smile. "My midwife tells me that long walks are a suitable exercise at such a time."

She was shocked at being referred to as madam, but she hid her surprise.

"Well, madam, please be aware that we're lookin' for some enemy soldiers 'round here. They may be wounded. They may be dead. Just watch yourself that you don't stumble over no bodies."

"I shall, sir. Thank you for the warning." Mary gave him a concerned look as she held onto her bundle.

As she wrapped one hand across her stomach, she felt the coat begin to loosen ever so slightly. The weight of it was making it difficult to keep everything in place, despite the tight knot in the petticoat.

The folded coat suddenly moved even more, now more obviously. She grabbed the bundle with both hands. She knew she must have a strained look on her face.

"Active little one. Must be a boy." An awkward giggle burst from her throat.

The soldier looked with surprise at the woman's belly. He was likely too embarrassed to question her, being a female matter and all. He shifted uncomfortably in his saddle.

"Fare thee well, madam." The soldier rode off in haste.

She waved at him with one hand until he was out of sight. She turned back toward her home and gave a huge sigh of relief. She realized now that her heart was racing and her forehead perspiring. The soldier probably assumed she was sweating from her pregnancy.

With the rider now out of sight, she retied the loosened knot in her undercoat. She gave the tie an extra tug to ensure there would be no premature delivery before she arrived home. She waddled faster this time, anxious for this charade to be over.

Dear Lord, do not let me run into anyone I know.

As she reached the farmhouse entry, she was breathing so rapidly she could barely speak. Her throat was as dry as cotton and she could not wait to drink something.

When Mary opened the door, her mother and Sarah were facing the fireplace. Widow Thomsen turned to look at her, but Sarah was otherwise occupied and not aware of Mary's presence.

Her mother's face revealed her shock when she saw Mary's "belly." It would have seemed laughable were it not so critical that Sarah not see her appearance. Mary motioned for her mother to distract Sarah, so she could slip into Daniel's infirmary.

As she closed the door to Daniel's room, Mary and the British soldier faced each other. It was difficult to know which of the two was more shocked: Mary at the sight of a clean-shaven Daniel in her father's colonial clothing, or Daniel seeing Mary apparently ready to give birth. When the astonishment faded, Mary struggled to keep from laughing.

"Mr. Lowe, please avert your eyes." She covered her mouth tightly to smother the giggles that kept arising in her throat.

Daniel continued to stare at her, causing Mary's cheeks to burn with embarrassment.

"Mr. Lowe, please turn away." She spoke more pointedly as her laughter faded. He looked up and then turned his back to her.

"I apologize, miss. I was just so dumbfounded… I could not fathom the situation."

Mary undid the knot in her petticoat and pulled out the scarlet garment. She pulled down the layers of her clothing and smoothed them back into place.

"Here, Mr. Lowe." She triumphantly held out the lost treasure. "I have your coat for you."

Daniel turned away from the wall and faced Mary. Drawing in a deep breath, she took a long look at the man's features. Shaving that rugged beard had revealed another hidden treasure — Daniel's handsome face.

Looking at his coat, his face contorted with emotion. He took the uniform out of her extended arms and looked up at her from the bed.

"Thank you." Tears fought their way to the brim of his eyes.

Mary realized this was a difficult moment for the escaped prisoner and she did not wish to embarrass him.

"I need to quench my thirst. I… I shall return in a few moments."

She left the room, while Daniel stared at his recovered uniform. Mary could not imagine the thoughts going through his mind.

⁓

Daniel kept gazing at the red coat, the material reawakening images of battle after battle. There were a few bloody stains on the scarlet material, which stood out against the dyed wool. Some of the blood was his own. Some was that of his fellow soldiers. And some belonged to his brother, Oliver.

It was all a painful reminder of the last several months.

As he wiped the tears away with the coat, a familiar thought stirred in his mind. This battered uniform that evoked sadness in his heart now exuded the soothing scent of lavender flowers. This time it was the lining of his coat, which had been touching Mary's perfumed skin.

It was the aroma of home.

Conflict

A loud knocking at the door of the farmhouse woke Mary with a start.

Who would be coming to their home this early? She inched her way out from under the quilts and set her feet on the cold wooden floor. She shivered as she pulled a shawl over her shift and went to answer.

"Miss Thomsen, we need your mother to come quickly!" It was young Richard Beal. The boy was perhaps nine or ten years old, with a puff of red hair on his head and large blue eyes that always seemed to look surprised. He was a sweet and sensible boy so 'twas no wonder his mother entrusted him to fetch the midwife.

"Of course, Richard. I shall wake her promptly." Mary stifled a yawn.

"Do you suppose your sister could come to keep me company, miss? I might need some help around the house watching the little ones while my mother is occupied."

"I suppose so, young man, but I shall have to ask our mother. Hurry along and tell your mother Widow Thomsen will make haste to your home." Mary struggled to smother a laugh. She knew Richard had a fancy for little Sarah, and he would make any excuse to visit with the girl. It didn't matter to Richard that Sarah was not much older than the little ones.

Mary closed the door. Far too much cold air had suffused into their home during the conversation so she hurried to the hearth to warm her hands.

"I heard young Richard at the door, Mary. I shall gather my things." Widow Thomsen threw off the quilts.

"The lad would like Sarah to go along, Mother."

Widow Thomsen harrumphed as she put on her woolen clothing.

"That boy will keep the gray hairs coming on my head if he keeps pining the way he does." She paused and looked thoughtful. "However, it would be a good diversion for Sarah to get away for the day."

"Thank you, Mother!" Sarah's voice piped up. "I shall be ready in no time."

Mary thought her sister was asleep. *She is a clever one. And always listening in.*

Their mother gathered her supplies, including wine, in case Martha Beal's supply of the drink had run low.

"Wouldn't want Missus Beal to birth a babe without some spirits. Put your cape on, Sarah, for it will be a very cold walk to their home without it."

Mary packed some bread, cheese, and apples.

"Here is some food for you both, Mother. This chilled air will make you hungry."

Widow Thomsen leaned over toward Sarah. "Now remember, we must not speak of Mr. Lowe. 'Tis our secret. Remember what can happen to disobedient children, Sarah."

The girl swallowed hard.

"They get put in the stocks in the middle of town?" she asked nervously.

"It could happen, young lady. So remember to obey." Her mother's look was stern.

"I shall." Sarah's voice dropped in volume.

"I almost forgot." Her mother turned toward Mary. "The wound. Can you change Mr. Lowe's dressing, Mary? It has to be done every day."

"Of course I shall, Mother. Now go. All will be well." She hurried the two on their way. It would not do for Missus Beal to deliver her babe unattended.

It had been nearly three weeks since they had brought Daniel to their home. Although his wound was healing, it was going to be a long and painful process.

"Such a wound can take weeks or months," her mother had said. She also told Mary in private that Mr. Lowe might always walk with a limp. Neither woman had divulged that fact to Daniel. No reason to hamper his recovery with difficult news.

The scarlet coat that caused such a stir just a few weeks earlier was now securely hidden in the barn toolbox.

Mary slowly walked back to the fireplace and stirred the burning coals. She added more wood to the embers, then stretched her arms out with difficulty. She sat down on her father's old chair next to the fire and felt the smooth wood beneath her fingers.

The touch reminded her of moments long ago when her small hands would glide over the newly finished wood while her father would read *Aesop's Fables*. The memory brought tears to her now grown-up eyes.

She made an effort not to reminisce about those she had once loved, now gone to eternity. This sadness only added to her physical pain. Her whole body ached from the pig killing of yesterday.

The annual slaughter of farm animals in November provided much of the family's supply of winter meat. She groaned thinking about the heavy labor of chopping pork for sausages with a spade—normally done by the men. Her hands still stung from salting the pork pieces she and her mother stored in barrels. Now, when she lifted her arms, her sinews ached from hanging the larger pieces in the smokehouse. She tried not to think about the chunks of lard they'd saved for cooking and soap making.

That will be another full day's work. She stifled a moan as every muscle in her body twinged in discomfort from the work.

With great effort, Mary rose from the chair to begin her day. She strode toward the chest of drawers and pulled out the petticoats and woolen gown that would complete her dress. Shivering from the cold, she slipped on her knitted stockings and tied the ribbons at the top of each so they would not slip down. She pinned up her hair tightly and set her cap in place. Last, she picked up the bottle of lavender water. The fragrant liquid would be smoothed underneath her nose and onto her arms to curb the stench of infection while changing the bandage, a nursing strategy her mother taught her.

But while her attire was ready for the day's work, she was not. She longed to lie back down on the bed and close her eyes just for a moment. And then she remembered Daniel. He would need her help.

Mary ladled out some warm cider for the patient and walked to the bedroom door. She gently knocked.

"Mr. Lowe?" She called in a hushed tone in case he was still asleep.

"Yes, come in." He sounded wide awake. He must have heard Richard at the door.

As always, Daniel appeared pleased to see Mary.

"I've brought your cider, sir." She noticed him staring at her, a pleased expression on his face. Then he frowned.

"Miss, you appear fatigued. Are you well?"

"Well enough. Yesterday was quite tedious and difficult." She handed him the tankard.

"Thank you. Please do not trouble yourself for my sake. I know you are weary."

Mary stifled a yawn. "My mother worked just as hard as I did yesterday, and she has gone to help Missus Beal deliver her baby. I think I can manage bringing you something to eat and drink." An embarrassed smile erupted . "I also need to change the dressing on your wound today." Mary was not looking forward to that intimate task, but she tried not to let her apprehension show.

"My wound is much improved. It is not as wretched as when you first tended to it."

"Mother says 'tis healing quite well. Would you like me to change your bandages now or later?"

Before Daniel could answer, Mary's attention was drawn to the window by a distant movement on the road leading to their home. A solitary soldier wearing the deerskin hunting shirt of his unit was approaching. For a moment, she did not recognize the bearded man. But she soon recalled that swaggering gait.

"Josiah!" Blood rushed to her face and her throat dried.

Josiah Grant was a friend of her brother James and was in the same company of Minutemen. His appearance was most unexpected — and most terrifying.

"Mr. Lowe, stay still and make no sound. And stay away from the window!" She ran toward the front door, grabbing her cape as she went. She opened the door and closed it behind her before the patriot could knock.

"Josiah, how good to see you." She tied the ribbon at the neck of her cloak with fumbling fingers.

The weary soldier was visibly refreshed at the sight of Mary. He took off his tricorne hat and bowed to her. His eyes scanned her form up and down with a familiarity that made Mary ill at ease.

"You've become quite the lovely woman, Mary. Can we not go inside where it's warm?" He gripped her hand and massaged her fingers.

"No." She startled at his attentive demeanor and attempted to withdraw her hand from his, to no avail. "My mother is acting as midwife today so there is no one home. 'Twould not be proper. Come, let us walk. What news of James?" She was anxious for some word about her older brother and hoped for less attention on herself.

He led her closer to the window in the room where Daniel lay. She faced the house so that Josiah would be looking toward her — and away from the British soldier.

"James is well. He sends his greetings and will come home when he can. I received news that my mother was ill and so I came home as soon as I could to visit her."

Mary noticed his blanket roll still strapped across his chest. The rest of his military equipment was also intact, as though he had just come from his field of duty.

"But you've not been home yet?"

Was he so concerned for his mother?

Josiah placed his musket barrel-side up against the house. Still gripping her hands, he closed the distance between them. His penetrating look made her feel uncomfortable — vulnerable. Exposed.

"I wanted to see you first, Mary. I was hoping you had changed your mind."

Josiah had made his strong feelings for her known before he went to war, but she had rejected him then. Her affections for him remained, as always, sisterly.

But his passion toward her must have grown with time. As he drew her closer toward himself, Mary tensed with fear as his breathing quickened.

"Josiah, I —" Mary started to reiterate her lack of romantic feelings for him, but he interrupted her. The look in his eyes terrified her. Josiah drew her body against his own and began to caress her.

"Mary, every night in the camps, I can think of no one but you. Your hair, your eyes, every part of you… I long to taste your lips on mine." As he said these words, he tried to experience the taste for himself.

Horrified, Mary drew back her hand and slapped his face as hard as she could. Josiah glared at her with raw anger and clutched her arms painfully.

"What kind of way is that to greet a soldier returnin' from war? I could force myself on you, you know, and you could do nothin' 'bout it."

"Is that what you want, Josiah?" Mary's voice trembled with icy rage. "To ravage a woman like the British troops do? Is that what the war has taught you?" She shook so hard her words came in fits and starts.

The soldier released his iron grip on her arms. He stared at her with fury and humiliation. Without another word, he stalked off toward his home.

Mary turned her back on him, her face enflamed with anger. Her relationship with Josiah, a friend since childhood, would never be the same. Tears forced their way to her eyes.

War changes people.

She stepped into the farmhouse, barred the door, and dried her eyes so Daniel would not see her tears. When her breathing slowed, she splashed water from the basin on her face and dried it with her apron. Mary reentered his room to begin the dressing change — but the patient was not in the bed.

"Mr. Lowe?" Where could he have gone?

"I am over here." His voice emerged from the floor on the opposite side of the bed. Daniel tried to get up but groaned in pain. "Are you all right?"

"I am. But you are not. What happened?" She put her arm around him and helped him back up to the bed. He fell onto the quilts, sweat pouring from his forehead.

"Is that b…" His voice seethed. "I mean, is that bloke gone?"

Mary looked at him in surprise.

"You heard Josiah speaking to me? I'm so ashamed…" Her voice trailed off as tears stung her eyelids once again. She looked down at the floor, too humiliated to meet his eyes.

"Did he hurt you?" His voice raged. "I wanted to cut his throat."

"No, I'm unhurt." She reeled at his harsh words. Her arms still ached from Josiah's forceful grip, but she saw no need to further inflame Daniel. She wanted to explain the situation to him lest he misunderstand.

"Josiah and my brother James grew up together. Josiah asked me before he left for war if I would wait for him. I said then that he was like one of my brothers — nothing more." Mary looked down and said through quivering lips, "I guess he did not believe me."

The British soldier scrutinized her.

"I wanted to help you but I could not bear weight on my leg." Frustration infused every syllable. "That's when I fell."

Mary stared at Daniel. She could see the humiliation in his eyes.

"You are getting stronger all the time. In due time you'll be able to walk again." She placed a gentle hand on his arm to reassure him. "Thank you for trying to help me."

Daniel still appeared furious. His hands closed in a tight grip as he stared down the road for any sign of the unwelcome guest.

"I shall go and get the medicinals for your wound, Mr. Lowe."

Mary left the room. She wanted to put this incident behind her lest she feel completely enveloped by fear. It was one thing to dread the enemy, but to be terrified by one of her own? The thought was too much to comprehend.

She returned to the infirmary with the clean linen bandages and the balsam apple solution.

"May I remove the quilt, Mr. Lowe, so I can reach your wound?"

His anger seemed to melt.

"You are always so polite, miss, and your voice so soothing. The nurses in the camp would have just torn off the blanket without thinking twice."

Mary looked at him and smiled.

"I am afraid I am not so forward." When she removed the blanket, she saw there was fresh blood on the bandage. "Mr. Lowe, you opened your wound when you fell." Mary untied the strip of linen holding the bandage in place and remembered with dread when she had changed this dressing in the wigwam.

Dear Lord, do not let me feel ill this time.

When she pulled at the bandage after dousing it with some wine, it came up easily, packing and all.

"That was much easier this time." She exhaled with relief.

Mary prepared the pledget of lint with apples in vinegar and placed it into the wound. The open crater was shrinking in size, much to her easement.

Daniel was so quiet that she looked up to see if he was all right. He stared at the ceiling, a pained expression on his face.

"Forgive me, Mr. Lowe. I did not offer you any spirits for your pain." She was appalled she'd forgotten so basic a care.

"Don't worry, Miss Thomsen. I would not have accepted such an offer today."

"Are you certain? I can get you something even now."

"I am quite certain."

Mary noticed him attempt to relax his grip on the bedding but his valiant efforts could not hide the extent of his discomfort. She touched his hand.

"I am sorry." It was then she noticed the old shirt that had belonged to her father. The faded linen shirtsleeve barely covered Daniel's forearm.

"It looks like your arms are a bit longer than my father's were." She tied the fresh linen over the dressing. Mary covered his legs with the quilt and looked at Daniel. "Perhaps I can add more material to the shirt for a better fit."

"Thank you, miss. Was your father quite tall?"

"Every man is tall when you're a girl of twelve. I know not his true height. My mother says that James is about his size and my brother is a good bit taller than I am."

"I'm sorry your father is gone." Daniel's brown eyes filled with compassion.

Mary gazed out the window. "I miss him a great deal. He was a good man, and always so kind. He could make me laugh even when things were not going well. I suppose though, were he still alive, he might not abide helping an enemy soldier. I remember how upset he was about the massacre in Boston. That happened just months before he drowned in the river."

Her thoughts wandered to the distant past, remembering her father's anger at the British soldiers who fired into the crowd.

"Massacre?" Daniel's voice had changed from tender to outraged. "I read the account as a lad in England. It was no massacre. The soldiers fired in self-defense!"

Mary's eyes narrowed as she glared at him with indignation.

"There were young boys killed that day, Mr. Lowe. Are not the troops trained to restrain their arms unless there is good cause?"

"There was good cause, miss." Daniel now used what sounded like his military voice. "The crowd provoked those men, harmed them even. One of your own lawyers from Massachusetts defended them and your fellow citizens acquitted those soldiers. They had a right to defend themselves."

"Tell that to the boys' mothers, Mr. Lowe. Tell that to the citizens of Massachusetts, who have been shackled by the King's men with tax upon tax. Many cannot support their families and our rights have been stripped away one at a time."

Anger constricted Mary's throat as she tightened her grip on the linens she held.

"The King thinks we must pay extra for the right to be defended during the French War. Would he have taxed your family in England for being defended from an enemy?"

Daniel started to speak, but Mary interrupted.

"The King wants the benefit of our labor without giving us the rights of citizenship. How does that make us anymore than the King's slaves? I suppose you think as little of us colonists as the Crown does." Mary's rage erupted like a volcano long believed dormant.

She turned and raced for the open doorway before turning once more toward Daniel. Her fury surged out of control.

"Perhaps you would prefer some Tory trollop to be your nurse."

She whipped around and stomped from the room shutting the door hard. As she leaned against the wood, she realized how vile her language sounded, and she brimmed with shame. She covered her mouth with her hand.

What must Daniel think of me?

Mary returned to the infirmary with remorse. Daniel sat in the bed, his mouth open in disbelief.

"I cannot believe that I used such an odious word, Mr. Lowe. Can you please forgive me?" She looked toward the floor.

Daniel's anger seemed replaced with amusement. "I... I was surprised that you knew the word, miss." His words seemed to tease her.

Still, she stared at the floor. "I heard my brother and his friends use it once. I had to ask James what it meant."

I'm confessing to an enemy soldier.

"Your honesty is tender, Miss Thomsen, and you are forgiven. But only if you forgive me for my impertinence. Friends?"

Mary slowly looked up to see his hand extended in a gesture of peace. She put her hand out to meet his and placed her long fingers into his large grip.

"Friends." She gave him an embarrassed smile.

Daniel held onto her hand for a long while. Finally she whispered, "I really must go, Mr. Lowe."

He released her fingers with a look of regret on his face. A moment passed in silence. "You called him Josiah." Daniel's gaze held hers.

Mary's brows furrowed. "What?"

"You called James' friend by his Christian name."

Was he offended?

"Well, I have known him since I was very small. He is... was... like another brother. I cannot imagine calling him by a more formal title."

"I see."

Is he jealous?

She tingled at the possibility.

"Perhaps one day I shall call you by your Christian name, Mr. Lowe." She cast a flirtatious smile before leaving. Before she closed the door, Mary heard him mumble, "I do hope so."

10

Nightmares

The night of the incident with Josiah Grant, Daniel's nightmares returned.

He had experienced a few blissful weeks of restful nights as he healed and regained his strength. But the rage over what happened to Mary rekindled the anger, fear, and terrible memories once again. And the demons visited his mind in full force during what should have been a restful sleep.

"Oliver, no!" he screamed out loud in the middle of the darkness.

Mary sat bolt upright in bed. Her heart raced while her breathing quickened; she thought she might faint. She looked over at the empty bed and saw her mother and Sarah had still not returned from Missus Beal's birthing.

She threw off the blankets and grabbed her shawl.

Is someone in Daniel's room? What if Josiah has returned? He could be attacking Daniel at this very moment. The very thought made her ill. She grabbed a large kitchen knife and trembled as she walked toward his room. She heard Daniel scream again and forced herself with shaking hands to open the door. There was no one in the room with the wounded soldier, but he yelled as though surrounded by enemies. And he kept screaming over and over for Oliver to take cover.

Mary's throat was so dry she could hardly speak but she resolutely walked over to his bedside.

"Mr. Lowe." She barely heard her own voice. "Mr. Lowe." She struggled to speaker louder.

Daniel's eyes were wide open and his face contorted in fear. He continued to yell at invisible ghosts. She put the knife out of his sight and placed one hand on his arm.

"Mr. Lowe, 'tis I, Mary Thomsen. You are in our home and you are safe." She stroked his arm but he pushed it off as though it burned him. She spoke again. "No one is harming you, Mr. Lowe. Please rest."

Daniel drifted back to sleep. His terrible memories returned to the dark places in his mind where they likely hid. Mary had heard of such wartime nightmares. She knew they could reemerge at any moment in the still hours of any given night.

Mary began to weep for this man, so far from home and all alone.

It seems so unfair, dear God. He has been through so much pain in body and mind. Why does he have to suffer so? What is Your purpose in all this?

The thought occurred to Mary, deep in her spirit, that God's Son had suffered the worst of pain when He died. And God had a definite purpose in that suffering. Mary understood in her heart that the Creator was doing His work in Daniel, molding him into the man God designed him to be.

I need to trust Your plan.

She squeezed Daniel's arm with the slightest pressure. Then she retrieved the kitchen knife from under his bed, and returned to her bed in the next room. As her tear-stained face dried, she fell into a deep slumber and did not awaken until dawn.

When Mary began her daytime chores, her mother and Sarah were still not home. Mary prayed everything was well with Missus Beal and the new baby. The knife from the previous night's occurrence still lay on the long wooden table. It was a chilling reminder of the terror that had come in the darkness.

Mary approached Daniel's closed doorway and knocked. No answer.

Opening the door as quietly as she could, she placed some warm cider near his bedside for when he awoke. She looked at him so peacefully sound asleep — a far cry from just a few hours ago. She smiled at his disheveled shoulder-length hair lying across the pillow, making a mental note to bring him one of Asa's leather hair ties. As she tip-toed back to the door, she heard him call her.

"Miss Thomsen." His groggy voice made her stop.

Mary turned toward him. "I'm so sorry, Mr. Lowe. I did not wish to disturb you. I was afraid I would be occupied in the barn and I wanted you to have something to drink when you awoke."

"It is quite all right, miss."

She went back toward the bed and picked up the tankard to hand it to him. He drank the warm liquid heartily.

"'Tis good to see you drinking and eating. If you're ready for corn gruel, I can bring it to you now."

Daniel took a few more gulps of the cider. "That sounds very good. Your porridge tastes like hasty pudding from back home."

"I am afraid our dish is not so hasty. It has to cook over a low fire all night. I shall serve you some." She looked at him shyly. "May I bring you something else?"

"Why, yes. Thank you." Daniel gazed at her with a warm expression.

She hurried out of the room and went to the special wooden box that held Asa's belongings. Mary searched through his books and clothes before finding the object of her search — the pouch that held the leather hair ties. Mary fingered the long soft strands of calfskin, holding them close to her face. She looked at them for a long moment before returning to Daniel.

"Here, Mr. Lowe. I thought you might want these for your hair." Mary handed them to the young soldier.

"I must look a sight, miss, with my disheveled appearance."

"On the contrary, sir. You look very handsome since you shaved your face." Mary stopped. "I am sorry, sir. I did not mean to imply that you looked badly before… I mean…" She stopped herself before she completely misspoke.

Daniel grinned. "You have most certainly seen me at my worst, miss. Thank you kindly for these hair ties. I shall always consider them a precious gift." He smoothed his fingers through his dark brown hair before tying the leather strands into a knot that held his locks in place.

She envisioned Asa wearing these same strips of leather in his light brown hair, and she grew quiet. Snapping out of her contemplation, she forced herself to tend to the needs at hand. But when looking at Daniel, she found it difficult not to admire him.

Just a few weeks ago he was a gaunt and scraggly man in need of food and shaving. Now he was gaining strength and vitality that shone through in his rich brown eyes. They highlighted the strong angular features of his lean, fine-looking face.

She took in a deep breath and said, "I shall go get the gruel, sir."

She returned with the hot cereal she had sprinkled with cinnamon. Daniel ate all the porridge with enthusiasm.

"Thank you, miss. For everything."

Mary began to speak but stopped herself.

"What is it, miss? There is something you wish to say?"

"Might I ask you a personal question, Mr. Lowe?"

"You may."

"Who... who is Oliver?"

Daniel's face grew white and he looked toward the window. Mary knew immediately she had touched upon a topic perhaps too painful to discuss.

"I regret now that I have brought it up, sir. Please do not feel compelled to tell me." She turned to leave the room, but he called after her.

"Wait." He looked deeply vulnerable. "How do you know the name, miss?" He looked at her in earnest.

She paused and then spoke. "You called out his name in the night."

A pained expression infused his eyes as he looked fully into hers. "Did I frighten you, miss?"

"Yes." She could barely swallow. "I thought someone, perhaps Josiah, was hurting you. When I realized you were alone, I knew it was a dream — a terrible nightmare. I spoke to you, but you were unable to answer me. You finally drifted off to sleep."

The two sat without speaking for what seemed an eternity. Finally, Daniel broke the silence.

"Oliver was my younger brother," he stated flatly. "He was killed near Saratoga."

"I am so sorry, sir," Mary replied in astonishment. "I had no idea you had someone from your family with you in battle. I am certain it was a comfort to him to have you nearby."

"I doubt it, miss." His voice rang with bitterness. "My brother hated me for the last several weeks of his life."

Mary stared at the soldier in utter confusion.

"Hated you? I cannot imagine why."

"Please, miss. I answered your question, but please do not delve further. It is too difficult…" Daniel's voice broke off.

Mary paused a moment. "I'm so very sorry to have stirred up your sad memories, sir. I shall not be so bold in my inquiries in future."

Daniel's eyes searched hers.

"You were not too bold." He could barely get the words out. "I would just like to put it all behind me, once and for all."

"We shall let your memories rest, sir."

When she reached over to reclaim his empty bowl, the sleeves of her shift slipped upward, exposing her forearms.

"What is this?" Daniel demanded. Purple bruises in the form of large fingers enveloped Mary's limbs. She winced in discomfort at the pressure of Daniel examining her arms. He drew her arms closer to get a better look at the injury. His aggressive action caused her to sit on the edge of the bed, stifling a cry.

"That bloody blaggart," Daniel exclaimed in anger. "How dare he put his wretched hands on you like that."

Mary did not know how to respond. She was so humiliated by the incident, remembering the ugly words and the pain of Josiah's grip. But mostly reliving the fear every time she laid eyes on those bruises. And now this friend, Daniel Lowe, had seen the evidence of her indignity. Mortification enveloped her.

She saw Daniel struggle to suppress his anger.

"Miss." His voice grew gentler. "I do not mean to frighten you with my harsh words. I am so angered that he hurt you this way. This vexes me so."

He looked at Mary, stroking her arms as if trying to erase the misdeed of the colonial soldier.

She looked down at the quilts on the bed, not wanting to meet Daniel's intent gaze.

"I... I never thought that Josiah Grant was a man of good character." Her voice grew distant. "All the other girls growing up in our village thought he was so handsome. But I did not trust his eyes. They say you can look into someone's soul through their eyes, you know."

The British soldier listened without speaking. He swallowed visibly and then dared to ask a bold question.

"And what do you see in my eyes, miss?"

Mary's gaze met his. Although her spirit was distressed, she felt comforted in his presence. "I see pain and fear. But mostly," she said almost in a whisper, "I see kindness."

She stood up from the bed.

"Thank you, Mr. Lowe." And then she left the room.

An overwhelming desire to go after her nearly made him forget his leg injury. He longed to take her in his arms and tell her that the nightmares would all be over forever — but he could not.

But there was something he could do — everything necessary to recover from this wound. He would work with all his might to strengthen his leg. He would once again be the strong man that could protect this woman from further harm.

Daniel Lowe did not ever wish to be found falling on the floor again when Mary Thomsen needed him.

Siblings

hen Ruth Thomsen returned that same day, her eyes focused immediately on Mary's bruised arms.

It took a rapid explanation on her daughter's part to convince her the marks had not come from Daniel's hands. She was enraged to learn it was caused by one of their own townsfolk.

"Josiah Grant will never be allowed near this home again." A skilled markswoman with the shotgun left by her late husband, Ruth was quite capable of carrying out that promise with force, if necessary.

Her demeanor toward Daniel became more positive after the incident with Josiah. She'd worried about the long absence from home when Missus Beal was in her lengthy labor but sighed with relief when she realized she could trust the stranger under their roof.

"When you are stronger," she said to Daniel that afternoon, "we would like to invite you to join us at table for the evening meal."

Daniel stared at her with surprise.

"I am grateful, ma'am, for your kind offer. But I feel I have already accepted far too much hospitality from you… far more than I deserve."

"'Tis not charity I'm offering you, young man. I am sure that once you are able to help out, you will make yourself quite useful. When you are well, you'll begin to earn your keep."

"Thank you." Daniel exhaled with a look of relief. "It is not in my nature to accept charity."

"Perhaps you would like a book to read while you are recovering."

"I would greatly appreciate the diversion."

"Our reading material is limited but I'm sure I can find something to suit your interest." She left the room and returned shortly with a large book. The heavy volume contained both text and ink drawings. "This is one of our family favorites. I hope you will find it pleasing."

"*Pilgrim's Progress*, by John Bunyan." Daniel read the cover aloud. He looked up at her. "I've never read it, although I've heard the title. Thank you, madam."

"You are quite welcome, Mr. Lowe. Now if you will excuse me."

When the widow left the room, Daniel carefully opened the front pages and saw an inscription written in a child's handwriting. "Asa Thomsen, received on December 12, in the year of Our Lord 1769."

Asa's book. He carefully turned the pages, reading the words that had fed the mind of Mary's younger brother many years before. Daniel was moved by the thought of this brother and son who was loved by his family. This young man who loved music — and who died in a terrible war.

Daniel forced these thoughts to the back of his mind as he read the opening words of Bunyan:

"As I walked through the wilderness of this world, I lighted on a certain place, where was a den; and I laid me down in that place to sleep; and as I slept I dreamed a dream…"

These words so intrigued Daniel that he read long into the evening, until at last, he could keep his eyes open no more.

During the next two weeks, Mary and her mother were hard at work catching up on the autumnal rituals.

The candle-making could not be delayed any longer. They scurried to set up two large kettles over the fire, each pot containing water and beef tallow provided by a neighbor. The candle rods were strung with the long wicks for dipping into the hot kettles. The coated wicks were then set to dry on long poles across two chairs. The candles slowly grew in size as they were alternately dipped and dried.

It was an all-day event transforming the bare wicks into the source of light that would provide illumination through the long winter nights.

Mary and Widow Thomsen spent another day making candles from the waxy fruit of a bayberry bush. These sweetly scented green candles were Mary's favorite. She was grateful for Aunt Prudence, who faithfully brought these berries every year from her home in Bridgewater.

When the candles were complete, the Thomsens set upon making the materials needed for clothing. While Mary spun flax fibers on the spinning wheel to be readied for weaving, Widow Thomsen carded wool from a neighbor's sheep into tufts ready to spin into yarn. They each worked long into the evenings, until they both fought to keep their eyes open.

While the Thomsens prepared for winter, Daniel prepared to strengthen his leg. He tried not to despair at the sight of the raw, pitted scar that covered much of his upper thigh. Part of the muscle appeared to be lost forever. He wondered if he could ever regain the use of his limb. Regardless of its appearance, Daniel determined to work with the muscles that were left. He resolved he would indeed walk again.

In between readings from Bunyan's book, Daniel spent hours each day working his way into a standing position. When he began, he could only manage a few moments of bearing his own weight. But as his strength and balance grew, he soon managed long periods of remaining upright.

One day, he decided to take a few steps by himself. This new skill was more difficult than he imagined, and he clutched the edges of the bed to keep from falling.

At that moment, Mary walked into the room with hot soup for him. She quickly placed the bowl on the small bedside table and helped him back onto the mattress.

"Mr. Lowe, we can find you a walking device that you can lean on. I did not know you felt ready to get up and walk about. My mother and I have been so busy. We should have realized your need."

"I do not want a crutch, miss," he replied stubbornly. "I want to carry my own weight."

Mary looked at him with amusement.

"There is a reason that the Bible says 'Pride goeth before destruction, and an haughty spirit before a fall,' Mr. Lowe. And your vanity will surely bring you down — right onto the cold floor. Please, let us find you a crutch. With all my brothers' youthful foibles and falls, I am certain we have something in the barn that will suit your needs."

"All right, then, I shall accept your advice. Not that I want to."

"That is quite clear." Mary smirked.

Daniel looked up at her with a defeated grin. Then he smiled more broadly as he saw her disheveled appearance. Her long hair was coming undone from her cap — a frequent occurrence when she was hard at work — and there were splotches of candle wax across her apron.

Mary lowered her eyes and attempted to push the escaping strands of hair into her mobcap. "I suppose that vanity is not my current dilemma. I should have improved my appearance before bringing you your soup." Her cheeks turned bright pink.

Handing him the bowl and spoon, she avoided his eyes.

"Miss Thomsen." Daniel waited for her to respond. When she finally returned his gaze, he continued. "Your appearance is always pleasing to my eyes. Thank you kindly for the soup."

"You are welcome, sir." She nearly stumbled going out the door.

Daniel stared after her for several moments. And he smiled at the thought of her arms around him as she helped him back onto the bed.

The weeks of hard work were paying off for the entire household, but Daniel was especially feeling victorious. He had grown strong enough to walk on his crutches to the main room. For the first time, he could share the evening meal with the family.

"I must say, Mr. Lowe, 'tis God's miracle you are doing so well," Widow Thomsen said.

Her hands were on her cheeks in astonishment as she watched him struggle toward the big chair by the fire. Daniel was out of breath by the time he reached his destination but he felt victorious despite his exhaustion. He had not walked this far since that first journey to their home.

"It is hard to believe that I used to walk long distances with ease."

"And you shall walk as well again." Mary's smile filled him with hope. Young Sarah jumped up and down and giggled.

"Would you like me to bring you a book to read, Mr. Lowe? May I sit on your lap for reading time?" The girl was out of breath with excitement.

As the words came out of her mouth, she started to climb onto Daniel's wounded leg. Both women gasped and shouted "No!" at the same moment. Mary grabbed her younger sister just before the girl put her weight on his lap. "Thank you," Daniel said gratefully to Mary.

"Mr. Lowe still needs to heal, Sarah. You cannot sit on his lap until he is fully recovered. And only if he says 'tis all right." Mary threw a stern look at her little sister.

Sarah gave a scowl, then strode angrily over to the fireplace to play with her doll. Daniel noticed the girl's displeasure and tried to ease her ill temper.

"Little miss, I shall be happy to read you a book if you sit in the chair beside me."

The young girl was so excited by the offer that she was not careful enough near the open fire. With horror, Daniel notice Sarah's apron catch the flame. Without thinking about his leg, he leaped to his feet to smother the kindled linen with his bare hands.

Sarah screamed and Mary and her mother rushed over to assist. The little girl threw her arms around Daniel's neck and began to cry. He held her tight for a moment, realizing how close this family had come to yet another tragedy. The thought elicited both terror and relief.

"Thank you, Mr. Lowe." Sarah spoke between sobs. And then the sobbing became more intense as she looked at his face and said, "I miss Asa."

Daniel clutched her close in comfort. "I know. I miss my brother as well."

Sarah leaned back and looked at the man with surprise. "Was he killed in the war, too?"

Daniel swallowed with difficulty. "Yes, little miss. He was."

The young girl twisted her face in hatred.

"Was he killed by a dirty Lobster, too?" Disdain exuded from her words.

"Sarah!" Mary's voice rang with horror.

"That will be enough hateful talk from you, young lady," said Widow Thomsen.

"But Richard Beal says —"

"I do not care what that young boy says. That is hateful talk. It has no place in a Christian home." Her mother's voice held no room for argument.

Widow Thomsen took Sarah from Daniel and carried the frightened child to the bed. She held the small girl in her embrace and rocked her slowly. It was as though she were a young babe in her mother's arms once again. "I am sorry," the widow whispered to Daniel, her eyes full of sadness.

Daniel stood there in shock, not knowing what to say. He felt like a beaten man who had suddenly aged ten years.

Mary put her hand on his arm.

"I… I think I shall retire for the night." Daniel grabbed the crutch and slowly made his way back to his room, his shoulders slumped in defeat.

Mary followed him back to his room and closed the door behind her. Daniel limped over to the window, struggling to catch his breath.

"How do I open this?" He breathed far too fast. "I need some air."

Hurriedly moving to the double-hung window, Mary pushed the lower frame upward and propped it open with a piece of wood. Daniel leaned on the sloping sill, taking in deep breaths of the freezing night air.

Mary paused a moment before speaking. "Sarah is just a child, Mr. Lowe. She does not understand. Please forgive her words so unwittingly spoken. She cares for you very much."

Daniel stared at Mary from the open window. "She would not care for me if she knew who I was."

Mary waited a moment before speaking.

"I know who you are, and I care for you."

"I do not know why, miss." Her words birthed warmth in his heart. And hope. When he became aware that she shivered from the cold, he turned to close the window. He grabbed one of the quilts off his bed and placed it around her shoulders.

He carefully sat on the edge of his bed and took in a long, deep breath. Mary sat down a few inches away from him and looked directly at his face.

"Tell me about your brother." Her voice was soft, caring. "Tell me what happened to Oliver."

Daniel stared into Mary's green eyes. She returned the gaze and he could feel the compassion emanating from her. It was the same kindness that he had felt in her presence since that day he met her in the woods. But now there was something more — a tender friendship that had grown between them, an alliance that transcended allegiance to any country or cause. At this moment, Daniel realized he could trust Mary with anything, even his very life. He could certainly trust her with the truth.

The story of Oliver unfolded slowly, like a small crack in a huge dam. But once the pressure of the distress had become too much for the edifice to bear, the tale poured out like a raging flood.

"Oliver was just seventeen when my father bought him a commission in the King's Army." Daniel stared out the window as he recollected the events. "I was one of the lieutenants, and my brother and several other ensigns were a part of the Twenty-first Regiment under Burgoyne. On the voyage across the Atlantic, Oliver became friends with a cocky ensign called Gray. I knew this blaggard was trouble from the start.

"When I spoke with Oliver about Gray, he told me I could stop playing the part of older brother. He was in the army now and he did not need me to look after him. I told him it had nothing to do with being family; it had to do with choices and falling in with the wrong company. He scoffed at my attempts to reason with him."

Daniel paused and took a deep breath.

"The real trouble began when we ran low on victuals in the countryside of New York. Our regiment split into companies and I was officer in charge at one farmhouse. We were told to obtain supplies of food from the barns — nothing more.

"Gray... Gray decided that he wanted more than victuals when he observed a young woman at the farmhouse. He started for the home where he had seen her run inside. 'Anyone else like some female company?' the idiot declared to the entire unit. Several recruits were more than willing to go along with the wayward ensign.

"I yelled for him to halt and return to the orders at hand. I loaded my Brown Bess with powder and ball. Gray ignored my demand, and I ordered him again, shouting, 'Halt or be shot.' Oliver could see I was serious and yelled for Gray to stop as well. When he kept proceeding to the farmhouse, unbuttoning his shirt as he went… I… I shot him. As he lay on the ground bleeding to death, all the others stood stock still. The look on their faces was utter disbelief. No one said a word. And Oliver… Oliver looked at me with such hatred in his eyes. I shall never forget his anger."

Mary's eyes widened with terror. She trembled.

"You must think me as cold-blooded as Oliver did." Daniel stared out the window.

"How could you think that?" He could see her struggle to hold back tears. "You were protecting that innocent woman at the farm —" She stopped. "I dare not consider what would have occurred without you stopping him…"

Daniel paused a moment before continuing.

"After that day, Oliver never spoke to me again. Until the battle at Freeman's farm, that is. Our unit held the right flank but then we realized we stood in the woods where we were open to surprise attack. I got ready to order another line of fire when I glanced over to my right and saw an insurgent rushing straight at Oliver with his bayonet. I yelled at my brother to take cover, but in so doing he turned to face a barrage of enemy balls. He was hit several times in the chest.

"I ran to him immediately. That's when a lead ball hit my own leg and I fell next to him on the field. I pulled him to me and held him as he was dying. 'I am sorry,' he kept saying. 'You were right, I am so sorry.' And then he was gone. He died with his eyes still open, and I had to close them for the last time."

Daniel began to weep. Mary's cheeks were also moist with tears, and she took his hand.

"I am so sorry."

Daniel wiped away his tears and continued.

"Then the strangest thing happened. A rebel soldier came at me with his bayonet held high. I knew it was going to be my demise as well, so I closed my eyes to wait for the end. But… it did not come. I opened up my eyes, and he was gone."

"What happened?" Mary's voice was incredulous.

"I know not." Daniel shook his head, still baffled by the event. "I suppose it was not my day to meet my Maker."

He stared at the clear December night sky, lost in the sight of thousands of stars pulsating in the darkness. They sat quietly for a few moments, Daniel overwhelmed by the contrast of the beauty of creation against the ugly tales of war. Mary finally broke the silence, her voice thick from crying.

"You must realize that Oliver loved you. He knew you had made the right decision when you stopped Ensign Gray at that farm. That is what he was trying to tell you before… he died."

"I had not thought so — until now. My father does not know about Oliver. The last words he spoke to me in England were 'Look after your brother, Daniel. See that he is safe.' I am certain I have disappointed him completely."

"Many men fall in war, Daniel Lowe. Only God decides who walks off the battlefield." Her words caught his attention and he stared long and hard at Mary.

"You called me Daniel." He felt his heart beat faster.

Mary seemed surprised by the revelation. "I suppose I did."

"May I call you Mary?"

"I suppose you may. But not when my mother is nearby."

Daniel could not help but smile as he wiped the rest of the tears from his eyes.

"It is settled then."

"Yes, 'tis settled." She looked at her lap and appeared nervous, then stood up from the edge of his bed and removed the quilt from her shoulders.

"I must go," she said.

Daniel held tightly to her hand.

"I wish you would stay." His hand holding hers became warm and moist. *I want to feel your warmth next to me.*

"I cannot. Although I wish…" Her voice trailed away. "I must go." He released her hand with regret.

She started to leave the room and turned again to face him. "You must feel very alone here, so far from home."

Daniel stared at her for a long while, shrouded in feelings he'd long since buried.

"I do not feel alone when I'm with you, Mary."

She walked toward the door, glancing back.

"Good night, Daniel."

"Good night, Mary."

As Mary climbed into her bed, her mother's voice spoke gently out of the darkness to her older daughter. "Do not set your heart on Mr. Lowe, Mary. One day, he will return to his home. I do not want you to be hurt."

Mary did not say anything. Her tears began to flow again, not just for the brothers lost in battle but at the thought that Daniel might return home one day. Then she would never see him again.

12

Thanksgiving

The group at the Thomsen supper table jumped in unison at a bold knock on the door.

"Hurry to your room, Daniel!" Mary's heart raced at the unexpected sound.

"Remember, Sarah. Not a word about Mr. Lowe being here." Widow Thomsen gave the girl a stern look before Mary opened the wooden door.

As she adjusted to the semi-darkness outdoors, Mary saw a young courier carrying a parchment. Fine flakes of snow covered his tricorne hat and his shoulders shivered beneath his overcoat. The man's horse was several yards back, grazing on a patch of dead grass sticking up from the snow.

The visitor's eyes were dark and moist. "Excuse me, ladies. A dispatch from the Continental Congress. May I come in and read its contents to your household?"

"Of course, sir." Mary's mother approached the portal and held the door wider. "Do come in out of the cold."

The courier turned his head for a moment and coughed several times.

"Excuse me, madam," he said. "Bit of a chill in my bones tonight."

"Have a seat, sir. Let me get you a warm beverage." Her mother drew up a ladle of hot cider and handed it to the man's trembling hands.

Mary could not contain her impatience. *What is in that dispatch?* Unable to contain her curiosity, she blurted out, "What news from Congress, sir?"

"Ah yes. The Thanksgiving Proclamation." The courier opened the rolled up paper and began to read: "Forasmuch as it is the indispensable Duty of all Men to adore the superintending Providence of Almighty God…"

It was a letter to acknowledge and to celebrate the victory of the Continental troops over the King's Army at Saratoga…

Daniel listened through the wall to the proclamation being read.

"It is therefore recommended to the legislative or executive powers of these UNITED STATES to set apart THURSDAY, the eighteenth Day of December next, for solemn THANKSGIVING and PRAISE: That at one Time and with one Voice, the good people may express the grateful Feelings of their Hearts, and consecrate themselves to the Service of their Divine Benefactor…"

Daniel sat down quietly on his bed and rubbed his forehead with his hand. He continued to listen to the courier extolling praise for the providence of Almighty God for the success in "the Prosecution of a just and necessary War."

Daniel stared out the frosty windowpanes, lost in conflicting thoughts. He knew the Thomsen women would want to celebrate this victory. Although Daniel was beginning to understand the colonists' quest for freedom, it did not change his own impassioned memories about his army's horrible defeat. For this family to commemorate the conquest caused him great distress. For the wounded soldier, Saratoga was a dreadful memory. But how could he express his struggle in the midst of their triumph?

As the visitor in the next room finished reading the proclamation, Daniel heard the man cough violently. Widow Thomsen offered the courier more cider before he would proceed on to the next farm. When the dispatcher was finished and the front door closed behind him, Daniel heard a gentle knock on the door.

"Come in."

Mary walked into Daniel's room. "Are you all right?"

Daniel turned his head toward the woman. The look on her face told him she understood the conflict going on in his mind. She knew the courier's resounding voice would have easily carried the message from Congress straight through the wooden walls to Daniel's ears.

He smiled with his mouth, but it did not reach his eyes.

"Yes, Mary, I am well enough. It is not surprising your Congress has proclaimed a day of celebration. It was definitely a victory for the colonies. We were overwhelmed in battle." The candle was not yet lit and he stared out the window at the stars. "It is amazing more of us were not killed."

"I do not know what to say, Daniel. I've so many confused feelings. Of course, I'm relieved and excited our troops have been victorious. But my heart aches for your loss as well." Mary looked down at the floor. "And it is my great comfort that you were not lost in battle."

She looked up at him, the turmoil evident in her countenance. Daniel gazed at her for a long moment, taking in her beauty in the moonlit room.

"There was a time not long ago when I did not care if I lived or died." His hands clenched, remembering his desperation and pain. "On your day of Thanksgiving, I shall be grateful for my life — and for you."

"I shall always be thankful for you, Daniel Lowe." He saw tears well in her eyes. "And I pray that you never despair so again."

As she turned to leave the room, she had an anguished look on her face.

"Good night, Daniel," she said, almost in a whisper.

"Good night, Mary." He wished she would stay longer. The usually calming scent of her lavender water could not quell the anxiety in his mind. He struggled with his intense feelings of attraction to her. The uncertainty about his future besieged his thoughts. The British soldier began to wonder just how committed he was to King and country and fighting for what appeared to be a lost cause.

He could never forget the outrageous horror of the frequent attacks on women and children during the campaign across New York. And Burgoyne — Gentleman Johnny, as his men liked to call him — seemed at times to be more interested in visiting his lady friend than seeing to the safety and well-being of his troops. These events and more had been a frequent source of consternation to him. He realized he had started his career with a naive belief in what it meant to be a gentleman officer.

Daniel was also surprised by the fervor with which the committed insurgents fought for colonial freedom. Were they so wrong in their quest for justice?

And then there was Mary. Just thinking about leaving her to return to his homeland evoked intense sadness. It was more disheartening than his deepest feelings of despair on the road to Deer Run. Yet how would he find a way to stay here in Massachusetts? How would the village accept him as one of their own once they realized who he was? And would they persecute her for being associated with a King's soldier?

These thoughts stirred his heart with sorrow. He lay down on his pillow and closed his eyes, hoping desperately that sleep would give him a respite from his heavy concerns.

The next morning, Daniel heard a flurry of activity in the next room. It sounded like Mary and Widow Thomsen were making preparations for a feast, with the widow bellowing orders.

"Sarah, bring those eggs to me. Mary, look sharp you do not burn yourself."

When Daniel appeared in the main room from his night's rest, Sarah ran over to him. "Mr. Lowe, did you hear we are having a Thanksgiving supper tomorrow?" She bounced with excitement.

"I can see that, little miss." Daniel smiled at the lively six-year-old, then turned to her mother. "Is there anything that I can do to help, madam?"

Widow Thomsen looked up from her task of bread-making.

"I cannot think of anything at the moment, Mr. Lowe. I cannot assign you too unwieldy a task, since you're still recovering. However, I think tomorrow you can help with cleaning the vegetables."

"I can do that." Daniel felt a pang of frustration at his still limited strength. "If you think of anything else I can do, allow me to assist you."

Mary mixed ingredients for something that included flour and sugar. She was so engrossed in her baking she seemed unaware that bits of the mixture were on her face. The flour gave her a ghostly glow. Daniel smiled at his industrious friend, who took more care in her work than in her appearance.

All at once, Mary stopped stirring and her mouth dropped open.

"Good heavens," she exclaimed. "I forgot Susannah!"

"Oh Mary, that is why I heard her bellowing a moment ago from the barn." Her mother sighed anxiously. "The poor cow must be miserable. But I am much too busy kneading this dough to stop and milk her. Can you do it?"

"I just started adding the butter to the sugar…" Mary began. All at once, both women looked at Daniel with expectation in their eyes.

"I can do it." His voice held more confidence than his heart. He had never done it before, but he wasn't about to let that stop him.

Mary and Widow Thomsen looked doubtful but they must have been desperate for they agreed.

"I shall show you where everything is, Mr. Lowe," Mary said.

Daniel noticed she had been careful not to call him by his Christian name within earshot of her mother. Mary picked up a buckskin coat from a wooden hook on the wall and handed it to Daniel. "You will need this in the cold."

"Was this your father's?" Daniel felt the softness of the deer hide as he put his arms through the sleeves.

"No. You've outgrown my father's clothing with your healthy appetite." Mary laughed. "This belongs to James."

Mary put on her woolen cape and placed the hood over her hair. They set out the front door for the barn.

There were a few inches of fresh snow on the ground, but the sun shone brightly. The reflection of light off the white landscape caused Daniel to squint.

"This is the first time I've been out of doors since I arrived here." Daniel tried to take some longer strides with his impaired leg. He found this new gait difficult to perfect and occasionally came close to falling.

Mary patiently kept pace with his awkward movements. "It must give you a sense of liberty to escape the confines of the farmhouse. I would feel like a prisoner if I'd been closed up in a house as long as you have been."

"I was a prisoner." Daniel struggled to walk more quickly. "Being in your home is nothing like that experience. But breathing in this fresh air — it is invigorating to the spirit to be sure."

As his eyes adjusted more to the brightness, Daniel looked at Mary. He took her arm to make her stop.

"Wait... if I may be so bold." He wiped the flour off her face. "There. We do not want your lovely skin hiding behind the sweet cake."

"I always do that." She blushed. "Mother says I need to cook more neatly."

"Well, if you did cook without wearing the food, I would have no reason to touch your face."

The sudden passion in his gaze startled Mary. Daniel stood so close that his buckskin coat touched her cape. Now that he could stand up straight, she was surprised at how tall he was. He gazed down at her with his warm brown eyes — brimming with more than just friendship now — causing her heart to race with excitement and turmoil. She swallowed and forced herself to remember her mother's words of caution.

"We had best get to the barn." She increased her stride.

The soldier followed her to the wooden structure. When they opened the door to the shelter, they were greeted with the loud bellowing of the unhappy bovine.

"I am so sorry, Susannah." Mary's voice crooned with apology. "I did not mean to forget you this morning."

The cow glanced over her shoulder at the newcomer while Mary handed the milk bucket to Daniel.

"Here you are, sir." She set the small stool next to the animal. "This should give you room to extend your leg out while you do the milking."

Mary started back to the farmhouse. She wanted to avoid being alone with Daniel.

"Wait." His voice sounded anxious. "What... what do I do?"

"Do not tell me you've never milked a cow before, Daniel?" Mary covered her mouth to keep from laughing.

"I've never even seen a cow being milked before." He was clearly embarrassed.

"So, who did the milking at your house, Mr. Lowe?"

Daniel turned red in the face. "The servants did."

Mary's eyes grew wide. "You never mentioned you had servants back at your home."

"You never asked." He shifted his feet and looked at the cow.

Mary smiled at this new revelation. "Well, 'tis never too late to learn. Watch what I do."

The young woman pulled the stool closer to Susannah and blew her breath over her hands.

"You always want to warm up your hands before touching her skin."

"Always sound advice, I am sure." Daniel blew on his hands.

Mary deftly grabbed at the teats hanging from the cow's udder.

"You use a squeezing and tugging motion alternating back and forth, like this." The milk began to flow easily.

"There." Mary stood up from the stool. "Now you try it."

Daniel moved the stool farther away from Susannah to accommodate his longer legs. He rubbed his hands together back and forth, and sat awkwardly on the small stool.

"Susannah does not know you. You might try talking gently to her," Mary suggested.

He turned and looked at Mary, his mouth dropping open. "Talk to a cow? You cannot be serious."

"But I am. Animals have feelings. She will cooperate with you far better if you treat her gently."

Daniel looked at her smugly. "I'm certain I can get her to give me some milk. I do not need to speak gently to a cow." He shook his head slowly.

Mary pursed her lips and said, "Well then, I shall leave you to your task." She left the barn to return to the farmhouse.

She glanced back and saw Daniel grabbing at the cow's underside with more fervor than technique. When no milk came forth, he applied more strength and less patience. Not even a drop squirted into the bucket.

"Blasted cow! Give me some milk!"

Mary sighed and proceeded back to the farmhouse when she heard Susannah bellow loudly and then the bucket being kicked over. A string of curses flowed out of Daniel's mouth.

Mary stopped in her path and shook her head.

"Try being kind to her, Daniel," she said under her breath.

Daniel hoped that no one had heard his foul language. He paused in his endeavor. Perhaps Mary knew what she was talking about.

"All right, Susannah." His voice was soft and calm. "Let us try this again. Please, can you give me some milk?"

He eased up his fervent grip on the unhappy cow and tried to imitate Mary's technique. Before long, the warm liquid began to squirt into the bucket and Daniel breathed a sigh of relief. And before he knew it, the bucket brimmed with the fruit of his — and Susannah's — labors.

Daniel awkwardly pushed himself to his feet and leaned over to pick up the bucket. The motion brought him closer to the animal's face.

"Thank you, Susannah." He stared into her large brown eyes. The cow just glanced at him, slowly chewing the hay that was in front of her.

When he entered the house, the Thomsen women seemed very impressed with the amount of milk Daniel had collected.

"Susannah must like you," Sarah said in amazement. "She never gives *us* that much milk."

Mary walked toward Daniel while her mother and Sarah were busy reading from the Bible together. She placed one hand on her hip.

"So, did your colorful language convince the cow to be so generous?" Mary kept her voice low.

Daniel's face grew enflamed and he looked away. "So you were listening in on our private conversation?"

"I could not help but hear." Mary raised her eyebrows and smiled tightly.

"I've been found guilty," Daniel said sheepishly. "I shall try to guard my tongue in future. Please forgive my foul outburst."

Mary smiled.

"You are forgiven." She glanced at the full bucket of milk. "It looks like Susannah has forgiven you as well."

⌒───◦

The day of Thanksgiving arrived with the smells of a mouth-watering feast. Daniel's appetite grew to a fevered hunger.

Upon entering the main room, he saw Sarah was in charge of twisting the twine tightly that held the wild turkey cooking over the fire. He watched her carefully observe the bird slowly untwist itself. Once it stopped moving, she spun the fowl once again. The young girl was an attentive sentry at her task.

When the six-year-old noticed Daniel watching her, she bubbled over with excitement. "Mr. Lowe, do you know how we trapped this wild turkey? We lined up kernels of corn to a turkey pen. The bird does not know he is heading for a trap. The next thing you know, the turkey is caught in the dug-out pen — and mother is looking for the axe!" She placed both hands on her hips and gave a self-satisfied nod.

"That is quite clever. And not a shot has to be fired."

"Unless the turkey refuses to be caught by hand. Then Mother gets her fowling piece to shoot him. 'Tis rather messy."

"Ah." Daniel attempted to smother a laugh.

He turned toward Mary, who reached for a bread peel. She maneuvered the long handled shovel to remove baked bread from deep in the oven. When she brought out the crisp loaf, Daniel inhaled the aroma.

"That smells worthy of a royal feast." He salivated with the smell.

"Or of a humble Massachusetts meal. 'Tis simply corn and rye bread." Mary's cheeks were bright red from the fire's heat and Daniel noticed how the color enhanced her beauty. As she removed her white apron, the red wool of her gown draped her in such a manner as to bring a long, admiring stare from Daniel.

Out of the corner of his eye, Daniel noticed the widow watching him. The mother's expression showed more than a little concern.

"Mr. Lowe." The widow's voice was terse. "Would you be so kind as to set out the linen tablecloth and napkins for us? This is a special occasion worthy of decorating our table board." She held out the cloth pieces toward Daniel.

"I'd be happy to make myself useful." He took the linens and awkwardly unfolded each piece, setting them out as best he could. "I hope I am doing this right."

"You are doing a fine job, Mr. Lowe." Mary's presence next to him, as well as her lavender scent, caused his heart to quicken. "Although I am assuming you have not set too many a table in your lifetime?"

"You are most correct, Miss Thomsen. Like many of my experiences here in Massachusetts, it is quite new to me." Daniel laughed at his clumsy attempts to set everything out neatly. He was relieved when the widow declared Thanksgiving supper was ready. As the group of four sat down at the table, Widow Thomsen led them in a prayer of thanks.

"Dear heavenly Father," she began, "we are Your humble servants who have come this day to give You thanks for the victory You have afforded our troops in our struggle for freedom." She went on to pray for the safety of the colonial soldiers, especially for James and those who fought side-by-side with her son.

"And Lord," she continued, "we are grateful for Your merciful favor upon Mr. Lowe, that You would bring him back from the brink of eternity and provide Your blessed healing upon him. For this we are thankful, dear heavenly Lord. Amen."

"Amen," Mary and Sarah echoed.

"Amen," Daniel said softly.

Everyone's eyes widened at the vast array of choices. There were sweet potatoes roasted in the ashes, peas, turnips, and carrots cooked in a kettle, several different kinds of beans, freshly baked bread, and of course, the fresh turkey. Daniel could not ingest enough of the women's hearthside endeavors.

"Save room for the celebration cake, Mr. Lowe." Mary laughed. "Although I must say, 'tis a joy to see your earnest eating."

"Do not fret, Miss Thomsen. I shall gladly make room for your cake."

"Well, I am relieved that Missus Stearns did not begin her travail before I could partake of this Thanksgiving bounty." The widow sat back from the table, obviously satiated. "She should be sending for me any day now."

"The husbands come home from war," Sarah interjected, "and nine months later they are calling for the midwife. That is what mother always says." Sarah resumed eating her cake, wiping crumbs off of her blue woolen bodice.

Mary's eyes opened wide and her cheeks turned bright red.

Widow Thomsen glared at her younger daughter and said tersely, "That is what we say in the company of females only, Miss Sarah."

"I am sorry, Mr. Lowe." The girl paused in her eating and stared at her lap. "I did not realize men did not know this was the way of it."

Everyone stifled a laugh and Daniel nearly choked on his piece of cake, so amused was he by this exchange.

"That is quite all right, little miss. I am grateful to be informed of the 'way of it,'" he said. He stole a glance over toward Mary, who looked even more lovely with the scarlet in her cheeks. "Your cake is delightful."

"Thank you, sir." Her voice was quiet.

"So, Mr. Lowe, do you have any family back at your home… up north." Widow Thomsen gave a sideways glance toward Sarah so that he would understand this was how they described his place of origin.

"I have a father and older brother, ma'am. That is all," he answered. "My mother died many years ago when my sister Polly was born. I was but seven."

"I am sorry, sir. So you have no wife or lady friend waiting for you?" Widow Thomsen asked.

Daniel saw Mary throw an angry glance at her mother. "Oh no, Widow Thomsen. I had an understanding with a young lady two years ago. But she decided she did not wish to wait for me to return from war. She took up with an older man who was quite wealthy. I heard that they married, but then she ran off with a younger man after only two months. I'm quite grateful I did not become allied with such a fickle woman." He gave a nervous laugh.

All three Thomsen females sat with their mouths open in astonishment. Sarah broke the uncomfortable silence.

"That is a sin," she gasped. "Leaving your husband for another man."

Daniel gave a half smile. "I suppose it is, little miss. I'm glad I was spared the hurt and humiliation."

He became self-conscious about this embarrassing revelation. He felt Mary's hand touch his ever so briefly under the table.

She somehow always knows when I need encouragement.

Daniel cleared his throat, anxious to change the subject. "So, tell me about your family. When did they come to the colonies?"

"We've been here since the first boat." Sarah nodded proudly.

"The first boat? You mean the *Mayflower*?"

Widow Thomsen sat up straighter. "Yes. My great-great grand-parents were on board that vessel. John Alden was the cooper on the *Mayflower*, one of the hired men. Priscilla Mullins was just a young woman traveling with her family to the new world. Sadly, Priscilla's entire family died within the year at Plymouth. Young Priscilla was left on her own. One of the families took her in to live with them."

Mary continued the telling of the tale.

"Half of the group of just over one hundred colonists died that year. 'Twas God's provision that any of them were saved at all. Some of the native Indians helped teach the survivors how to live in the new land. We still plant our corn according to the Indian ways."

"John Alden," the widow added, "was the only hired man on board who stayed behind here in Plymouth. The rest of the crew set sail back to England. John had to learn how to become a farmer in the new world, just like the rest of the colonists."

"The man must have been quite taken with Miss Mullins to have given up his life back home." Daniel looked at Mary. She glanced down at her hands in her lap.

Sarah gave a deep sigh, caught up in the romance of the story.

"He was smitten with her beauty." Sarah then whispered to Daniel, as though she were sharing a deeply guarded secret, "That is what my Great Grandmother Sarah said. I am named after her."

"You do not say?" he whispered back. Daniel stared at Mary again, well imagining the young John Alden being smitten with the beautiful Priscilla.

"Well then, enough talk of family," Widow Thomsen interrupted the moment. "Let us clean up the table and sit by the fire for some reading."

The group stirred from their seats at the table at the widow's prompting. Daniel helped to cover the leftover food with linen cloths before limping over to the chair near the fire.

Mary and Sarah huddled together on the bricks near the fire with a warm quilt covering their shivering shoulders.

Widow Thomsen handed *Aesop's Fables* to Daniel so he could read out loud. As he began to recite from the book, the tales of foxes and frogs and lions seemed to capture the minds of the satiated group. When Daniel looked over at the sisters, they were fast asleep, propped against each other in the glow of the fire.

Daniel's heart warmed at the sight.

"I believe I have lost part of my audience," he said to Widow Thomsen.

"I believe so." She stared into the fire and then focused her eyes on Daniel. "Mr. Lowe, these words are difficult to say. But let me be direct, sir. I know that my Mary is drawn to you and that you appear to be setting your eyes upon her as well. You seem to be a fine man, but I am concerned that Mary might get hurt in this matter. We are at war, sir, and I do not want your feelings or Mary's to put you both at risk."

Daniel swallowed hard at these words. At length he replied.

"Widow Thomsen, I shall never do anything to endanger Mary or any of your family. Please believe me when I say that I would rather die than put any of you in harm's way."

Widow Thomsen looked long and hard at Daniel.

"I believe you mean that, Mr. Lowe. But Mary has borne much hurt in this last year. I could not bear to see her so despondent again." She paused. "Nor could I bear the thought of her risking her life."

Daniel's heart sank at the widow's words. For the last few weeks, he'd struggled with his attraction to Mary and felt like he was losing the war with his emotions. How many times had he envisioned embracing the woman and feeling her heart beat next to his? Feeling his lips press against hers. Now the widow's words were a jolt back to reality — and he mourned the loss of feelings begging for fulfillment, as though a bud about to bloom was cruelly cut off.

After a few moments, he spoke with great difficulty.

"Nor could I, ma'am. And… I will do my best not to reveal my affection for her."

"Thank you, sir. I know this is difficult for you both."

"Yes. Now… if you will excuse me, madam, I think it is time for me to retire for the evening." He stood up and placed the book on the chair.

"Good night, sir."

"Good night, Widow Thomsen."

Daniel limped back to his room. When he shut the door, the reality of the woman's words hit him full force. He stretched across the bed and covered his eyes with his hands, as hot tears rolled down onto his pillow.

How he would hold back his feelings for Mary, he could not imagine. But he had promised her mother he would. And though it broke his heart, the possibility of endangering Mary stabbed at his conscious. If anything happened to her, he would never forgive himself.

13

Influenza

The next morning, it was obvious to Mary that something was wrong with Sarah. Usually full of energy upon awakening, she had stayed in bed without attempting to move.

"My head hurts, Mother." Sarah's voice was pitiful.

Widow Thomsen hurried to her bedside and felt her crimson face.

"You are burning with fever," her mother said. "Let me make you some tea, Sarah."

Sarah began to cough. Mary had heard that same harsh sound coming from the courier a week before. Fear infused her mother's eyes.

"The dispatcher must have been carrying contagion with him. None of us should go anywhere today if it can be helped."

Their mother walked over to the cabinet of herbs and teas and pulled down the jar with hyssop leaves. She spooned a small amount into a pewter cup and added warm water from the kettle.

"This is no ordinary cold. The grippe takes a powerful hold upon a body." Her mother spoke under her breath as her lips trembled.

Mary saw the rising panic in her mother so she placed a comforting touch on her arm.

"Sarah will recover, Mother. She is strong. Why do we not say a quiet prayer for her?" Mary tried to be encouraging, even though she herself was concerned.

Mary lifted Sarah's health up to God and prayed for strength and healing for her little sister. Mary also asked for comfort for her mother in this time of trial. No sooner had they finished the prayer than there was a loud knock at the door.

"I shall get it, Mother. Take the tea to Sarah." When Mary opened the door, she saw the anxious face of young Nathaniel Stearns.

"Please, miss." The handsome thirteen-year-old shivered in the fresh falling snow. "My mother… well, the baby is coming. Can the midwife come quickly?"

Mary's heart went out to Nathaniel. He had been carrying a man's work at home since his father went to war with the other Minutemen. The patriot's son was trying to be brave, but it was obvious his burden was heavy. The impending birth seemed to be causing the young man even greater distress.

"My mother will be there very soon. Please do not fear. Do you wish to come in to warm yourself?"

"Oh no, miss, I'd best get back to Mother. I shall tell her the midwife is coming with haste." With that, Nathaniel left as swiftly as he had come.

Widow Thomsen was with Sarah and obviously distraught. "Of all the times to be called away." Her mother's lips quivered.

"Mother," Mary said, "you know that I will look after Sarah. We do not want Missus Stearns delivering her little one alone. We certainly do not want poor Nathaniel to have to assist her."

Widow Thomsen smiled at her words. Mary breathed in relief to see her mother's expression brighten.

"Thank you, Mary," Widow Thomsen said. "I know that you can look after Sarah. 'Tis just difficult to leave one's child when she is ill." She looked down at Sarah and smoothed her long hair, which lay across the linen-covered pillow.

"I shall return as soon as the Stearns' baby is birthed, Sarah. It should not take long. Mary will give you the best of nursing care while I am gone. She will tend to your every need. Please rest, little one, and be well." Widow Thomsen gave Sarah a tender kiss, then left her bedside.

Sarah looked like she was about to cry, so Mary went to her side. "Let me help you with your tea, Sarah, and then I shall read to you if you like. You can close your eyes and rest — no chores today." Mary hoped to put a smile on the girl's face.

Mary watched her mother gather her supplies and her woolen cape.

"'Tis snowing outside, Mother. Please be careful."

Widow Thomsen brightened as the words were spoken.

"How often have I said those very words to you, Mary? I shall hurry lest the snow become worse. And I know you will take good care of Sarah."

Mary watched her mother leave the warmth of the farmhouse, trudging bravely against the freezing December wind.

She turned her attention back to Sarah. "Let's try two more sips of Mother's tea, shall we?"

The door to Daniel's room opened and the young soldier emerged with dark circles under his eyes. He looked far more tired than usual. When he saw Sarah in the bed looking poorly, he gave Mary a questioning look.

"Is Sarah ill?"

"Yes. She appears to have the grippe and she is burning with fever. It so happens Missus Stearns is in travail, so my mother had to go assist her. I told Mother I would nurse Sarah."

"What can I do to help?" Daniel looked at Sarah lying so still in the bed. Her cheeks were a bright red, a stark contrast to her normally fair skin.

"You could gather snow from outside to help cool her fever, Daniel."

When he returned with the basin of snow from outdoors, Mary scooped some of the white flakes onto a piece of linen and placed it on the girl's forehead. Then she scrutinized Daniel.

"Are you not well? You look weary this morning." Mary worried he might also come down with the contagion.

Daniel looked away.

"I am well enough. I did not sleep soundly… that is all." His voice sounded cool and he avoided meeting her eyes.

Mary bit her lower lip. She did not understand this sudden change in his demeanor. The way he had looked at her yesterday — the passion in his glances — had made her hope that perhaps he would not go back to England. But now, his seeming indifference toward her caused her heart to skip a beat.

Maybe he does not care for me after all.

Perhaps he had just been caught up in the festive spirit of the large meal and the heady wine her mother had served. Perhaps he was thinking fondly of his former lady friend. How could such a simple colonial woman as herself compare with a lady of fine clothing and finer skills? She silently chided herself for thinking she could be the object of his serious intentions. Mary felt hot tears begin to well.

I am a foolish farm girl.

Her thoughts were interrupted by the small voice of Sarah.

"Mary, would you sing to me?"

"Sing to you?" Singing was the last thing Mary wished to do. "I've not sung in many months, Sarah. I'm not certain I remember any songs."

Though trying to appear lighthearted, Mary's heart weighed heavy. Not only was her sister very ill, but their mother was not here to be her nurse. And as far as Mary could ascertain, Daniel did not have feelings of affection for her. Mary was more likely to cry than sing.

"Please, Mary," she asked again. "You never sing like you used to. I miss it. Your songs will help me feel better."

Mary looked at her frail sister and held back her tears. How could she ignore such a simple request?

"All right." Mary sniffed back her tears. "But only because you asked so sweetly."

Sarah's eyes lit up in anticipation.

"Could you sing 'Aylesbury'?" Sarah coughed several times again. "'Tis one of my favorites."

"I shall see if I can recall the words."

Mary stroked Sarah's blond hair across her forehead. It was with just such a comforting touch that Mary had soothed Sarah since she was a baby.

Mary started to sing the words of the favorite hymn.

"The Lord my shepherd is, I shall be well supplied Since He is mine and I am his, what can I want beside?

He leads me to the place Where heav'nly pasture grows, Where living waters gently pass, and full salvation flows.

If e'er I go astray, He doth my soul reclaim, And guides me in his own right way, For his most holy name.

While he affords his aid, I cannot yield to fear; Though I should walk through death's dark shade, My shepherd's with me there."

When Mary sang the last verse, she could hold back her tears no longer. Sarah had drifted off into a fitful slumber, and Mary continued to stroke the child's forehead.

Daniel sat by the fireside, staring in wonder at Mary. Her voice had taken him by complete surprise. Both the words of the song and the soothing sound of her voice mesmerized him. His desire for Mary was both exhilarating and troubling. After all, he'd made a promise to Widow Thomsen. He swallowed with difficulty and then spoke.

"That was beautiful." Daniel admired the young woman across the room.

Mary glanced at him, a surprised expression on her face. "Thank you, Daniel." She swiped the tears off her cheeks.

"I... I've never heard that song before. I walked through death's dark shade when I was in the woods, but I do not think there was a shepherd there with me. There was an angel, though." Unbidden emotion filled his voice. "I opened my eyes and I saw your countenance staring at me with compassion."

Mary regarded him. "There was a Shepherd with you, Daniel." Her voice filled with tenderness. "But I am not an angel... just one of God's earthly helpers. I believe the Shepherd sent me to you."

Daniel listened to her words thoughtfully.

"Perhaps you are right. But I do not understand why the Shepherd would pay me any mind. I have not served Him nor acknowledged Him, nor afforded Him a place in my life. Why should He concern Himself with my well-being?"

Mary studied him a moment before speaking.

"That is like asking why a mother loves her infant. The child has done nothing to deserve the love of the parent. He has even caused her great duress in birth. But her heart is awash with a love so deep that nothing the child does could possibly cause the mother to stop loving him." Mary paused for a moment then said, "That is how God loves every one of His children."

Daniel considered each word she said. He remembered something he had not thought about in many years. It was the memory of his own mother just prior to giving birth to his sister Polly. She was sitting in her favorite chair, reading from her Bible to him. He was just seven years old at the time. She told him how much God loved him and encouraged him to give his heart to the Lord.

Tears began to well in Daniel's eyes. After a long pause, he said, "I shall contemplate what you have said."

At that moment, Sarah woke up, her voice trembling.

"Mary," she cried. The child shuddered, chills ravaging her body.

Mary climbed onto the bed and picked up Sarah in her arms. She held her close, trying to warm the shivering child.

Daniel got up from his chair quickly. He grabbed some quilts off the bed and wrapped them securely around Sarah. As he did so, his arm found its way across Mary's shoulders. They looked at each other so closely, it was all he could do not to kiss her. He thrilled with desire and could barely breathe.

"Thank you, Daniel." Her voice shook him back to reality.

"I hope this helps to warm her." His words seemed awkward, considering what he longed to say. He reluctantly stood up and moved away from the two sisters.

"It shall."

How he wished that his arms had stayed upon her shoulders, even just a moment longer. Walking with a limp to the chair across the room, Daniel beheld the pair. Mary rocked Sarah in her arms and continued humming the melody from "Aylesbury" to comfort the girl.

The wind howled, grabbing Daniel's attention. He looked at the supply of wood near the fireplace to be sure there was enough to provide warmth through the snowstorm. By the sound of the gale outdoors, this would be a powerful blizzard.

Three days had passed, with Mary tending to her ailing sister. Sarah be-came worried about their mother, who was still not home from the birthing.

"I am certain Mother will be home as soon as this terrible storm ends. She'll be safe indoors with Missus Stearns and her family."

But Mary was concerned as well. She knew their mother would not take any risks in this weather. Her long absence from home and this unending winter storm were worrisome.

Mary appreciated Daniel's attempt to distract them from becom-ing fearful. He read to them and told ridiculous jokes that made them giggle. Daniel smiled whenever Mary laughed.

She was grateful for Daniel's presence, not knowing how she would have managed without his help.

Because of the storm, he had strung a rope from the farmhouse to the barn so he could find his way each day to do the milking. He brought in fresh supplies of wood for the fire several times a day. He even killed one of the chickens in the barn when Mary had expressed a desire to make some broth for Sarah.

Stretched across the bed in exhaustion on that third night of Sarah's illness, Mary's heart lifted as she envisioned the sight of Daniel covered in snow and chicken feathers, holding up his prized kill. She remem-bered his sweet grin as he handed her the precious offering.

Had his hand lingered on hers a moment longer than necessary? She smiled at the possibility. So consumed were her thoughts about Daniel that she barely noticed the aching in her limbs.

I must be especially tired from all the extra chores, she thought, as she drifted off to sleep.

When Mary awoke before dawn on that fourth day, something was not right. Her head throbbed so hard she felt it would burst. She had thrown off her quilts during the night but was still covered in sweat, causing her shift to cling to her damp skin. When she tried to stand, dizziness and nausea overwhelmed her. She thought of Sarah.

I've got to help my sister.

Mary tried to get up to make tea for the child, but she couldn't walk straight. She nearly fell. Pain ravaged her body and she craved something to drink.

"Daniel," she whispered, barely able to swallow. She tried to call his name again, but all that emerged was an unintelligible croaking sound.

Mary held on to furniture and then steadied herself against the wall as her bare feet struggled to find the way to Daniel's room. She leaned on the door and tried to call his name again. The fevered woman began to panic. She wondered if she even had the strength to open his wooden door. But she knew she must find the resolve. She threw her last ounce of energy into grabbing the door handle and pushed as hard as she could.

She fell headlong onto the floor before the darkness took over.

⁓

Daniel awoke with a start. He was not sure what the sound was outside his door. When it opened suddenly and he saw Mary fall to the floor, fear gripped him.

Throwing off his quilts, he hurried toward her. She mumbled something but her words were not coherent.

"Mary! Mary!" She did not respond. He tried not to panic as he picked her up in his arms and carried her to her bed. The fevered woman was covered with perspiration and her cheeks were flaming red. Intense heat radiated from her.

"Snow." He spoke aloud to himself, trying to keep his thoughts focused. "I need to get snow."

He opened the door of the farmhouse and was assaulted by the frenzied storm outdoors. The cold air whipped at him as he stooped over to grab some of the newly fallen white flakes. His warm hands turned frigid in the short time it took him to collect the snow.

"Blasted, horrible weather." He squinted his eyes against the winter onslaught. It took all his strength to shut the door against the wind when he returned indoors.

Sarah awoke in the meantime and sat up in bed. Her fever had finally broken and her color had returned to its normal tone. She was still very weak from the influenza. When the girl saw her sister in a fevered state, she began to cry.

"Mr. Lowe, what is wrong with Mary?"

Daniel glanced at the young child and forced himself to be calm.

"Your sister is just a little fevered — that is all. I shall cool her down with some snow."

He rubbed the snow-packed cloth across Mary's forehead and brushed her hair back from her face with his fingers. Her eyes occasionally opened, but she did not appear to be awake. Mostly she kept her eyes closed and appeared to be in a fitful state.

Daniel massaged the cool cloth across the insides of her arms, as he had seen Mary do for Sarah. He stared at Mary's lean limbs in his large hands.

Recalling how she had helped him walk to the wigwam so many weeks ago, he wondered in awe at how such a frail-looking young woman could possibly have borne his weight to bring him to shelter. His hands smoothed across her forearms where Josiah Grant had once left his mark upon her skin. The bruises were gone now but the memory of that event rekindled his outrage. Daniel was beside himself with worry.

He had never felt as helpless or fearful as he did at this moment.

How can this be happening?

Only last night she had been laughing and teasing him about his "triumphant hunting catch." He could still see her radiant smile as she took the small chicken he had slaughtered and plucked it for the soup.

Sarah's small voice broke into his anxious musings. "Shall we pray for her, Mr. Lowe?"

Daniel heeded the girl and rubbed the hair away from his forehead.

"Yes, little miss. I think that would be an excellent thing to do. But let us get you back in your side of the bed. You are still not recovered yourself."

He laid the cold cloth back on Mary's forehead, then helped Sarah back under the quilts on the far side of the bed.

When Sarah was under the covers, she closed her eyes and folded her hands. She was waiting for him to say a prayer.

Daniel paused awkwardly. "Perhaps you could say the prayer, little miss — just the way your mother likes to say it." He was not worthy of making requests to the heavenly realm, but he saw no reason to tell Sarah this.

Why would God answer a prayer from someone such as me?

"Dear heavenly Father," Sarah began in her small voice, "please make my sister well. She has always been a good sister and always loved her family. Please, dear Lord, do not take her from us." Sarah's lips trembled. "I would miss her greatly. In the name of your Son, Jesus Christ, amen."

Sarah opened her eyes and focused on Daniel.

"You are crying, Mr. Lowe."

He swiped away the tears from his face.

"It was a beautiful prayer, little miss. Now, let us try to rest. I shall bring you some broth."

What am I doing? What am I supposed to do?

The difficulty of the situation was beginning to reveal itself. He realized he did not know what else to do for Mary's fever.

"Do you know what kind of tea Mary makes for you when you are ill?"

"I am not sure. But there is a book over by the medicinals that Mary and my mother use sometimes." Sarah pointed to the cabinet across the room.

Daniel walked to the pine cupboard and looked at the numerous bottles marked with such names as Linseed, P. Bark, Parsley, and Plantain Leaf. He was confused by the numerous selections. Then he found the book that Sarah referred to.

"*Every Man His Own Doctor.*" He read the title out loud as he opened the small edition that described a variety of ailments and what could be done to provide care.

He found the page entitled "Fever" and was horrified to see instructions to "bleed 20 ounces, without loss of time." Daniel's breath caught in his throat.

Bleed Mary?

He had seen it done in the camps for fevered soldiers, but the thought of bleeding his friend caused him great distress. But the book had said without loss of time and Daniel's fear was causing him to waste precious moments.

He found a knife and prepared for the procedure. His hands trembled, which made it difficult to accomplish the bleeding without dropping the bowl and cloth that he would use. When he had gathered all the necessary supplies, he looked at Mary tossing and turning on the pillow. His resolve disappeared as he grappled with the idea of letting blood from his sweet friend. He turned away from looking at her face and picked up her limp arm. His hands shook.

What if I cut her too deeply?

As he struggled to calm himself, sweat began to pour off his forehead onto her arm. He wiped away the perspiration, which was blinding his view. He was finally ready to make the incision on her arm and held the knife against her smooth skin.

"Stop, Mr. Lowe!" Sarah cried. "Mother does not let out the blood. She says 'tis too dangerous and many die from it."

Daniel looked gratefully at the frightened child and breathed a deep sigh. He laid Mary's arm down on the quilt.

"Thank you, little miss. I did not want to do a bleeding. I was following the instructions in your mother's book, but I'm so relieved you stopped me."

"Mother says doctors are wrong to bleed. She says plants are the right way to help a body. That is why she uses teas."

"I shall remember that." Daniel wiped his damp forehead with his sleeve. "Let me put these things away and I shall get you some broth."

Overwhelmed with relief, Daniel shuddered at what he'd nearly done. He busied himself with ladling the broth for Sarah and tried to put the troubling thoughts out of his mind.

When Sarah was finished with the soup Mary had made the previous day, her eyes grew heavy. When Daniel tucked her back into bed, she looked up at him.

"Do you think God heard my prayer for Mary, Mr. Lowe?"

"Yes, little miss. I'm certain He did." He tried to reassure her with a smile.

The girl yawned. It was still morning, but Sarah appeared as tired as if it were bedtime. The fever had taken a toll.

"Good night, Mr. Lowe."

"Good night, little miss."

By the time Daniel returned to the other side of the bed to tend to Mary, young Sarah was already fast asleep.

Mary began to shiver now and Daniel placed extra quilts from the bed upon her. He went to the fireplace and added more logs to encourage the flames to send out more heat. Despite the increasing temperature in the room, Mary shuddered from chills that racked her body. The woman's reddened eyes opened up and she recognized her friend.

"Daniel." Her voice rasped. "I'm so cold." She could barely get the words out. Her body was at the mercy of the influenza.

He picked her up, quilts and all, and carried her to the chair by the fire. He held her close and Mary clung to him, pressing her shivering body against his warmth.

Daniel stroked her head, hoping the touch would bring her comfort. Soon he perceived the tension in her body lessen as the trembling ceased. He could feel her hand rest gently on his chest, and he covered her fingers with his. Her head relaxed and fit snugly into the notch of his neck.

For a short while, the illness seemed to relent and Daniel took momentary relief in the consolation of his friend. But the comfort was only temporary as the fever soon returned. This time, it raged with greater fury.

Daniel placed Mary back in the bed. He tried to cover her with a quilt but she kept kicking it away. Sweating profusely, her cheeks flamed red. He spoke to her, not sure if she could hear him.

"Mary, I must get more snow to cool you." He heard the panic in his voice.

Facing the treacherous outdoors once again, Daniel brought in a basin brimming with snowflakes. He resumed his attempts to cool her from the persistent fever, applying the snow-covered cloth on her forehead, then on her arms and neck, and then back to her forehead again.

Frantic and exhausted all at once, he sat down on the cold floor next to her bed and rested his head on the edge of the quilts.

I'll just close my eyes for a moment.

Sometime later, Sarah's urgent voice stirred him from his slumber.

"Mr. Lowe." Sarah sat straight up in bed. "Mary is calling Asa's name. I'm frightened."

Daniel got up as quickly as his wounded leg would allow him. Mary's eyes were open, but she was staring at nothing in particular. He leaned in closer to Mary's lips and heard her whisper Asa's name.

"Mary! Mary, please wake up." He grabbed at the linens in the basin only to find that the snow had long since melted.

"You fool," he berated himself. "How could you let yourself sleep?" He rushed out to the snowdrifts a third time and brought in a heaping basinful. Mary still stared in a trancelike state, her fever making her cheeks as red and hot as the flames in the hearth.

Daniel scooped large handfuls of snow onto a cloth and held it against her skin. She gasped at the sensation as he moved the ice from one part of her body to another. He lifted her arms up and wrapped them around his shoulders as he put more snow on the back of her neck in an attempt to halt the fever's progress. The sudden change of temperature on her neck seemed to rouse Mary's consciousness, but it did not awaken her; she appeared to be in a dream.

"Do not go." Her voice barely whispered. Daniel laid her head back on the pillow and he had to lean closely to discern her words.

"What is it, Mary?"

Tears formed in her eyes as she stared at the ceiling.

"Daniel," she whispered again, "do not leave."

"I'm here, Mary. I've not gone."

He stroked her face. She closed her eyes and went back into a fitful slumber. Overwhelmed with sadness and fear, Daniel sat on the edge of her bed and wept.

What if Mary dies?

He could not bear the thought of losing her. He'd never felt such strong feelings for a woman before and he despaired she might slip away from him. He was doing everything he could, yet it did not seem enough.

Filled with hopelessness, Daniel sought the only source he could think to turn to for help. He began to pray.

"Dear God," he sobbed. "I know I've no right to ask anything of You, but I ask this for Mary. I ask that You would heal her of this infirmity and bring her back to us. We need her." He paused before continuing his prayer.

"I need her." He bowed his head and stayed there for a long time.

The next two days were a blur of activity. Daniel brought tea and broth to Sarah, more snow to cool Mary's fever, and more wood for the fire. He made sure the cow was milked each day and that the food over the fire was stirred frequently. And he prayed.

On the morning of the third day, Daniel's head was in his usual sleeping position on the edge of the bed while he sat on the floor next to Mary. As dawn broke, he finally heard what he had been waiting and hoping for — the voice of the woman he loved.

"Daniel."

I must be dreaming.

He felt a hand touch his unshaven face and stroke his scraggly beard.

"Daniel."

His eyes opened wide and he grabbed at her hand. He kissed her palm several times and held her hand against his face. Tears of relief rolled down his cheeks and his voice thickened with emotion.

"I have missed you." He wanted to embrace her but knew she was frail.

"Daniel. I thought you'd gone away." Mary began to cry.

Squeezing her hands with both of his, he kissed them again. "I'm here," he said in a whisper. "I've not gone away."

"Please," Mary said still crying. "Do not leave me."

He gently kissed her forehead and looked at Mary tenderly. "As long as you need me, I shall not leave you. That is my promise."

14

Healings

*A*s if reflecting the outbreak of joy within the cabin, the sun broke through the clouds the next morning with no hint of a storm.

When Daniel looked out the window, the reflection of the light on nearly three feet of fresh snow was blinding and energizing.

"Look at all the snow." Sarah touched the layer of ice on the inside of the window. "May I go out and play in it, Mr. Lowe?"

"I think you'd best stay in a bit longer, little miss, until your cough has ceased." He ladled a bowl of gruel for Sarah and placed it on the table.

"Thank you kindly, Mr. Lowe." She glanced over at her sleeping sister in the bed. "Do you think Mary would like any?"

"I think I'll make her some slippery elm tea, instead." He remembered how soothing that brew had been when he was so ill not long ago.

Daniel went over to the cupboard of herbs and spices and found the bottle of elm bark. He crushed a small amount and placed it in a pewter mug, then added some cinnamon, just as he remembered Mary doing for him. After making sure the water from the kettle was not too hot, he poured some into the cup. He brought the tea over to her bedside and pulled a chair up close. He placed his hand on Mary's shoulder and gently squeezed. He would have preferred to let her sleep, but he knew she desperately needed sustenance.

"Mary, I've made you some tea."

Mary opened her eyes, squinting against the brightness shining through the windowpanes. She held her head as if in pain. Daniel hurried toward the source of discomfort, closing the curtains to dim the light.

"Thank you, Daniel," she answered with her eyes still closed. There was not a hint of color in Mary's cheeks.

She appeared to move her arms with great effort as though there were heavy weights attached to each limb. She tried to move her head and shoulders to sit up for the tea, but seemed too weak for the effort. She let her head fall back to the pillow, then opened her eyes in dismay.

"How long have I been ill?"

"Three days," Daniel replied. "Let me help you sit up."

He wrapped his arms around her shoulders and easily pulled her to an upright position against the pillows.

"Not too fast, Daniel. It makes me dizzy." She closed her eyes again. When she was able to open them, she looked with fear at Daniel. "Where is my mother?" The effort of the question obviously taxed her and caused her to cough deeply.

"I'm certain she is safe at the Stearns' home. No one would dare venture out in such a storm. She's probably enjoying cradling that new baby even as we speak."

"I hope you are right."

Sarah hurried over to Mary's bedside and hugged her tightly.

"I prayed for you, Mary. I was so afraid when you would not wake up." Daniel watched Mary touch her sister's face.

"Thank you, Sarah. God heard your prayer."

"Our prayer," Sarah corrected her. "Mr. Lowe prayed for you, too."

"You did?" She sounded surprised. "Thank you, Daniel."

Mary stared at him with gratitude in her eyes.

Daniel looked down at the drink in his hand. He was self-conscious about this revelation and he struggled to find the right words.

"I think the Shepherd heard our prayers." He shifted in his chair, then changed the subject. "You must drink this tea, Mary."

Sarah released her sister from her embrace and returned to her bowl of gruel at the table. Daniel held the mug to Mary's lips and she took a sip. It must have tasted right because she anxiously took the cup a second time and swallowed several gulps.

"That is all for now, Daniel. I'm so grateful to you… for everything." She coughed hard before speaking again. "I feel as if I've been battered about."

"You must rest, Mary. Sarah and I will see to the needs of the farm."

He took her hand and she returned his touch. They gazed into each other's eyes for a long while. No words were spoken, but Daniel knew their friendship had grown more deeply in these past few days. He smoothed her disheveled hair back from her face with his free hand.

"I must sally to the barn," he finally said. "I am sure Susannah is quite irritated with my tardiness. And I am quite certain she is anxious to have you return to the milking. I know she prefers your touch."

He smiled at Mary as he stood up and released her hand.

Mary watched him grab the coat and milk bucket, and go out the door to the barn. Shivering from the cold air that wafted her way, she pulled the quilts up around her shoulders as Sarah returned to her sister's bedside.

"Mary, I heard Mr. Lowe praying for you in the darkness when he thought I was asleep."

"You did?"

"Yes. And then… then he started to cry."

Mary was so moved that tears welled in her own eyes.

"Thank you, Sarah." She embraced her sister. "Thank you for telling me."

Mary released her and she returned to a book she had started to read. Mary closed her eyes and drifted into a deep sleep. When she awoke much later, the sun coming through the windowpanes had dimmed. Daniel was reading in the chair next to her bed. When he saw her awaken, he hurriedly put the book on the floor and smiled.

"Let me bring you some gruel."

"Just a small bowl, please. What have you been reading?" She attempted to see the words on the book lying on the floor.

"*Pilgrim's Progress*. I'm nearly finished."

Mary stared after him as he ladled the corn gruel into the bowl. He brought the steaming porridge to her bedside.

"Be careful, it's quite warm."

She smiled at him and took the wooden bowl.

"The warmth feels good on my hands. Thank you." She stared down at the volume on the floor. "What do you think of Asa's book?"

Daniel paused before answering.

"It's an amazing allegory, Mary. But I wanted to ask you about something that Asa wrote in the margins on one of the pages."

He opened the large book to page thirty-four and noted Asa's handwriting. The script was not the youthful markings found on the inside cover when he first opened the volume. This inscription was written just three years prior, dated January 29, 1775.

"What does this mean? I'll read it to you." He began. "On this day, Asa Thomsen released the burden of sin upon his back and obtained mercy and favor from his Lord Jesus Christ."

Daniel looked at her with questioning eyes. Mary placed the bowl on her lap and wiped the tears away from her eyes.

"That must be the part in the book where Christian goes to the cross of Christ and the Lord releases him of the oppressive load upon his back — the burden of sin we all carry. I remember the day Asa told me he'd surrendered his will to Christ. His eyes shone more brightly than ever." Mary looked out the window as the tears continued to flow.

"I'm sorry to have brought up such a painful memory, Mary."

"No, I am crying tears of relief, because I know that Asa is with God. Of course I miss him so very much. But I know he is safe with Jesus."

Daniel was quiet for a few moments. "Surrendering to the enemy is not a pleasant affair. But I know that God is not my adversary." He looked down at his hands. "I think… I need to spend some time with the Shepherd."

He slowly got up from his chair and looked at Mary. He touched her hand and squeezed it. "I shall be back in a short while."

Mary watched him go into his room and close the door. She wept more tears of relief and joy, for she knew Daniel was answering the call to his heart. She could almost hear the heavy burden on his back falling away.

15

Motherhood

uth Thomsen finally came home two days later, thanks to the assistance of a neighbor and his horse.

"Thank you kindly, Mister Eaton." She slid off the large brown animal. "Can I repay you with a cup of warm cider, sir?"

"No thank you, Widow Thomsen," Mr. Eaton replied. "'Tis kind of you to offer but I've much work at home feedin' my livestock. Take care now, ma'am."

The gray-haired man tipped his hat to her and his eyes crinkled when he smiled. She returned the friendly grin as he rode back home, his horse plowing expertly through the snow.

Ruth hurried inside, anxious to check on her daughters. When she opened the door she saw Sarah setting out bowls for a meal. Daniel stirred the food over the fire.

"Mother, you are home!" Sarah excitedly threw her arms around Ruth's waist.

She hugged her younger daughter and looked around. "Where is Mary?"

Daniel greeted her. "She's been gravely ill, ma'am." The young man paused as he served up the warm soup. "Mary is recovering, but she had Sarah and myself quite concerned."

Ruth hurried toward the bed and stared at her older daughter. Mary was sound asleep.

"Good heavens, Mr. Lowe. How long has she been ill?"

"Several days, ma'am, but she's eating some now and seems to be doing better."

Mary's eyes opened.

"You're finally home, Mother." Her voice was so weak. Mary reached out to her and Ruth hugged her for a long while, then looked at her pale daughter. Mary was nearly as white as the linen sheets.

"Thank the Lord you are recovering." She looked up at Daniel with gratitude. "And thank you, Mr. Lowe, for taking good care of my Mary. When I left here more than a week ago, 'twas only Sarah that weighed on my heart. I did not imagine both my daughters would be in such need of my prayers."

Daniel glanced at her and smiled while stirring the soup over the fire.

"Mr. Lowe never left her side, Mother," Sarah said. "He was just like a doctor."

"I hardly think my skills in medicine would be sought after by most." Daniel gave a sheepish grin. "I did the best I could, but my endeavors were sometimes pathetic. I was quite out of my element."

"Well, you obviously were successful in helping her to recover and I am beholden to you, Mr. Lowe."

"We prayed for her, Mother. Mr. Lowe and I did." Sarah clung to her apron.

Ruth was surprised. It was the first time she was aware of Daniel acknowledging his Maker.

"God is always the best healer, is he not?" She hugged Sarah.

"Yes, ma'am. He is."

"Let me help serve up these victuals. It seems as if you are due for some relief, sir."

"I shall gladly hand over the ladle to you, Widow Thomsen." In jest, he bowed formally.

"Thank you, sir." She couldn't resist laughing at his formal gesture.

Daniel limped over to Mary at her bedside.

"And may I bring you some fine victuals from the Thomsen hearth, miss?" he asked her.

She watched Mary's face light up.

"Why yes, sir, if you would be so kind." Her voice held the same mock formal tone. They both laughed as he brought her a bowlful of the warm soup.

Ruth's smile faded as she heard this playful interaction between the two. After stirring the soup, she turned in time to see Daniel take one of Mary's hands as he passed the bowl into her other. She noted the look of devotion on Mary's face toward the man. Ruth turned back toward the fire, her brow furrowed.

"Oh dear," she whispered to herself.

The next morning brought more cold air but sunshine instead of storms. "At least 'tis not snowing." Ruth sighed as she glanced at the rays streaming through the curtains.

She pulled herself out from under the quilts to start her workday. While she was grateful to be back home and grateful her daughters were well, her thoughts were fraught with concern about Mary and Daniel. She looked over at her two sleeping daughters. She moved carefully so she would not awaken them as she grabbed the milk bucket. But before heading for the barn, she decided to check the embers in Daniel's fireplace. She lifted two large logs and carried them into his room without knocking. She shivered from the cold air as she placed the logs on the dying fire. While stoking the ashes, she noticed Daniel had fallen asleep reading the Bible.

Ruth glanced at the passages from James where his fingers lay.

"Blessed is the man that endureth temptation: for when he is tried, he shall receive the crown of life," she whispered. She looked at the young man peacefully sleeping.

"Keep enduring that temptation, Mr. Lowe," her voice mumbled. "Keep working on that crown."

She sighed deeply as she left the room and closed the door.

Ruth checked on her sleeping offspring once more before heading out the front door of the farmhouse.

As she opened the door to the barn, she greeted the cow as though she were visiting an old friend.

"Well now, Susannah. How have you been doing while I've been away?" The cow looked over at her and mooed its reply.

"Yes, I feel the same way." She pulled the milking stool over next to the bovine and plopped down in weariness.

"So Susannah, you've been tended to by our Mr. Lowe these days. And what do you think of the gentleman?" The cow was eating her hay and ignored her voice.

"I suppose he is a fine enough man, but… we barely know him. He is just a stranger." She paused and looked up at the animal. "You are a mother… would you let your daughter take up with an unfamiliar bull that suddenly showed up in your pasture one day? I should say not."

Ruth kept up the rhythmic motions on the cow's teats, producing great streams of fresh milk.

"But I shall tell you something more, Susannah. He is no ordinary suitor. No, this man is a soldier of the King. The enemy. And he's making eyes at my daughter."

She paused thoughtfully for a moment.

"And she is making eyes at him." She gave a deep sigh before resuming the milking.

"I do wish my husband James were here."

Susannah continued eating.

"I shall never forget when I met my husband. I offered him some cool water at the barn raising. I confess I'd been eyeing him from a distance. He looked at me, sweat streaming off his forehead, and his handsome green eyes looked into mine." She sighed again.

"I knew when I saw those eyes that James Thomsen was the only man for me."

For a few moments the only sound in the barn was the splash of the milk into the bucket.

"I do not object to Mr. Lowe himself, Susannah. He has taken care of my daughters better than most men would. But there are no secrets in this village, and soon everyone would know the truth about Daniel Lowe. At the very least, they would run him and my daughter out of town. Mary and Daniel would have to move far away, perhaps even to Halifax, where the Tories have fled. I might never see Mary again. And if the townspeople were cruel…" Tears pushed past the brim of her eyes. "I have already lost a child… Could I bear the hurt of losing another for a man that she thinks she loves?"

She paused in the milking long enough to consider this.

"But what if she really does love him? No amount of interference from her mother could change her heart. And without Mr. Lowe, my Mary might not even have survived." She stopped for a moment, furrowing her eyebrows.

"Now," she said with vehemence, "the man is praying and reading the Bible. Is this supposed to sway my feelings on the matter?"

She stood up from the milking stool, her chore complete. She looked up to the rafters of the barn and closed her eyes.

"Dear heavenly Father," she prayed, "this turmoil is far beyond my ability to discern any possible solution. But Lord, You have designed the heavens and the earth — surely You have the answer to this plight. Help me, Lord, to trust in Your creative resolution. Amen."

She started to carry the full bucket toward the house, but paused for another moment to look heavenward.

"And please, dear Lord, keep Daniel reading the Bible — especially those verses about temptation."

16

Longings

"Hold still, Daniel." Annoyance edged Mary's voice.

She stood on a chair with him in front of her.

"Mary, I've work to do finishing the lock. I've been trying on this smock for several days now. These constant fittings are tiresome." He shifted his legs. "Ouch! You've stuck another pin in my shoulder!"

Mary knew she worked hastily but it was already February.

She needed to complete this shirt before spring — before Daniel would be outdoors, where visitors would see him. The more his clothes looked like they'd been tailored for him, the less suspicious he would appear.

"It would be easier to avoid sticking you if you would not move so."

"But my leg, Mary." Daniel rubbed his thigh near his war injury.

She put her hand on his shoulder. "Are you in pain, Daniel?"

He turned and grinned at her.

"No, but it was worth the lie to hear the tenderness in your voice."

Mary was doubly annoyed now and threw her hands into the air.

"I surrender. We are finished for today."

She shook her head in exasperation and started to climb down from the chair. Before she could get very far, Daniel lifted her in his arms and swung her to the floor in front of him. "That was the best part of the shirt fitting right there." He winked at her and flashed the grin that always took her breath away.

"Daniel, let me go." She whispered and nodded toward Sarah. Mary did not want her little sister informing their mother about her close encounters with Daniel.

He released her, but he continued holding her with his eyes. She returned to the hand-sewing in one of the chairs near the fire.

Mary never tired of new linen. She stroked the precious fabric that took months to process and weave, then resumed her careful stitching.

"I shall complete this shirt despite your wily behavior, Daniel Lowe."

She tried to look stern, but her sparkling eyes must have given her away. She could never stay annoyed with him for long and he grinned at her emerging smile.

He returned to his chore of repairing the wooden brace used to bar the Thomsen door.

"I noticed this ill-fitting hardware weeks ago. And the wood is swollen. Anyone could enter your home as they pleased."

"Well so far, all our visitors have been welcome. But thank you for fixing the faulty device, Daniel."

As Mary watched him return to his task, her mother unexpectedly arrived home from a neighbor's labor and delivery. She had only been gone for a few hours.

"That was a fast birthing, Mother." Mary completed stitching the collar.

Widow Thomsen rubbed her cold hands together.

"Yes, it was one of the fastest I've attended. Sometimes it works quickly when it is not the first — and this child was number seven."

"Seven?" Sarah's eyes grew round with wonder. "What a great many babies! Was it a boy or a girl?" Sarah usually wanted to know the details.

"'Twas a boy, a big healthy one at that. Started eating right away. Quite the sturdy little patriot." Her mother gave a satisfied nod. "I just stayed long enough to make sure all was going to remain well with Missus Burk, and long enough to catch up on some news."

"What news, Mother?" Sarah stopped playing with her doll.

"Well, let us see." Widow Thomsen took off her cape and hung it on a hook. She sat wearily in a chair that was opposite Mary's near the fire. "Oh, that warmth is so good on my feet."

Her two daughters looked at their mother expectantly.

"Yes? Go on, Mother." Mary tried to be patient but news was rare in these farm communities. She had already fixed some tea for her mother and set the warm cup into her cold fingers.

She knew Daniel would be listening in as well. He was always curious to hear news of the war, although he sometimes told Mary he'd prefer to forget about the military conflict just miles away.

"We have a new name for our country." The widow declared the announcement with pride in her voice. "The Congress has decided to call us the 'United States of America.'"

"The United States of America," Mary repeated. "Then we are to be called... 'Americans'?"

"That is correct, Mary. We are no longer just a separated group of colonies looking out for our individual interests. We are a nation."

Widow Thomsen sighed in awe. The entire group pondered the ramifications of such a pronouncement. Daniel seemed speechless.

The colonies were now declaring themselves a separate country from England! Never before had settlements in the New World done so. *What must Daniel be thinking? Does this give him hope or fill him with despair?*

"So what other news did Missus Burk have for you, Mother?" Mary was anxious for news about the American soldiers.

"She said that our army is taking shelter at Valley Forge through this miserable winter. The snow and cold there has been even more treacherous than here in Massachusetts." Her mother's brows furrowed.

"Where is Valley Forge?" Mary had not heard of it.

"In Pennsylvania," Widow Thomsen said. "Not too far from Philadelphia. It has been a dreadful winter there. Many of our troops have died of disease and starvation. But that General Washington... he has stayed right there beside his men encouraging them to stay the course." She always spoke highly of General Washington. Her mother admired his commitment to the troops and to the fledgling nation.

"Missus Burk also brought out a letter from her son Robert." Her eyes sparked with hope. "He has been asking about you, Mary. He speaks fondly of you and hopes to visit when he returns from the war camp." Her mother sipped at her tea and hummed a hymn under her breath.

Mary glared at her.

"I am certain I do not know what you're talking about, Mother. Robert and I haven't been friends nigh these many years."

"Ah, well, war has a way of tugging on one's heartstrings for the people we hold most dear." Widow Thomsen stretched out her feet before the hearth.

Mary glanced at Daniel and saw the anger in his eyes. She did not know how to refute her mother's insinuations. How would she explain this entire conversation about her childhood friend?

"I think I shall work out in the barn for awhile." Daniel's voice was as frigid as the air outside. He pulled on the deerskin jacket and shut the door behind him.

Mary gave her mother an icy stare.

"What was that all about, Mother?" Mary tried to smother her rage.

"I was just repeating the information from Missus Burk's letter — that is all, Mary." Her mother's feigned innocence did not fool her.

"That is not all you were doing, Mother. You have made every attempt to dissuade me from setting my heart upon Daniel Lowe. And now you have made me appear to be a flirtatious woman who would throw a man's feelings into the mire. I am not that kind of woman, and you know that."

Widow Thomsen stared at Mary drawing her lips into a thin line. "I am merely watching out for your best interests, Mary. I do not want you to be hurt."

"*You* are hurting me, Mother. My heart longs for Daniel and you are treading upon my deepest affections. Please, do not make me choose my allegiance between Daniel or you." Mary scowled at her mother. Grabbing her cape, she followed Daniel to the barn, slamming the door as she went. Her cheeks burned with anger.

How could Mother be so hurtful?

⁘

Mary raged with indignation as she approached the barn door. When she opened it she could see Daniel taking out his frustration by planing the wooden bar from the door lock. He glanced up at her.

"So, is there any more news about lonely soldiers awaiting your embrace at their homecoming?" Daniel's statement dripped with sarcasm and his deep-set eyes blazed with fire.

Mary's face heated with embarrassment.

"Daniel, I have no one away at war that I am longing for. Please believe me."

"Your mother does not appear to believe so."

Mary looked down at the hay-strewn floor and moved the straw with one foot.

"Please do not be angry with my mother. I am furious enough with her for the both of us." She looked up as his eyes met hers.

"Well it is quite obvious she does not approve of me taking an interest in her daughter." He continued planing the piece of wood with rapid and forceful thrusts of his arms, then stopped suddenly. "And just who is this Robert Burk person that she was talking about? Another soldier who wanted you to wait for him, like James' friend did?"

"No, Daniel, nothing like that. Robert and I were friends when I was thirteen or fourteen. I've not seen him except at Sabbath meetings in many years." Her eyes pleaded with him to believe her.

His demeanor began to soften slightly.

"And I suppose this soldier has some special memory from age fourteen that is still in his thoughts?" There was still a hint of lingering annoyance.

"Well, let me ponder that." Mary giggled and flirtatiously hugged herself with her cape. "I do remember him kissing me once secretly behind the meetinghouse." She stared innocently up at the rafters of the barn, waiting for Daniel's reaction. She did not have to wait long.

Daniel stopped his work as his face fell.

"He kissed you?" He appeared crestfallen.

"On the cheek, Daniel." Mary laughed. "I was only fourteen. If I remember right, I went home and washed my face."

The young man set the planing tool down on the wood and walked over toward Mary, wiping his hands on his jacket. He came up close, held gently but firmly onto her arms, and stared deeply into her eyes.

"So," he said, his voice thick with emotion, "is this how he kissed you?"

He leaned toward her and touched her cheek lightly with his lips.

Mary's eyes widened and her pulse quickened as she looked up at him. "Actually, 'twas this cheek." She pointed to the opposite side of her face.

He leaned even closer and kissed that cheek slowly and tenderly.

"Like that?" He whispered right next to her ear and nuzzled her cheek with his lips.

Her heart raced now and she could barely speak.

"No." Her voice was a hoarse whisper. "Your kiss is much sweeter."

This time Daniel leaned in toward her lips. He met them gently at the beginning. As she eagerly returned his tender kiss, she sensed his growing passion that sent chills through her spine. Mary was breathless when he pulled away and she saw the earnest look in his eyes.

"I've been longing to do that since we met." He held her close, and she could feel his trembling hands squeezing her shoulders as she rested her head against his chest. She looked up at Daniel as he held her face and caressed her cheeks. His eyes reflected love and… something more. They were filled with hope — hope for a future with Mary.

17

Questions

aniel heard the front door close.

It must be Widow Thomsen returning from the Beal's home. She had been summoned there for illness instead of a birthing this time.

The final light of yet another cold March day offered no hint of spring. The weather only added to the somber mood of the Thomsen house. Daniel sensed everyone worried about the illness of the Beal baby. He closed the Bible he had been reading and walked into the main room. When he saw the widow's face, he knew the news was not good.

"How is Richard's little brother?" Sarah's voice expressed hope as she helped her mother remove her cloak.

Widow Thomsen looked at the eager face of her young daughter as she plunked into the chair by the fire.

"Come here, Sarah." The widow's face seemed sad, disheartened.

"He is all right, is he not? He is such a sweet baby." Sarah climbed into her mother's lap.

The widow took a deep breath and spoke slowly.

"Sarah, God has seen fit to bring young Adam home to heaven."

Sarah looked at her mother with a quizzical expression.

"I do not understand, Mother." The young girl glanced at Mary, who stirred a pot of soup over the fire. Daniel noticed Mary put her hand over her mouth. Tears began to roll down her cheeks.

"The babe has passed away, child. I stayed with his mother long enough to comfort her and lay out the child in fresh clothing." The widow said these words with great difficulty.

Daniel knew the sadness this would bring Sarah. She'd been at the baby's birthing and spoke often of holding and rocking the newborn. The impact of his short life would leave a deep mark upon her heart.

"No, Mother. This cannot be. Why?" She began to sob great loud wails that shattered the previous quiet and gave voice to everyone's mood.

Mary dropped the spoon she was using, grabbed the milk bucket and her cape, and raced outdoors, covering her mouth as she went.

Daniel grabbed a coat and hurried after her. He saw the door to the barn ajar. When he entered the chilly building, he could not see Mary but heard her crying over near Susannah. He walked over toward the stall and gently put his hand upon her shoulder. She clutched a wooden post with a grip that turned her knuckles white.

When she was unable to stop sobbing, he put his arms around her shoulders and held her close. After a few moments she pulled her head from his chest and spoke through her tears.

"The Beal baby has died."

"I know. I am terribly sorry."

"He was so young and full of life not two weeks ago. The child's father is away at war and will not even know about his son's passing." Mary looked up at Daniel with reddened eyes as he wiped the tears off of her cheeks. "It seems as if, even when there is hope for new life, it gets taken away. Will death always triumph over hope?"

She rested her head back upon Daniel and clung to him. Without lifting her head, she added, "And will this dreadful cold never end?"

Both stood in silence, letting her tears slowly subside.

"I was just reading about hope," he finally said. "And about difficult times. Something about glorying in tribulations because they lead to patience and patience to experience. The experience then leads to hope which makes us not ashamed, because the love of God is shed in our hearts."

He looked at Mary and stroked the hair away from her face.

"I am sorry about the baby. It must be so painful to lose one's child." Mary pulled away from his chest once again.

"Yes," she said in a flat tone. "I feel… numb. Overcome by sadness. It… overwhelms my spirit 'til I feel… nothing." Her breathing stuttered from crying.

Daniel lifted her chin slightly so he could look into her eyes.

"When I was reading in the book of Romans about tribulations leading to hope, my thoughts were consumed with the memories of the last several months. My injury and then escape, your rescue and nursing care, my healing, your sickness… so much has happened that has been such hardship. And yet there is still hope, just like the words say."

Mary listened in thoughtful silence. When she did not say anything, Daniel continued.

"I am so very grateful for all that you have done for me. I never could have survived without your assistance and I shall be forever beholden to you."

Mary drew away from his embrace and looked up at him. "I see."

He could sense her heart pulling away from him.

"You need not thank me further, Daniel, and you are not beholden to me." She took a step backward. "I suppose you are planning on leaving when spring arrives. I suppose you are bidding me an early farewell?"

Mary's words wounded his soul. His face contorted in confusion.

"Bidding you farewell? I am trying to express my deepest regard for you."

He moved toward her once again and held both her arms with a firm but gentle grip. He tried to calm his voice.

"I fear I'm not making myself clear. I know I am far more adept in the ways of war than of love."

He now had her full attention and he nervously moistened his dry lips.

"Mary, you have captured my heart completely and I am a willing prisoner of your affection." Daniel trembled. His eyes widened with apprehension about Mary's possible response. He bravely continued on, more fearful of her eyes than of an entire column of cannons on the battlefield.

"When you walk into a room, I cannot take my eyes from you. You have made me laugh and you've moved me to tears. You have been my true friend and I wish for you to be my true love." He touched her cheeks with his moist hands. "I do not know all the answers to our uncertain future. But I do know one thing." He swallowed hard, his voice barely more than a whisper. "I do not wish to have a future without you by my side. Please, Mary, will you be my wife forevermore?"

There was a look of total surrender in Daniel's eyes as he waited for her response.

Mary gazed at him for a moment before slowly touching the cleft in his chin. She smiled softly and reached up with both of her hands to draw his face toward hers. She kissed him on his lips and she felt him respond in kind.

The kiss continued as their embrace became impassioned. Her heart fairly burst with joy as her blood raced through her veins. When she finally drew away, Daniel started to kiss her neck. His warm lips made her tremble with each encounter.

"I love you, Mary." His voice mumbled in between his caresses. "From the first time I saw you, I loved you."

"I love you so much, Daniel."

He suddenly stopped kissing her and looked at her strangely.

"You never answered my question."

She looked at him and touched his face.

"Yes," she whispered into his ear. "Yes. I shall be your wife, Daniel Lowe. I shall be your wife forevermore."

Prudence

Spring had not truly arrived each year at the Thomsen farm until Great Aunt Prudence came on the scene. Mary thought Prudence a formidable woman, with a wide face and tightly wound hair beneath a too-tight cap.

"'Tis a wonder her head does not ache from the constriction," Widow Thomsen had once said of her aunt. But Prudence always insisted that it was the only way to keep her hair neatly confined. The cap, in addition to an unpleasant smelling pomade, kept every lock in perfect order. Mary never had the courage to ask the woman what the source of the oily substance was.

Aunt Prudence had never been married. She had long ago had the opportunity when she was engaged to a merchant in the town of Bridgewater. But the woman's commanding presence could be intimidating. Before the planned wedding could take place, the slightly built groom-to-be closed up his shop and disappeared. He was never heard from again.

"I think she frightens men away with her imperious attitude," Widow Thomsen had said. Mary could well imagine.

Despite her overbearing demeanor, Prudence had a good heart when it came to helping others. And ever since Mary's father had died, Prudence came faithfully every spring and fall to bring two of her servants to help with planting and harvesting.

"What is a successful farm without the strength of men?" Prudence had said matter-of-factly.

The great aunt had a very profitable farm that she managed well. She was the sole heir of her father's land and was adept at finances and agriculture. Her independence as a farmer was secure as long as she remained single.

"If I had married that no-good Mr. Crowell, I should never have had such freedom," she once said, referring to her absconded fiancé.

As Mary saw Prudence approach the Thomsen farm earlier than expected that April morning, she hastened to the barn to warn Daniel. She berated herself that she had not thought to caution him of her aunt's impending visit.

"Daniel, Aunt Prudence is here." Mary was out of breath from running. "She is not someone who will keep her silence. You must hide or you will face her interrogation."

He had been sharpening the tools to prepare for planting.

"I'm confused. I thought we'd decided to explain to everyone I was wounded in the war and am helping with the farm in exchange for food and shelter. I did not think I needed further seclusion."

"Please, Daniel. You do not know my Great Aunt Prudence!"

"Alright then. Where should I hide?" He set the hoe against the barn wall.

"Under the hay. Quickly!" As Mary threw large piles of hay over him, she said, "I feel like Rahab hiding the spies, like in the book of Joshua."

Daniel looked at her with feigned shock.

"Mary! Was not Rahab a harlot?" He looked at her with a grin partially covered with straw.

Mary glanced at him with exasperation. "You have a very selective memory from the Bible, Daniel Lowe." She fought the urge to grin.

"I must say, it is quite shocking my future wife should compare herself with a woman of such dubious occupation." His eyes danced with mirth.

Mary rolled her eyes at him and threw one last pile of straw over his face.

"Hush before my aunt hears you," she whispered.

Mary left the barn and walked toward Aunt Prudence, who approached on horseback. The visitor was accompanied by two servants driving a wagon brimming with supplies.

Future wife. A smile emerged on Mary's countenance. Yes, she would soon be Daniel's wife.

But there was one obstacle that overshadowed Mary's joy — Daniel still had to speak to her mother. It was a conversation Mary had begged him to put off until spring, but the season was now upon them, and she would have to allow him to approach her mother to ask for her blessing.

But Mary had already made a firm decision. Should her mother reject Daniel's request, Mary would elope with him. As difficult as leaving her home would be, Mary could not imagine the pain of losing this man that held her heart. She prayed desperately that her mother would consent.

"Hellooo, Miss Mary." The stout woman waved vigorously at Mary as she approached the party of travelers.

"Welcome, Aunt Prudence." Mary immediately noticed the tight cap upon her aunt's head. "And how are you this fine April day?"

"Well enough, my dear." Prudence's brash manner grated on Mary. "I have brought my servants Jubo and Gibb to help out with the spring planting."

Mary approached the two men managing the reins of the horses drawing the wagon.

"Welcome, sirs. We are grateful for your help. And how are your wife and family, Jubo?" Mary had known this man and his family since she was quite young. Gibb had only been with Aunt Prudence a short time.

"They are doing well, Miss Mary," Jubo said. "My wife says to thank you for the blanket you made last year for our newest baby."

"You are most welcome, Jubo. I hope the baby is doing well."

Widow Thomsen and Sarah came out of the farmhouse and approached the three visitors from Bridgewater. Sarah was far more subdued than usual.

Mother likely gave strict instructions to Sarah about not divulging Daniel's presence.

Her little sister's enthusiastic chatter could reveal too much information to their always-inquisitive relative.

Aunt Prudence heaved her generous girth off the saddle of Dash, her large brown mare. The overburdened animal seemed to exhale in relief.

Poor Dash, Mary thought, gently stroking the animal's nose.

"Aunt, may I take Dash into the barn to feed her?" The animal gently nuzzled Mary's hand. *Dash remembers my offerings of hay and apples.*

"Yes, of course," Prudence said. She turned to the two servants and raised her voice in a stern command. "Jubo, Gibb. Unload these supplies and carry what's needed to the fields."

The men began the work of lifting and unloading the crates and barrels.

"I've brought new tools for you. And a barrel full of salted cod for your table, Ruth."

Sarah covered her ears from the bellowing announcement.

"Thank you, Aunt Prudence." Widow Thomsen seemed beside herself with joy. "You know how much I miss the ocean bounty. 'Tis a welcome luxury so far inland."

"Miss Mary," Aunt Prudence called to her great niece. "Make Dash at home in one of your stalls. He is going to be staying here. Your mother needs his swift legs to deliver those babes, especially in the cold of winter."

Mary grinned at the prospect of keeping the horse and hugged its neck.

Widow Thomsen's jaw dropped. "Aunt Prudence, I could not accept such a gift."

"You are doing Dash a favor," Aunt Prudence said. "She is not getting any younger and I am not getting any leaner. She will live a longer life underneath your smaller frame, I am sure." Aunt Prudence gave the widow a smile that said the discussion was finished.

"Thank you." Widow Thomsen threw her arms around her aunt.

After Aunt Prudence brushed off the widow's show of affection, the visitor carefully scrutinized Mary as she led the horse toward the barn. Mary's face burned as she felt the woman's inspection.

"Speaking of small frames, your Mary seems to need a few extra pounds upon her bones."

Mary cringed, hearing these comments.

Before Widow Thomsen could intervene, the resolute aunt marched toward Mary with long, forceful strides. "Miss Mary." Her aunt called out with a voice that could rival the tenor of musket fire.

Mary flinched at the command. She paused in her steps as she neared the open door of the barn.

"Yes, Aunt Prudence?"

What advice will she have for me this time?

Prudence took stock of Mary's figure. "You seem to have some potentially fine flanks and hindquarters for child bearing, my dear. But perhaps a few extra spoonfuls at each meal would serve you well." The horsewoman squinted with a critical eye. "When those lads come home from the war, they will wish to court the women with ample figures to feed their babes."

Mary's face warmed with embarrassment. Had her aunt realized there was a gentleman within hearing distance, naturally she would not have spoken so frankly. But Mary knew that Daniel was nearby and she was mortified. The situation was even more humiliating due to the older woman's annoying habit of discussing one's physical appearance as if she were livestock.

"I shall keep that in mind, Aunt Prudence." Mary's cheeks grew hotter by the moment.

"Well then, I shall see you back at the house." Prudence strode back to the farmhouse with the same forceful steps with which she had approached Mary. If she noticed Mary's intense embarrassment, Aunt Prudence never acknowledged it.

Daniel watched through a small opening in the hay as Mary led Dash to the stall next to Susannah's. He immediately recognized Mary's discomfort, and as much as he wanted to laugh at Prudence's amusing advice, he thought better of it. When he heard the door to the farmhouse close behind the visitor, Daniel moved the hay away from his face.

"Is it safe to come out yet?"

She looked over at him, her face bright red.

"You heard, did you not?" She appeared to be on the verge of tears.

Daniel stood up, his linen shirt and breeches covered with bits of hay. He walked over to his intended and put his arms around her.

"I think you are perfect."

"I am mortified." She turned away from him.

"Look at me, Mary." He lifted her chin upward. "If you were as large as your Aunt Prudence, I would be fearful you might injure me."

Relief filled Daniel when she began to giggle.

"Can you imagine, Mary?"

"You can always find the humor."

"Mary." Daniel touched her hair and caressed her cheeks. "You awaken deep feelings of desire within me." He kissed her lips and drew her closer. "I cannot wait until we are married."

Mary slowly pulled away. "I had best go inside before I lose myself in your kisses." She released herself from Daniel's embrace and walked back toward the farmhouse, looking back at him for one last glance.

Daniel stared after her and took a deep breath. He slowly exhaled, trying desperately not to think about her flanks and hindquarters.

When Mary opened the door to the farmhouse she was still trying to recover from the sweetness of Daniel's kiss. Her ears were suddenly assaulted by the resonant voice of Aunt Prudence. The visitor was discussing the Revolution, marriage, and patriotic responsibilities.

"'Tis the duty of every citizen to do everything possible to promote our revolutionary cause." Prudence's hand swung up and down like a hammer, as if to emphasize her words. Her other hand held the tankard of cider and rum she had requested from her niece, Widow Thomsen.

The visiting relative looked up at Mary.

"Ah, yes, just the person we were discussing. Have a seat, miss."

Widow Thomsen looked at Mary as if to apologize for the impending verbal onslaught. Aunt Prudence took a long swig of her drink and then a deep breath before starting.

"So, Miss Mary, I was telling your mother that it is the duty of every young woman in these colonies to marry and replenish the supply of citizens that have been lost in the war."

"Duty? Replenish the supply of citizens?" Mary gulped.

"Yes, miss. How else will these United States of America flourish without its citizens being fruitful and multiplying?" Aunt Prudence took another long swallow of brew.

Mary cleared her throat. "Well, I am certain that will happen naturally as young people fall in love. Do you not think so, Aunt Prudence?"

Aunt Prudence's eyes narrowed and the imposing woman leaned forward in her chair. "Love?" The woman looked aghast. "I am not discussing love. I am talking about the duty of every patriot. If a farmer needs more livestock in the field, he just brings in a few stud animals and lets nature take its course."

Mary was speechless for a moment but finally found her voice. "But Aunt Prudence, we are more than animals. We are humans with a need to love. Marriage is a gift from God." Mary tried to sound brave.

Aunt Prudence harrumphed.

"If we wait for every citizen to fall in love, we shall run out of time to replenish the American population. And leave it to the Thomsens to dwell upon God and love. I tell you, there is more to life than following the Good Book, as you call it."

"I disagree, Aunt." Widow Thomsen spoke up. "There is much wisdom to be gleaned from reading the Bible. And marriage should be based on love as well as suitability." She looked over at Mary.

Mary stood silent, but hoped her mother perceived the look of gratitude in her eyes.

Aunt Prudence was not to be dissuaded from her intended goal.

"So 'tis love you are after, is it?" Aunt Prudence smirked at her niece. "Are you telling me there are no men in your town suitable to provide a caring home for you, Mary?"

Sarah rose from her chair and began to answer the question but was interrupted by Widow Thomsen, who firmly squeezed the girl's arm and pulled her back in the seat. Sarah folded her arms tightly and pouted.

"Most of the young men are away at war," Widow Thomsen explained.

"Well, what about the older widow men? I'm certain they'd appreciate the fine withers of a strong girl like Mary."

There it was again — another comparison to equine anatomy. Mary looked pleadingly at her mother.

"I am sure that Mary will set her eyes on a proper husband who will sire many children for the sake of America, Aunt Prudence." Widow Thomsen spoke with a firm voice.

Mary knew Aunt Prudence would not so easily be disarmed.

"So, Mary, is there a young man whom you have set your heart upon who could help you in this patriotic cause?"

Mary's face blushed and she was afraid her demeanor would invite more pointed inquiries.

Sarah again rose from her chair but was once again halted by her mother's firm grip upon her arm.

When the widow glanced at Mary, her discomfort brought a look of sympathy. Widow Thomsen turned resolutely toward her aunt.

"I think that Mary will use good judgment in whom she chooses to father her children," her mother said. "There are several men who are suitable and would be more than willing to offer their help as patriots."

"Good!" Aunt Prudence finally seemed satisfied. The great aunt raised her tankard of drink for a toast.

"To mother's milk for the Revolution!" She took one last swig and belched heartily. "Well, I must start my journey back to Bridgewater before I lose the light of day. I shall return in a few weeks to collect my servants."

The sizeable woman stood up and straightened out her rumpled clothing. As she started for the door, no one asked her the obvious question about her safety traveling alone. Mary knew that no one would dare harass Aunt Prudence — not even someone as brave as General Washington.

While standing in the doorway watching their mother say farewell to Aunt Prudence, Sarah tugged on her older sister's arm.

"Mary," she whispered. "Why did you not tell Aunt Prudence about Daniel? He loves you and would make many patriot babies for the cause." Sarah had a wounded look upon her face.

Mary bent down toward her sister and hugged the girl. "I think you have a good suggestion, Sarah. 'Twas just not the right time to tell Aunt Prudence."

Mary watched her aunt drive off in the wagon and wondered when it would be the right time. She prayed that soon there would be no more need to keep so many secrets

19

Decisions

ary leaned over the slightly greening gray spikes of lavender. The leaves were just starting to awaken on this sunny April morning. It was a reminder that winter was finally over.

"My favorite plants are coming back again." Mary turned toward Daniel and gave an affectionate tug on his arm.

It had been two days now since Aunt Prudence had returned to her farm in Bridgewater. Spring planting was well underway, with Jubo and Gibb tilling the soil in the flax field.

Mary breathed in the fresh air, which carried the scent of warm earth and sun-drenched grass. The straw bonnet that shielded her from the bright sun shifted a bit. Her fingers quickly redid the ribbon into a tighter bow. She moved on toward the field readied for the corn seed. A pouch of kernels hung over her shoulder and she toted a tall planting stick.

"The pointed end of this tool will allow easier planting of the corn seed, Daniel. After these are in the ground, I'll show you how to place the beans and pumpkin seeds around the corn."

"I'm looking forward to spending the day outdoors. It's been a wearisome winter." Daniel tipped the brim of his felt hat to keep the glare out of his eyes. "The sun feels like a balm on my skin. Of course, I relish the thought of working alone with you, Mary."

Mary beamed. "I do as well. But let us keep on the task at hand."

"First you take the stick to poke the hole in the mound and then drop a seed corn inside. After each seed has been put in the ground, we will plant pumpkin seeds and beans that will grow around the stalks. We learned this from the Indians."

"Why is there such a large mound of dirt around each spot for the corn plant?" Daniel stared at the rows of mounded earth.

"The Indians say it represents fertility — like the belly of a woman with child." Discussing such an intimate explanation caused her to feel self-conscious. She looked at the ground, pretending to focus on the work.

"I see." His words edged with mirth.

Mary ignored his tone and continued moving up and down the long rows. When he began, Daniel seemed awkward with this unfamiliar work, but he quickly caught on to the maneuver. Soon, he was right across from Mary on the adjacent row.

"So you have caught up with me."

"I will do whatever it takes to be close to you, Mary Thomsen."

Mary grew more serious, and paused. "Daniel, I think 'tis time to speak with my mother."

He placed one last seed into the ground and returned her gaze.

"I know." His voice sounded sober and worried. He stared into the distance toward the pale green leaves just beginning to emerge on the maple trees at the edge of the field. After a moment he turned back toward her. "And what if she says no?"

Mary took a deep breath. She looked straight at him and said with resolve, "Then I shall go away with you."

Daniel seemed taken aback by her reply.

"You would leave with me if I have to go?" he said incredulously. "But your life is here. I have nothing to offer you."

Mary set the stick down and came next to him. She took his hand. "My life is with you." Her lips trembled. "I know it would not be easy. But Daniel, I cannot let you go without me." Fresh tears washed over her face.

Daniel reached out to her and held her closely to himself without speaking a word. He did not know what to say. How could he convince Mary — the woman that he loved more than life — to stay behind if her mother refused them permission to marry?

Mary had always been taken care of by her family. How could he provide a home for her when he had no skills other than being a military man? And would she resent him if he failed to be a proper husband? He shuddered at the thought.

Somehow, he would have to convince Widow Thomsen that he would make her daughter an acceptable husband — a suitable American husband. Somehow, he must make her understand how much he loved her daughter. He hoped and prayed that would be enough. Daniel finally broke the silence.

"I shall speak with your mother as soon as I find the right opportunity. I shall speak with her by tomorrow."

Mary shivered. "All right." She looked up at him with eyes of devotion. "I love you, Daniel."

Daniel picked up both of Mary's hands and kissed them tenderly. "I love you more than I have ever loved another person." Daniel worked his jaw hard to control his emotions. He let her hands go with regret and they both returned to their task.

The day went by slowly. The weight of this decision lay heavily on his heart. When the sun began to set on the horizon, Daniel brought the tools back into the barn. He noticed Jubo and Gibb staring into the toolbox. They pointed at something and seemed distressed.

Fear gripped Daniel. *My red coat.*

Mary had stored it in the toolbox for safekeeping. In the ensuing months, it had long been forgotten. Now it was discovered by two strangers, whom he did not know if he could trust with this secret.

Daniel looked at both men with fear and trepidation. Jubo and Gibb looked at each other and then at Daniel. Daniel knew they'd been told he was wounded in the war. But now they would know which side he'd been fighting for.

Gibb spoke excitedly to Jubo in his native African tongue. Jubo responded in the same language, which was completely foreign to Daniel. The two servants spoke loudly and with excited hand gestures for several moments.

Daniel's breathing quickened and he mentally devised a plan. He knew if they shared this information with Prudence, she would turn him over to the rebels without hesitation. His anxiety caused his heart to race and it was difficult to concentrate on a reasonable course of action because he now had so much to lose. If he left the farm, that would mean leaving Mary. He could never take her with him if he were being sought by the Continentals.

Just when he thought all was lost, Jubo began to speak to him in English. His words were simple but powerful.

"Miss Mary has much feeling for you, Mr. Lowe." Jubo looked directly into Daniel's eyes. "If you are her friend, then you are our friend, too."

Daniel was speechless. He looked at the two men with deep gratitude and did something he had never done before to a man from Africa. He held out his hand in friendship.

"Thank you." He grasped Jubo's fingers with relief.

The two men returned the gesture and then went about their work as if nothing had happened.

Later, Mary brought out supper to the three men and they all ate until they were full. She gathered the bowls and turned to Daniel.

"Tomorrow?" Hope brightened her luminous green eyes.

"Tomorrow." Daniel touched his fingers to his lips as a sign of his love to her. She touched her own fingers to her lips as well and returned to the house.

He settled into his new sleeping area in one of the barn stalls. With the arrival of the warmer weather, Widow Thomsen had suggested it was time for him to sleep in the outer building with the other workers. He knew without her saying so, this was a way for her to keep him at a further distance from Mary.

He hoped to shorten that distance after speaking with her mother tomorrow.

20

Intruder

aniel was restless and he did not know why.

The long day of planting should have been suffi-cient reason alone to put him into a deep slumber. But his rest was disrupted when Widow Thomsen was called away for a birth at a neighbor's. Daniel had helped saddle Dash for the midwife and watched her ride away down the dirt road toward her patient's home. He hoped she would not be delayed too long. He did not want anything to interrupt his plan to speak to her the next day about Mary.

Even when he lay back down, however, sleep still escaped him. He tossed about under his blanket and his eyes opened wide when he heard an owl in one of the nearby trees. Occasionally, he felt the hair on the back of his neck stand up. He listened intently but heard no obvious sign of danger.

Probably just nervous about speaking with the widow.

He took in a deep breath and tried to relax.

Before she rode off on Dash, Widow Thomsen had cautioned Mary to set the bar that locked the door. She checked it once more before settling in for the night.

Both of the Thomsen girls were in their night shifts, ready to retire from a long day of work. Mary was tempted to open one of the windows to let in the balmy night air, but she thought better of it.

It will probably get too chilly later on.

Mary tilted her head to one side while plaiting her waist-length hair into a single braid. Before blowing out the candles for the night, she noticed a reddened spot on her foot from walking down the long rows of corn earlier that day. She sleepily made a salve from the slippery elm bark and rubbed it over the abrasion.

Sarah was in a giddy mood, which was a sharp contrast to her own fatigue. Sarah, enlivened by the spring weather, chatted with excitement about seeing her friends at church meeting on Sunday, which was still two days away. The warm season always brought out the mischievous spirit in the girl and this April was no different.

"Settle down, Sarah," Mary chided her gently. "It's way past your bedtime and morning will be here before you know it."

Sarah repeatedly tossed her cloth doll up in the air and caught it. One time she threw it too high and it fell on the floor out of sight. She climbed down on the floor to look for it. There was a gentle knock on the door.

What did Mother forget this time?

As she opened the door, instead of seeing a friendly face, she was confronted by a large man wearing a red coat. The intruder looked with evil intent at Mary and pushed her to the floor. The look in his eyes was unlike any Mary had seen before. It frightened her to her core.

The man's hair hung in greasy strands onto his shoulders. His uniform was filthy, the smell of the man nauseating. Mary could barely breathe, much less scream. She slowly crawled backwards to get away from this frightening apparition. She pulled herself up by the bedpost and moved away from this lone soldier, who eyed her like a wild animal encircling his prey.

"Well now, lovely lady. Your husband gone to war, is he?" The man sneered, revealing blackened teeth. "Gettin' a bit lonely are ya? I could take care a that." The stranger began to pull his dirt-covered shirt out of his breeches and unbutton his waistcoat. Mary's breathing quickened. Nausea overwhelmed her while spots of light danced in front of her dizzy eyes.

"I've been known to satisfy a lady or two," he said. "Just wait 'til you experience the pleasure, ma'am."

Despite her anxiety, Mary had a moment of clear thinking. She remembered something her brother James had told her before he left for war. At the time, she'd not wanted to listen to his words — they were embarrassing and fearful. But James had insisted.

"Listen to me, Mary," James said. "In case anyone tries to attack you, you have your best defense by kicking him between his legs. If you cannot use your legs, use your knees or hands. And be harsh about it, not gentle. It may give you enough time to get away."

She wished desperately her older brother were here now. Even though he wasn't, his words guided her actions.

As the man narrowed the distance between them, she decided her knees were the best choice for defending herself. Using all the strength she could muster, Mary thrust her upper leg into the man's groin and he bent over in pain. As she sped past him, he grabbed at her shift and pulled her back next to his body, more determined than ever to carry out his intentions.

Mary scratched at his face, but he grabbed both of her arms and held them down.

<hr />

Daniel heard a noise that sounded like the door of the house opening. He had fixed the lock weeks ago but maybe the spring rains had swollen the wood. Perhaps the bar no longer fit.

I'd better check on it. He was exhausted but still on edge.

As Daniel walked toward the front door, he saw a small figure running toward him.

"Sarah?" His legs nearly stumbled in alarm. He'd never seen such a look of terror on the child's face. She sobbed and pointed toward the house.

"That man… that man." Her eyes seemed frozen with fright. Daniel's heart pounded. "Go to the barn. Stay with Jubo," he ordered as he ran toward the house.

Though he still had a pronounced limp, Daniel raced frantically to the front door without faltering. What he saw in the house chilled his blood. The man had Mary pressed against the wall with his entire body.

He tore her shift although she seemed to fight him with every ounce of her strength. Daniel lunged toward the intruder, grabbed him around the neck, and pulled him off of Mary. Enraged, he swung at the stranger with powerful fists. Daniel's hair came undone from the ties and his face dripped with sweat.

The intruder now bled from his mouth. After being punched with several precise blows, the intruder seemed to realize he was not facing an ordinary colonial farmer. The attacker shoved him away and pulled out a knife from a sheath hidden beneath his coat.

"Daniel!" Mary screamed.

The terrible nightmare continued as the intruder swung his knife at Daniel. One of the thrusts of the weapon connected with flesh, leaving a bloodied mark on Daniel's cheek.

While feeling the warm blood run down his face, his eyes sought anything he could use as a weapon. When he saw the Thomsen's butter churn near the fireplace, he knew he'd found his opportunity. He lunged for the long wooden handle and spun around, smashing it against the intruder's ear. The man dropped his knife on the floor as he cried out.

Mary ran to get the knife and the enraged attacker slapped her hard across her mouth. "You bloody trull," the attacker screamed at panic-stricken Mary.

Rage surged through Daniel. He grabbed the knife from the floor and with a firm thrust of his arm, set it deeply into the man's neck. Just as suddenly as the attacker had made his frightening assault, he now slid to the floor without further motion.

For a moment, Mary's fitful breathing was the only sound Daniel heard. He made sure the man was dead before looking over at her. What he saw twisted his heart with wrenching pain.

She stared at the floor, one cheek red and swollen, struggling to cover herself with her torn shift. Daniel ran over to her and placed one of the quilts from the bed around her bare shoulders. He did not speak but put his arms around her. As she clung to him, she glanced up and saw the intruder sitting upright against the far wall.

"Daniel, he is still here!" she screamed.

"Mary, he'll not hurt you. He's dead." Daniel kissed her head and wrapped his arms protectively around her. He smoothed her disheveled hair away from her face. His hands trembled. He finally was able to get the words out that he feared saying. "Did he... did he harm you?" He forced back angry sobs.

"No. He tried, but he did not. Daniel..." She wept with gut wrenching sobs.

She looked up after a moment with alarm in her eyes. "Where is Sarah?" she screamed.

"She is safe with Gibb, Miss Mary," Jubo said from the doorway. Daniel looked up and saw that the man wept silently.

"Thank you, Jubo." Daniel's voice shook.

The night's event made his heart race with fear. He was not unused to fighting, but he had never before fought to protect the woman he loved and he was deeply shaken.

Mary touched Daniel's cheek. "You are hurt."

Daniel hugged her close to himself, afraid to let her go. Just then he heard the sound of a horse's hooves. Fear still running high, he stood up and placed himself in front of Mary to protect her.

"It is Widow Thomsen," Jubo said to the frightened group.

The door to the house was wide open and Mary's mother appeared on the threshold.

"Jubo? What has happened here?" Widow Thomsen turned toward Mary and Daniel. Intense anger twisted her countenance.

"I never should have left you two here, Daniel Lowe." She headed for her musket but then saw the dead intruder propped up against the wall. "Good heavens!" Her eyes widened with horror. "Daniel, I am so very sorry." The widow sobbed, then focused her eyes on her bruised and frightened daughter.

"Mary," she barely whispered. She wrapped both of her arms around her daughter's shoulders as if trying to protect her from further injury.

But for tonight, the harm had already been done.

"Let us get this pathetic creature out of here." Daniel wiped the blood from his face with the back of his hand and limped toward the dead intruder.

He and Jubo carried the body out of the house. They laid it outside, where Sarah could not see it when she returned. Jubo ran to get Gibb, who brought Sarah to her mother. Widow Thomsen clung tightly to both of her daughters, rocking them slowly as they all sat quivering on the edge of the bed.

"We will take this man to the river, Mr. Lowe," Jubo said. "The water will carry him away and no one will know where he was killed."

"Thank you, Jubo." Daniel looked gratefully at his new friend as he fought tears that welled in his eyes. He turned back toward the open door of the house and saw Mary and Sarah clinging to their mother. They were all crying for what they had lost tonight — the naive belief that perhaps danger would never come right to their own door.

He saw a glint of metal lying on the ground. It was the intruder's firelock, which he had set down before breaking in.

The man was a deserter, Daniel thought in disgust. All the prisoners of war with the British Army had been forced to give up their arms along the banks of the Hudson River. This rogue left his regiment still armed, long before any surrender. How many other women had he terrorized from New York to Deer Run? The thought made Daniel sick to his stomach.

He picked up the Brown Bess musket and sat down just outside the front door with the weapon at the ready. He would make sure there would be no more intruders this night.

Trauma

aniel had not slept for a moment all night, as his mind wrestled with the terror of the previous evening.

What if I'd ignored the sound of the door opening and delayed getting up? What if Sarah had not made her escape when she did? What if Mary had not fought back? What if...?

Daniel had to stop the whirlwind of panic rushing through his mind. His heart raced with fear every time he allowed these alarming questions to run free.

The truth was that Mary was alive. God had protected her from the intruder carrying out his wicked intentions. Despite this realization, all of them were greatly traumatized in their hearts by this malevolent encounter. And Daniel and Mary both bore physical pain from it as well.

The door to the farmhouse opened up and Widow Thomsen came out with the milk bucket in hand. Her eyes were as fatigued and swollen as Daniel's felt.

"Let me get that for you." Daniel reached for the wooden pail. "Perhaps you should stay with Mary."

The widow looked at him, her manner subdued.

"Thank you, Daniel." She handed him the bucket.

Widow Thomsen watched the weary man place the Brown Bess against the outer wall of the house. It seemed clear where the musket had come from. The look on her face revealed her repulsion at the previous owner.

"We should keep that inside by the bed in your room," the widow called out to Daniel.

He turned back to look at her and gave her a questioning look. "Inside?"

She looked up at him, shielding her eyes from the early morning sun. "Yes. The barn is too far away."

The exhausted-looking mother went back into the farmhouse, and Daniel stared after her for a moment before heading back to the barn.

His wounded leg ached this morning, made worse by the night's struggle. He winced with each step, making his way slowly to the outer building. Jubo was already awake and setting up the supplies for the day's planting. He stared at Daniel.

"How are you, Mr. Lowe?"

"I am grateful we are all alive, Jubo," Daniel looked squarely at his new friend. "And I am grateful to you, sir, for your help last night." Daniel fought back the tears once again as he began to milk Susannah.

"Is Miss Mary all right, sir?" Jubo's voice trembled.

"I hope so, Jubo. I've not seen her yet today." He resumed the rhythmic pulling at the cow's teats for a moment and then stopped and looked down at the straw-covered floor. "I thought I was finished with killing when I left this war." He rubbed at his eyes and smoothed the hair back from his head.

"Killing a man is never a good thing, Mr. Lowe," Jubo said. "But sometimes it is the right thing."

Daniel was silent for a moment. "Please call me Daniel, sir."

Jubo looked at him and smiled. "Yes, Mr. Daniel."

Gibb and Jubo headed out toward the field to start their day's work. Daniel had just finished the milking when he heard the voice of a child. It was the same neighbor who had come last evening with the false alarm. The young boy raced up to the house and called for the midwife. Widow Thomsen opened the door and was greeted by the frantic youngster.

"Please, Widow Thomsen, we truly need you right away this time. My mother asks you to come with haste!"

"I shall come directly, Amos," the midwife said.

Daniel set the bucket down in Susannah's stall and went over to saddle Dash for Widow Thomsen. The woman came in a moment later, her supplies in a pouch she carried over her shoulder.

"Thank you, Daniel, for preparing the horse. I have barely finished helping Mary this morning — she is so distraught and too bruised to even brush her hair without great pain. Can you stay with her while I'm gone? I fear for her well-being."

Daniel had never heard the widow so anguished. He swallowed with difficulty. "Of course." He despaired at the widow's description of Mary.

"Widow Thomsen…" he began, then hesitated. "I know this is probably the worst possible time, but I have promised your daughter that I would speak to you today."

The widow stopped in her frantic preparations and looked at Daniel, her eyes full of understanding.

"About declaring your love for her, Daniel?"

He swallowed with nervous energy. "Yes… I love your daughter, ma'am, and I am asking you for your blessing."

Widow Thomsen stepped off the horse block used to reach the saddle and faced him. She looked weary and somehow much older this morning.

"God and I had a long conversation last night," she began. "Actually, it was a one-sided conversation — He spoke to my heart and I listened. I have judged you unfairly from the start, Daniel. All I have been able to see is your red uniform rather than your good heart and your integrity.

"Mary has seen you quite clearly. She's known you to be a good man and she loves you deeply. And if it were not for you… if it were not for you, I might not even have a daughter." She quickly wiped away the tears that began falling down her cheeks. She paused.

"And so, Daniel, I will defend you and your reputation to the most ardent colonial patriot. And yes, you have my blessing. I only ask that you go slowly with Mary as she recovers from her wounds. The bruises will heal faster than her heart."

Widow Thomsen climbed up onto the sidesaddle with ease and looked down at Daniel.

"And I thank you, sir, for saving my daughter."

With that, the widow prodded Dash into a fast canter so the new babe would not be born before she could get there. Sarah came running out of the house after her mother.

"Do not leave me here, Mother." Sarah wailed pitifully.

The woman halted her horse and made a quick decision. "Daniel, please help Sarah up onto the saddle with me."

Daniel limped as quickly as he could to the child and lifted her up onto the horse in front of her mother.

"Tell Mary we will be back as soon as the child is safely birthed."

With that the two riders set off down the dirt road. He stared after them until they were out of sight. He should have been relieved and elated at hearing Widow Thomsen's words of blessing.

But her words had come with a price. Daniel feared that Mary's heart would be deeply wounded by the events of last night.

He slowly opened the door to the farmhouse and walked inside. Mary looked like a frightened child suddenly alarmed by the sound.

"It is I, Mary." Daniel spoke with a soft voice.

When she saw who it was, her expression relaxed.

Her mother had helped her clean up and Mary was now dressed in a clean shift. Daniel noticed the fresh scent of lavender in the room, no doubt meant to eliminate the horrible stench of the intruder. Mary's left cheek was swollen and dark purple from the stranger's cruel blow. Mary huddled on the edge of the bed in silence, hugging herself with a woolen shawl.

Daniel walked over to her and sat beside her on the edge of the bed. He went to take her hand and noticed she was holding a brush. He remembered her mother saying that she was in too much pain to brush out her hair. Her long locks that flowed to her waist were disheveled and matted.

"May I brush your hair for you?"

She looked at him with mild surprise. Her eyes were moist and full of despair. After a moment's hesitation, she handed him her hairbrush. He began at the lower edge of her locks, gently brushing each section and slowly unraveling the twisted strands.

"I used to brush my sister Polly's hair." Daniel broke the silence. "She would sometimes get upset because the servants were too busy to do her hair carefully. They pulled too hard and made her cry. She would plead with me to take over the task because I took more time to unravel the strands. Our mother was long gone by then."

Daniel's eyes moistened thinking about these losses in his life.

He could see Mary's shoulders begin to relax. Daniel kept his voice soothing and quiet. By the time the brush had reached the crown of her head, she closed her eyes, the tension falling from her face.

Daniel smoothed her soft locks with his hand. "There. Your hair is lovely."

When he put the brush down, Mary turned to look at him. She touched the dried blood on his cheek, which made him wince.

She furrowed her brow and stood up, walking to the medicine cabinet. When she returned, she cleaned off the blood and applied slippery elm to the long but shallow knife wound.

Daniel took her hand and kissed her palm slowly.

"Thank you, Mary. I'd quite forgotten it was there."

Mary stared at him with hollow, pain-filled eyes. "I should not have opened the door." Her lips trembled and the tears began.

"What?"

She took a deep breath in between shuddering sobs.

"The door. It was locked and I thought it was Mother returning. I should not have opened it." Her tears spilled forth like a river flowing over a burdened dam. Daniel looked at her with tenderness.

"You did not know, Mary. How could you know? This was not your fault."

He held her close and let her sobs subside. When she was finished crying, he looked at her and wiped her tears with his linen shirtsleeve.

"Come sit with me, Mary." He led her to the chair by the fire. It was the same chair he'd held her in when she had been so ill with influenza. It was the same place of comfort when she could not get warm. He sat on the wooden seat and held out his arms to her. She gingerly crawled onto his lap and curled up in his arms.

"Rest your head on my shoulder," he whispered. She found the familiar notch in his neck that seemed to be made just for her. She placed her hand on his chest. He once again covered her long fingers with his large hand.

Without lifting her head, she spoke, this time without crying. "I love you, Daniel."

He struggled to contain his own emotions as he answered her in kind. "I love you too, Mary."

The exhausted couple closed their eyes and rested for the first time since last night.

Daniel could finally relax. He knew deep in his heart Mary would one day be able to put aside the horror of the intruder's heartless touch. She would instead remember the tender embrace of the man who loved her. He prayed it would be so.

22

Friends

It took weeks for the purple mark on Mary's cheek to fade, but the terror from that night continued to plague her. She felt it every time someone walked through the front door unexpectedly.

Sarah seemed deeply afraid ever since that night, as well. She had become far more nervous about letting their mother out of her sight. Widow Thomsen was patient with these fears. She allowed Mary and Sarah to recover slowly, offering each ample love and attention.

One day when Mary thanked her mother for her understanding, she placed her arm around Mary's shoulder. "I have faith that with time, God will bring healing."

It had been over three weeks now since the dreadful incident and no one had attended meetinghouse during that time. But on a bright sunny morning in early May, Widow Thomsen surprised Mary with an unexpected question.

"Who wishes to go to the meetinghouse today for Sabbath services?"

Mary and Sarah looked at each other and then back at their mother. Mary was anxious for life as it once was, although she knew it would never be completely the same. She would now carry with her the memory of coming face-to-face with evil.

But Mary desperately wanted to put this incident behind her. What better place to do it than at church, where she could worship God and be surrounded by friends?

"I shall go — if Daniel comes as well." Mary looked over at her intended.

It was just after dawn, and Daniel had come out of his room only a moment before. He still had the partially open eyes of someone just awakening.

"The meetinghouse?" He seemed suddenly alert but with apprehension in his tone. "Would this be imprudent of me?"

Widow Thomsen served trenchers of gruel. "There will be more conjectures made about you if you do not come as a part of our family. Besides, Mary has just completed your new waistcoat and you will be dressed quite smartly for worship."

"Waistcoat?" Daniel paused before sitting at the tableboard. "I was not fitted for such a piece of attire."

He stared at Mary with a questioning look. A shy smile emerged on her face. "I used your old one from your uniform. It guided my sewing. I worked on it when you were out in the fields every day." Mary went to the wooden chest of drawers where she had been hiding it.

"Do you like it?" She held up the vest.

Daniel looked at the richly dyed garment of blue linen she had pieced together each day. Every stitch was evenly placed, each button gleaned from his old waistcoat carefully covered with the same blue material to match the garment. He looked at it with admiration.

"This is as splendid a piece as any I've owned." His expression beamed.

Mary smiled with relief.

"Why do you not try it on?"

Daniel slipped both of his arms into the holes and buttoned the indigo-dyed vest. The fit was perfect, and very flattering to his appearance. He had never looked more handsome to Mary.

"Perhaps you should not wear this to the meetinghouse today," Mary teased.

Daniel's face fell. "Why not? It is perfect and exceedingly well done."

"Because, Daniel Lowe, other young ladies may set their eyes upon you when they see how handsome you look in this waistcoat." Mary's eyes flirted with him.

It was the first time she had spoken to him in a playful manner since the incident. Daniel grinned, walked over to her, and kissed her on her cheek, right in the presence of her mother and sister.

"I only have eyes for you, Mary Thomsen."

Sarah covered her mouth and giggled.

Mary blushed but was grateful that at last she and Daniel could show regard for one another in front of her mother. She only wished the fear in her heart would leave for good. Her recollections of Daniel's tender moments of endearment brought tears to her eyes. In her prayers, she pleaded earnestly that God would remove the memory of the intruder. She longed to set the time for her wedding to Daniel but did not want to be fearful of his embrace on her wedding night.

Thankfully, she couldn't have asked for a more patient man than her future husband. He gave her the time she needed to recover, and his devotion was obvious and constant. This made her love him all the more.

They each hurried through the morning chores so they would arrive at the meetinghouse early. Mary knew there would be much curiosity about Daniel, and they wanted to address the issue prior to the worship. All the townsfolk would speculate about his presence.

Everyone from Deer Run posed the same questions about Daniel: "Who is he?" "Where be he from?"

Mary watched her mother answer each curious congregant. "This is Mr. Lowe from up north. New York colony, I believe. Yes, he was injured in the war. Yes, he has been helping us out at the farm with our work and we are so grateful for his assistance."

There were a few raised eyebrows among the congregation. After all, Daniel Lowe was a complete stranger to them, and in such a small village, strangers were often seen as a threat. But the townsfolk knew the Thomsens well. They had been a respected family in the community for many years and there was no cause to mistrust any friend of the family.

When they finally settled in their pew, the Thomsens and Daniel breathed a collective sigh of relief. All that is except Sarah, who still did not know the details about Daniel's origin. The young girl appeared oblivious to the tension Mary and the rest of them felt. Sarah just seemed grateful to be back at church with all of her friends.

As the singing of one of Isaac Watts' hymns began, Mary smiled. It was the same song Sarah had requested last winter when she was ill. The song had inspired both admiration from Daniel and a discussion about the shepherd who guards his flock. Mary glanced at Daniel and noticed he was looking at her. She smiled at the memory.

Reverend Phillips began his sermon; today's topic was forgiveness of our enemies. The subject had been a struggle for many colonists as the war waged on between the King's army and General Washington's. With the onset of warmer weather, the battles would likely increase, and all the residents appeared tense. As Mary scanned the faces of each congregant she read fear in their eyes. Missus Burke wiped a tear off her cheek, and Missus Stearns struggled to maintain her composure. Nearly everyone fretted for a loved one at war, and Mary knew they were each wondering if their family member would be the next casualty.

She looked down at her hands and wondered about James. *Lord, please protect my brother.*

When she looked up from her prayer of supplication, her thoughts were suddenly distracted by what she perceived as a completely different kind of threat — the persistent glances of the Howard sisters looking straight at Daniel.

Buxom and brash, Hettie and Matilda Howard had an "interesting reputation," as Widow Thomsen would say. They had much to offer a man's desire and were not afraid to flaunt it. Even in so sacred a setting, they seemed more interested in earthly desires than heavenly ones. Mary wished she could discreetly offer each a kerchief to cover her endowments — not that either would accept such assistance in the cause of modesty.

The two sisters whispered back and forth and giggled, casting several glances toward Daniel. He did not appear to notice the two young women. Instead, he listened intently to the preaching. Mary tried to focus on the reverend's words as well, but she could not ignore the lascivious young women.

In exasperation, Mary shifted her position on the pew closer to Daniel. This caught Daniel's attention as her leg was touching his own. He looked over at Mary in mild surprise but seemed pleased. He touched her finger with one of his own, which made Mary smile. She circumspectly stroked one of her fingers across the back of his hand, which made him both grin and shift his weight on the pew.

Daniel's occasional glances warmed Mary's heart, and she soon forgot about the Howard sisters. She could not wait to be alone with him later. When the sermon was finished, the congregation paused for a time of eating. Since the weather was warm, many had brought blankets to place on the lawn of the meetinghouse. The Thomsens had brought simple fare of cheeses, breads, and dried fruit, and they all ate vigorously.

"Why does going to church make one so hungry?" Sarah asked. The ravenous group nodded in agreement.

When every last bite of their meal was consumed, Mary's friend Hannah White walked over and greeted all of them warmly.

"'Tis so good to see you, Mary. And Widow Thomsen and Sarah. You are all looking well." Hannah was twenty years of age, with light hair and kind blue eyes. Her soft manner of speaking occasionally made it difficult to hear her words. Mary suspected that her overbearing father was the source of Hannah's shyness.

Mary stood up and hugged her dear friend.

"You look very well also." She pointed toward Daniel. "Hannah, I would like you to meet Mr. Daniel Lowe. Daniel, this is Miss Hannah White. Her father is one of the Selectman from our town."

"'Tis so good to meet you, Mr. Lowe."

"It is my pleasure, Miss White." Daniel rose to his feet.

"May I speak to you in private, Hannah?" Mary asked.

"Of course, Mary." She had a questioning look.

They stepped aside and spoke in quiet voices.

"Hannah, I wanted to speak to you first — to tell you my news. Daniel and I are to be married."

Hannah's smile could not have been wider. "Dear Mary, I could not be happier for you." The long-time friends hugged. "I can see your love for him in your eyes. 'Tis the first time I've ever seen you this happy. When will the event take place?"

"Soon. I'll let you know. Thank you for being happy for me. I know 'tis difficult awaiting news from James."

Hannah's face sobered. "Have you heard anything?"

"No. He may have tried to write but his letters can be intercepted. I assume you've received no correspondence as well?"

"Nothing." Hannah's eyes welled. "Every day I await the postrider and every day there is no word from him." She paused and straightened her back. "But I shall continue to wait for him, as he asked me to before he left."

Mary touched her friend's hand. "I know he will come back to you, Hannah — to all of us."

Hannah gave a brave smile and then they both returned to the group awaiting them. Her friend looked at Daniel.

"Sir, you know that you have won the heart of the most sought after young woman in Deer Run, do you not?" Hannah kept her voice low so as not to alert others nearby.

Daniel grinned and responded in a hushed voice. "I do not deserve such a treasure as Miss Mary Thomsen. But she has agreed to my request to become my wife, and I am a most fortunate man."

Mary's heart warmed at his words, and her cheeks grew hot.

"I think 'tis my friend who feels fortunate." Hannah bid them all farewell before returning to her father.

Mr. Myles Eaton approached the group. The robust widower with the hearty laugh grinned at Widow Thomsen and tipped his tricorne hat. His success in raising healthy livestock was well known in the community and he generously helped out many who were in need.

But Mary noticed his spirit of giving seemed especially focused on one neighbor — her mother, Ruth Thomsen.

"Would tomorrow be a good day to bring those little piggies over, Widow Thomsen?" the farmer asked. "They're a fine lot this year, ma'am."

"Why yes, Mr. Eaton, tomorrow would be an excellent day. We shall have the enclosure ready for them. I thank you, sir."

He tipped his tricorne hat once again.

"After a bit then, ma'am." He walked back to his large horse.

Her mother grinned like a schoolgirl. "That's the same horse that took me home last winter after the blizzard."

Mary didn't want to think about cold weather. Winter was a distant memory today as they sat in the balmy breeze that carried the scents of lilacs and apple blossoms through the air.

After everyone had had a chance to rest, the congregation returned to the meetinghouse for afternoon service. Mary walked closely to Daniel, steering him clear of the Howard sisters whenever it seemed they might approach.

The preaching resumed for several more hours. Mary noticed many in the sedate group struggling to keep their eyes open. When their attempts failed, one of the ushers would faithfully bring the long pole with the squirrel's tail on the end to tickle the nose of the dreamer. The sight of this always made Mary laugh. Daniel seemed to find the practice quite amusing as well. They locked eyes and grinned at one another.

When the church meeting was finally over, the sleepy congregation slowly made their way out of the wooden building. The Thomsens were in somewhat of a hurry this afternoon as Aunt Prudence would be arriving at any time. She was coming to pick up Jubo and Gibb and bring them back to Bridgewater. The Thomsens bid farewell to their friends at church, explaining their need to hurry home.

Mary and Daniel walked together, followed by Widow Thomsen and Sarah. The mile-long hike was mostly uphill, and they walked as briskly as they could. They arrived home just in time for Aunt Prudence's arrival. This would be the woman's initial introduction to Daniel, and Mary did not know what to expect from her aunt. She did not have long to wait for the answer.

"Your intended?" Aunt Prudence said with obvious delight. "So you have taken my advice! Good lass!"

While Daniel shook Jubo's hand and then Gibb's, Aunt Prudence sized up Mary's future husband. Prudence leaned over to her great niece and whispered in Mary's ear. She was aghast at her aunt's carnal comment and felt her own face burn with embarrassment.

"Aunt Prudence!"

The older woman smiled and continued to stare at Daniel as the wagon pulled out of the farmyard. Daniel waved good-bye to her as she drove off. He looked at Mary with a confused expression.

"What did she whisper to you?"

Mary glanced at him and then looked away.

"Nothing that I shall ever share with you." She walked toward the house with her eyes looking downward.

∽⸺⸱◦

The next morning, Daniel watched Widow Thomsen hasten through the morning chores. Mr. Eaton was expected at any time and the pigpen needed cleaning.

"I can clean the pen, Widow Thomsen."

Mary raised her eyebrows in surprise. "Daniel, you've no experience with this foul-smelling chore. I had best help you."

They walked out toward the field behind the barn. The enclosure was as far from the house as it could be placed but still close enough to easily tend the little piglets.

"Why is the pen so far out back?" Daniel looked at the lengthy distance to the house.

Mary looked at him and stifled a laugh. "You've obviously never smelled a pigpen before, Daniel Lowe."

"It has been quite some time. By the way, Mary Thomsen, why were you tempting me at meetinghouse yesterday? I was trying to concentrate on the reverend's words and you were doing your best to distract me."

She took hold of his arm. "I was doing my best to distract you from the glances of two sets of ladies' eyes."

"And I missed that? Were they pretty?" He grinned.

"Daniel, you are incorrigible." She placed her arm around his waist.

"And you," he said, taking her in his arms, "are far too beautiful for me to be tempted by any other woman."

"And you will be judged by your Maker for speaking such lies."

Daniel grew serious. "But I am not lying." He drew her close to himself and kissed Mary's lips. She did not pull away but allowed his mouth to linger on hers. When his kiss became more impassioned, he could feel Mary's arms become tense. He immediately stopped, seeing fear flash across her face. Silently, he cursed the intruder.

Mary began to tremble. "I am sorry, Daniel."

Daniel held her close. "You've nothing to apologize for. There are times when I wish I could kill him all over again. And yet, I know that is wrong and I pray God will forgive my unforgiving heart."

"You are a gift to me, Daniel Lowe. And I know that soon, I shall be able to forget that man's touch — because I long so for yours."

They held each other for several moments before resuming their task. The two had no sooner finished cleaning out the pen than Mr. Eaton's wagon came down the road. They could hear the squeals of the little animals coming from the crate in the back. Widow Thomsen and Sarah came outdoors to greet the man and his noisy cargo.

"Look at them, Mother." Sarah bustled with excitement. "Can we name them?"

The widow and Mr. Eaton looked at each other. Their faces seemed to envision the child's pet being turned in to Sunday sausage.

"Probably not the best idea, miss," Mr. Eaton replied.

Sarah, Widow Thomsen, and Mary each picked up one of the squirming piglets and laughed at their active antics. They each placed a piglet over their left shoulder, much as they would a human baby, and carried them out to the pen. The two men stared after the women.

"Some hideous-looking babies on those ladies' shoulders, eh?" Mr. Eaton jested. "Looks like Queen Charlotte's brood."

Daniel tried not to laugh but nodded in assent. He and his fellow soldiers in the camp had often discussed the plain look of their country's queen.

"You have a quick wit, Mr. Eaton."

Mr. Eaton continued to stare at the ladies. "Now that's a handsome woman."

Daniel looked at Mary. "Yes, she is, sir," he said with admiration.

Mr. Eaton looked at him and slapped his shoulder in jest. "I was talking about the widow, Mr. Lowe."

Confusion flummoxed Daniel's thoughts.

"Widow Thomsen?" His eyes narrowed.

"You young lads cannot imagine the beauty us old men see in a woman like her, can ya?"

"So… you are setting your eyes on Mary's mother?" Daniel tried to wrap his thinking around this unexpected conversation. "Are you married, sir?"

"Was. Been widowed some years now. Looking out for your lady's mother, are ya? Good lad." Mr. Eaton looked thoughtful. "These long winters get mighty cold, sir, if ya know what I mean."

Daniel did not know how to respond. He was completely bewildered by this exchange. There was much he was trying to comprehend.

Mr. Eaton became serious. "So I understand you have set your heart on Miss Thomsen. She is an admirable young woman."

"Yes, sir." Daniel smiled as he looked up at the field where Mary, her mother, and her sister were laughing at the piglets.

"You've been at war, Mr. Lowe. To be blunt, sir, I hope you've not brought home any peculiar diseases from the ladies in the camps. Wouldn't want to see Mary getting hurt now, would we?"

Daniel looked at Mr. Eaton squarely. "I have not, sir. I stayed away from the trulls and doxies. It's not that I was not tempted, but I saw enough of my friends suffering from one night's pleasure that it did not seem worth the cost."

Mr. Eaton paused for a long moment to look at the ground. He stared downward for so long that Daniel began to get nervous. *Trulls and doxies!* He inwardly groaned. *You are a fool, Daniel Lowe. Your own words have betrayed you.*

The former British soldier tried not to panic, but he felt a sweat beginning on his brow. When Mr. Eaton finally looked up he put his hand on Daniel's shoulder.

"Widow Thomsen told me how you took care of Mary when she had the grippe last winter," Mr. Eaton said. "You're a good man, Mr. Lowe."

The farmer started to unload the hay he had brought for Widow Thomsen's horse and cow. "I figure the way to a woman's heart is through the stomach of her livestock." Mr. Eaton laughed.

He paused in his work and looked again at Daniel. Mr. Eaton must have noticed the look of terror on Daniel's face and placed his hand on Daniel's shoulder in a fatherly manner.

"Any friend of Widow Thomsen's is a friend of mine as well. Any secrets you may have, lad, are safe with me."

Mr. Eaton became a regular guest in the Thomsen home that summer — much to Mary's dismay.

"Mother, why must he come to our home for dinner so often?" Mary did not try to hide her annoyance.

"Mary, you know how lonely he has been since his youngest daughter married last winter. He now has no one with whom he can share his supper. 'Tis the least we can do for the man in return for all he does for our family." Widow Thomsen made it clear the matter was settled.

Still, Mary wondered about this blooming friendship between the older couple. She asked Daniel what he thought about it when they were walking toward the town square. They were going to the second anniversary celebration of the Declaration of Independence. It was early evening and the mosquitoes were having a feast on them both. Daniel seemed to ponder Mary's question before he replied.

"I think Mr. Eaton is quite fond of your mother." He swat at yet another insect and kept his voice low, since the widow and Sarah were not too far behind.

Mary seemed startled. "Fond?" She repeated the word quite loudly, then remembered to keep her voice low as well. "How can that be? My mother is far too old for such affection, do you not think?"

"I think," Daniel said slowly, "that your mother and Mr. Eaton are free to decide if they want to become friends or even develop a strong attachment for one another."

Mary grew silent as she contemplated his words. The thought of her mother setting her eyes on another man was disquieting, not to mention unexpected, but she knew Daniel was right. Both her mother and Mr. Eaton were widowed and they were certainly free to pursue one another. However, it would take Mary some time to get used to this idea.

As the group of four approached the festivities, they saw the object of their discussion approaching.

"Good day, Mr. Eaton." Widow Thomsen's face brightened. Mary wondered if her mother was always this animated around the older man. Her mother's cheeks even seemed a deeper shade of red when she looked at him.

"It's a good day when we can celebrate the freedom of this new country of ours." Mr. Eaton seemed in fine form.

It seemed the whole town of Deer Run had come out for the celebration.

"I'm feeling quite nervous." Daniel expressed his anxiety quietly to Mary. The heat induced volumes of sweat from everyone, Daniel most of all.

"Will you be all right, Daniel?" Mary noticed the strain on his face.

"Perhaps I'd best practice looking relaxed."

Mary took his arm. Her demeanor and touch calmed him while he limped beside her amongst the townsfolk who raised their ale tankards and sang loudly about freedom from "bloody King George."

Several of the men in the town set up wood for bonfires. These would be kindled in celebration of the United States of America declaring its liberty. The fires would be lit simultaneously right after the reading of the Declaration of Independence by Selectman Jonathan Grant.

Children ran everywhere. Some of them played Ring around the Rosie around the village liberty pole. Most villages in Massachusetts as well as other colonies had set up these wooden poles in prominent positions in the center of town. They were a silent declaration of their support for the troops fighting in battle and their own wish for freedom from England. Mary explained that a ribbon was attached to the pole for each Minuteman from Deer Run. Asa Thomsen's ribbon was now a black one.

Since most of the younger men were off at war, there were not the usual sporting events included in the festivities that often accompanied town celebrations. Instead, clusters of older men and young teenagers stood around discussing the affairs of the struggling nation. When they saw Daniel approaching arm-in-arm with Mary, they drew him in to the conversation.

"So, Mr. Lowe." A gent with long, thinning hair pulled him into the group. "What is your take on the French getting involved in helping our troops? Those bloody frogs were the enemy not so many years ago, and now we're lookin' to fight side-by-side with 'em." The villager wiped sweat off his forehead while awaiting an answer.

Daniel tried not to appear surprised, for he had not yet heard of this alliance with France. He weighed his words carefully before replying.

"I think that, in the course of time and various circumstances, those who were once our enemies can just as quickly become our friends. Much to everyone's surprise." Daniel attempted to hide his anxiety from these Colonials. All the men in the group stared at him while they pondered his words.

The silence was abruptly broken by another gentleman with thick gray hair and a tankard of ale. The liquid spirits kept spilling every time the excitable man spoke.

"See," he said, "I told you it could work."

Everyone began to talk at once and Daniel felt Mary's arm encouraging him away. She seemed to understand this was not a comfortable setting with so many strangers, and he with so much to hide.

"Ah, that Miss Thomsen already has her hooks in you, Mr. Lowe." The men teased him as they left the group. Daniel looked back at the group of men and smiled.

When he turned around again he took a deep breath and whispered, "Thank you. You are a rock of strength to me."

"We can go back to the farm, Daniel. We can make up a plausible excuse."

"No, I shall be all right. This is something I must do if I am to be a part of your life here."

She gazed at him with affection. "I hope you know how deeply I love you, Daniel Lowe." Her lips enticed him.

"If you keep talking that way, Miss Thomsen, I shall have to kiss you passionately right here in front of this whole town." He spoke under his breath and only half teasingly.

The town bell rang out thirteen times, each ring representing an American colony. She and Daniel watched as a group of thirteen men with muskets fired toward an empty field. Each gun was loaded and shot thirteen times as a salute to the new nation.

It was late in the day, so everyone began to gather outside the meetinghouse for the reading of the Declaration of Independence. It was a somber moment full of emotion, as the words of Thomas Jefferson were read by Selectman Grant, a veteran of the French and Indian War. When Daniel heard the man's name announced by Reverend Phillips, he looked over at Mary inquisitively. Mary looked at him and nodded.

"Yes," she said, "that is Josiah's father."

The older man was similar in appearance to Josiah, but the resemblance ended there, as the father had a more humble demeanor in both his countenance and his speech. He read the Declaration with a clear, audible tone, obviously moved by the passion underlying the text. It was easy to understand why Mr. Grant had been chosen to do the reading.

"When in the Course of human events, it becomes necessary for one people to dissolve the political bands which have connected them with another, and to assume among the powers of the earth, the separate and equal station to which the Laws of Nature and of Nature's God entitle them, a decent respect to the opinions of mankind requires that they should declare the causes which impel them to a separation.

"We hold these truths to be self-evident, that all men are created equal, that they are endowed by their Creator with certain unalienable Rights, that among these are Life, Liberty and the Pursuit of Happiness. — That to secure these rights, Governments are instituted among Men, deriving their just powers from the consent of the governed, — That whenever any Form of Government becomes destructive of these ends, it is the Right of the People to alter or abolish it, and to institute new Government..."

The speaker continued with the words that listed the "long train of abuses" King George had levied against the colonies.

Daniel listened in awe at the words. He'd never heard this document read before or seen it in print. The colonists' message of outrage and their fervor to obtain justice for the people of America awakened his understanding of the Revolution.

Sunset was upon them. Unbidden tears worked a path down Daniel's face. Mary placed her arm around his waist and rested her head against his shoulder. His spirit was unexpectedly moved by the whole event as he put his arms around her shoulders.

Mr. Grant slowly and fervently read the final line to the audience of listeners: "And for the support of this Declaration, with a firm reliance on the protection of Divine Providence, we mutually pledge to each other our Lives, our Fortunes, and our sacred Honor."

Selectman Grant rolled up the parchment and slowly walked off of the meetinghouse steps.

There was not a dry face in the group of onlookers who stood in silence. The mood was so somber that none seemed of a mind to move. Everyone knew what this document had already cost, and they all knew they were not yet finished paying the price of this Revolution. Many had already paid with their lives.

All at once, one of the town leaders shouted out, "Light the bonfires!" The flames were lit in the three piles of wood simultaneously. It was a splendid sight, as the glow from the fires glimmered across the tear-stained faces in the crowd. The whole town stood watching the flames for several moments in silence.

Gradually, hushed conversations began in a few small groups while other townsfolk began their walk home. The Thomsens were in this latter group, somberly heading back toward the farm. Mr. Eaton approached Widow Thomsen and offered to drive them all back to the farm on his wagon. Sarah was beginning to fall asleep, leaning against her mother, and the widow gladly accepted the ride.

Mary spoke up. "I think Daniel and I will walk back, Mr. Eaton, but thank you for your kind offer." Mr. Eaton gave an understanding smile to the young couple.

"Don't get lost on the way." He winked.

When the wagon pulled out of sight ahead of them, Mary looked at Daniel. "You look troubled."

He stopped walking for a moment. Now that they were out of sight of the townspeople, he took her in his arms and kissed her. She responded in kind and they held each other for a long while.

When they resumed walking, Daniel finally spoke.

"For the first time today, I've begun to understand this Revolution. Not just in my mind but in my heart as well. It both excites me and grieves me, as I feel as if everything I've been doing for the past few years has been for naught." He paused. "The arrogance of the King had become my arrogance. I have been a part of hurting innocent people, forcing them to submit to the Crown."

His words caught in his throat. "It was wrong. I was wrong."

Mary paused in mid-step and took his face in both of her hands.

"You thought you were doing the right thing." She met his eyes. "I know you, Daniel. You are a man who would choose the honorable way."

He put his arms around her waist.

"But it was not always honorable. I… I can still hear those words read from the Declaration: 'sent hither swarms of Officers to harass our people, and eat out their substance.' I was one of those officers, swarming like a hornet, following the King's orders." He paused, struggling to contain his emotions. "It is unforgivable."

He looked off in the distance down the hill, observing the lighted bonfires still glowing dimly in the darkness.

"Nothing is unforgivable in the eyes of God." Mary drew his face to look at hers.

"But can you forgive me for my part in this war?"

"Yes, Daniel. You do not need my forgiveness. But if you are asking for it, yes, I forgive you."

She stood on her tiptoes and kissed him. He held onto her as never before and wept for so much that he had lost, and for all that he had gained but did not deserve. They embraced in silence, and then just as silently, resumed the walk up the hill toward the farm.

Mr. Eaton had already passed them on the way back down the hill. He waved to them both in his friendly manner, winking at Daniel as he drove by. When they reached the farmyard, Daniel noticed the outdoor fire from earlier that day. The widow and Mary had been doing washing in the huge kettle over those flames and there were still a few embers glowing in the darkness.

"Please wait here." Daniel walked over to the barn and after a few moments walked out with something in his hands. As he drew closer to her, recognition of the object dawned on Mary's face — his red coat of the King's army. He also carried a powder horn.

Daniel walked over to the glowing coals. He took one last look at the stained scarlet wool, sprinkled a small amount of gunpowder on the material, and threw it on the fire. He drew Mary away from the flames. As the fibers fed the embers, it quickly ignited in a rupture of energy that made Mary gasp. Placing his arm around her, they watched the uniform disintegrate. All that remained were the silver buttons. The deed was done.

Mary turned and looked up at Daniel. They kissed with a passion that encompassed so many thoughts and emotions. Their embrace had never lingered for so long and Mary's heart raced as never before. She felt Daniel holding her closer than he'd ever done and she had a sudden and surprising realization. Not only was she no longer fearful of the intruder's touch — she did not want this embrace to stop.

In a moment of clear thinking, she pushed Daniel away. His lips were moist and his eyes heavy. He stared at her and seemed out of breath.

"You are no longer afraid of me." He seemed more than a little pleased.

"I'm only afraid I will not stop." Her voice trembled but she smiled and took a step away from him.

"Can we marry soon, then — so we do not need to stop?"

"Yes." She nodded with vigor. "The sooner the better."

24

United

I don't know what she sees in that face, Daniel Lowe." He studied his reflection in a small looking glass. "You look quite the ragged bloke to me."

It was July 28, the day of the wedding. He'd spent little time perusing his appearance in the last few months. As he stood in the barn observing his reflection, he was once again disconcerted to see the long red scar on his right cheek — a permanent reminder of the intruder's knife. But Daniel also had an older look about him — lines etched in his skin that reflected the last two years of pain and struggle. Anyone might have easily mistaken him for a man several years older than his twenty-three years of age.

As he shaved away the last remnants of facial bristle, he went too close to his skin, causing a small cut.

"Blasted razor!" He wiped away the blood as best he could and started to put on his white linen shirt. He realized how nervous he was as his fingers trembled while buttoning up the garment.

Daniel began to think about his father back home in England. Here Daniel was about to be wed, yet his parent had no idea the event was taking place. There were so many things he would have liked to ask his father, but communicating during the war was too much of a risk.

"So how is the future husband doing this morning?" The voice of Mr. Eaton broke into his thoughts. Daniel turned to look at him. "I see you've been wrestling with an angry razor there," the older man said.

"I am all thumbs this morning." Daniel tried to finish up the last of his shirt buttons.

"A bit shaky there, lad?" Mr. Eaton patted Daniel on the shoulder. "You'll be fine. No regrets about this wedding?"

Daniel looked at the man in surprise. "Regrets about marrying Mary? Good heavens, no. I still cannot believe she will have me. Just look at me." He pointed to his scar. "And that is not the worst of the lot. My leg wound is hideously scarred — I hope it does not frighten her."

Mr. Eaton stared at him. "If you think Mary Thomsen would be terrified by a mere scar on a leg, then you do not know your future wife. She is made of much hardier stock than you know, lad. Besides, I've seen the way she looks at you. I've never seen her look at another lad like that before. You're a lucky man, Daniel Lowe."

Daniel beamed. He took his blue waistcoat off of a hook on the wall and slipped his arms through the sleeve holes. He turned toward Mr. Eaton. "May I talk to you… man to man, that is?"

"Aye, be happy to." He grinned and rubbed his cheek with his hand. "Never got to have a weddin' talk with a young man before. Had all girls, we did… seven of 'em!"

Daniel's eyes widened. "Seven lasses?"

"Aye. Got 'em all married off now. Lots of grandbabies, too."

"You must be quite proud." Daniel hesitated for a moment and took a deep breath. "So… were you and Missus Eaton… happy?"

"You mean under the quilts?" Mr. Eaton laughed. "Aye, very happy. And those seven daughters? They didn't all start out in this world as my idea, if you know what I mean." The older man slapped him heartily on the shoulder.

Daniel smiled nervously. Mr. Eaton regarded Daniel with a look of sympathy. "I remember my own weddin' day, lad." He put his arm in a fatherly gesture around Daniel's shoulders. "Come. Take a walk with me."

The two men were in a deep conversation in the distance when Mary looked out the window from the farmhouse.

"I wonder what Daniel and Mr. Eaton are doing?" She scanned the distance with narrowed eyes. "You don't suppose Daniel has changed his mind and Mr. Eaton is trying to talk him into staying, do you?" Mary clutched a lace cap and twisted it nervously back and forth in her hands. It was the cap she would be wearing for the ceremony.

"That is not likely, dear." Widow Thomsen shook her head in exasperation. "Mary, you will ruin that lace if you keep twisting it like that. Please sit back down and let me finish your hair."

Mary wore the same indigo-dyed dress her mother had worn on her wedding day. It was made of soft linen fabric that felt cool and comfortable on this warm summer morning. The lace kerchief that draped below her neckline matched the cap that would complete her attire. Mary kept pacing the small room that was to be hers and Daniel's. She had waited so long for this day. Now she feared something would interfere with the wedding.

"Mary, please sit down!" Her mother's voice sounded exasperated.

Mary resigned herself to sitting still and placed herself on the edge of the bed. She sat at an angle so her mother could reach her hair. "Where are the blue and green quilts, Mary?"

She turned to her Mother with a mischievous smile. "'Tis a surprise... for Daniel." Mary offered no further explanation and her mother did not press for details.

"Mother, I am a little nervous." Mary turned around as the last hairpin was placed. "Weren't you at all... fearful?"

Her mother smiled. "I remember my own wedding day. I was terrified," she admitted, "but I was so in love with your father, the fears slowly melted away." Widow Thomsen swept a piece of Mary's hair that had loosened from its pin back into its position. "Your father was a gentle man and... I think he was as nervous as I was."

"But... what if I do not please him? What if he is not happy with me?"

Widow Thomsen put her arm around her daughter. "Let us have a talk."

⌐~◦

The wedding was a simple event with very few guests. Daniel was so relieved that Mr. Eaton was there, encouraging him with an occasional smile.

Hannah White had come at Mary's request, holding the bouquet of lavender flowers and roses for Mary while she and Daniel said their vows.

Mary's eyes were locked upon his as they promised to love and cherish one another through sickness and health.

Reverend Phillips officiated the ceremony. He grinned at them as he read the words that would unite them as husband and wife.

Widow Thomsen and Sarah wore their best linen dresses. Daniel noticed Mary's mother fighting back tears at the sight of her daughter becoming a married woman.

As Daniel took Mary's hands, he noticed hers were as moist as his own. He looked at her long fingers remembering the first time he had laid eyes upon them back in the woods. It seemed so very long ago. So much had occurred since then. But he could still remember the feel of her fingers smoothing away the sores on his hands and her gentle touch offering him comfort.

Mary glanced down at Daniel's hands holding hers. She thought of his comforting touch when she had been so ill. She recalled his protective grip on her after the assault by the intruder. These were the hands that had held her, loved her, cared for her.

They both looked at each other's eyes as they completed their vows.

Their words affirmed in front of this small gathering that the couple had decided, no matter what, that their love would endure. They would not allow anything in this world to tear them apart. No war, no set of ideals, no government would ever come between them.

"I now declare that you, Daniel, and you, Mary, are married in the eyes of God and according to the laws of the Commonwealth of Massachusetts," Reverend Phillips concluded. He looked over at Daniel. "You may now kiss your wife."

Daniel hesitated just a moment before leaning down to her with trembling lips. Hers were trembling as well, but she eagerly returned the kiss.

This is really happening. We are truly husband and wife. Her heart skipped a beat with a joy she could hardly describe.

The hugs and handshakes of congratulations began. Wine was poured for all, except for Sarah, who had turned seven in June. She was given some cider instead. Mr. Eaton continued to pat Daniel on the back, giving him an occasional mischievous wink. Hannah, though clearly happy, occasionally wiped away an errant tear from her eye. Sarah danced around the room, asking for another piece of the spicy wedding cake her mother had made.

But Daniel and Mary had eyes for only each other. When they felt they had lingered an appropriate amount of time with the guests, they looked at each other and slipped out the door.

Widow Thomsen sat across from the reverend. She discussed Daniel's plans to build a log cabin on the road to Deer Run. It was a section of the Thomsen farm she was deeding over to the couple as a wedding gift.

"I was just telling Mary... Mary?" Widow Thomsen began looking around the room for the new bride. The reverend's back was to the window and she was relieved, because at that same instant she saw Daniel and Mary running off into the woods. Her eyes widened at the sight and her face grew hot. This prompted the reverend to follow her gaze toward the window.

Before he could see the couple escaping amongst the trees, she gently grabbed his arm and said, "More wine, Reverend Phillips?"

Daniel and Mary were out of breath from running and laughing. When he knew they were out of sight of the farmhouse, Daniel pulled on her arm to stop her. He drew her close to himself and started kissing and embracing her more freely than he ever had before.

Breathless, Mary pushed against his chest. "Wait." She laughed.

Daniel was crestfallen. "Wait?" he said in confusion. "Why?"

"I have a surprise for you. Meet me at the wigwam." Mary backed away from her husband a few steps and pulled off her lace cap. She then untied the kerchief at the neckline of her low bodice, removed the lace accouterment, and threw it playfully at Daniel. She smiled flirtatiously and then ran off into the woods.

"You are a cruel wife." Daniel called after her as he struggled to keep up with his new bride. His leg ached and he had to slow down his pace. This gave Mary the advantage of arriving there several moments ahead of him.

When he finally came to the familiar bark enclosure, he slowly opened the door. What he saw made his heart race.

Mary had set up their marriage bed. She had placed piles of fresh straw on the ground — bedding she had carried one armload at a time from the Thomsen farm. On top of the straw, she had laid two clean quilts. A flask of wine lay next to the quilts and bouquets of lavender flowers were everywhere, permeating the wigwam with their sweet aroma.

His new bride had taken out every pin from her hair. Her waist-length locks enveloped her shoulders, which were covered only with her sheer night shift.

Daniel could barely breathe as he began to fumble with the buttons on his waistcoat.

Mary drew close to him. "Let me help." She carefully undid each button she had lovingly sewn. She touched his chest and looked up at him.

"Welcome home, my husband."

He leaned over to kiss and embrace her — and bask in the warmth of her touch. Daniel paused only long enough to close the wigwam door.

25

Letters

Dawn was breaking that late August morning when Daniel awoke. The opened window allowed a soft breeze to cool the humid air. In the distant woods, Daniel heard the mournful cooing of a pheasant looking for its mate. Susannah gave a gentle bellow in the barn as if to hurry up the hands that would milk her, and Dash whinnied.

The smell of the maturing crops in the field wafted through the open window, competing with the aroma of lavender water that was the scent of the woman lying next to him. He snuggled in closer to the back of her neck and kissed her skin and hair.

Mary stirred slightly but did not awaken. Daniel held her close, still marveling at the circumstances that had brought them together at such a time and place. On occasion, he rubbed his eyes to make sure he had not just imagined Mary was his wife.

He caressed her skin and nuzzled her shoulder. She started to move slightly and opened her eyes sleepily.

"Happy birthday, Mary." Daniel spoke in hushed tones so as not to awaken Widow Thomsen and Sarah in the next room.

Mary smiled dreamily and turned to face her husband.

"Thank you, Daniel."

He leaned over his young wife and pressed against her lips. As the kiss became more passionate, they heard Widow Thomsen close the front door on her way to milk Susannah.

He looked mischievously at Mary, then threw the quilts over them both and enveloped her in his arms.

When they emerged from their room, Mary saw that Sarah still slept. Mary walked toward the hearth to stir the porridge.

Her mother returned from milking Susannah. "It's going to be another hot day, I'm afraid." She wiped the perspiration from her forehead, then stopped her morning activities while grinning at Mary.

"Happy birthday, Mary." She gave her a hug. "Twenty years of age. It does not seem possible."

"Thank you, Mother."

"Yes, Mother Thomsen, thank you for having Mary." Daniel placed his arm around her. "I cannot imagine my life without her."

"Nor can I imagine life without you." Mary kissed him slowly on the lips before returning to the hearth to stir the gruel.

Sarah sat up in bed rubbing her eyes and yawning. "Happy birthday, Mary. When do we get to eat your cake?"

"Later," Widow Thomsen said, "after we have our supper. Hannah is coming to join us."

Hannah White had shared Mary's birthday dinner with the family every year for as long as Mary could remember. It had been at her fifteenth birthday when James took notice of Hannah. James was seventeen then and could not take his eyes off the young farm girl. His obvious stares of appreciation for Hannah's beauty finally forced Widow Thomsen to send him out to do some chores.

"Mother, do you remember when James tripped and fell?" Mary laughed at the memory. "He was so taken with Hannah at my fifteenth birthday party that he completely missed the step outside when he went to milk Susannah. Poor James turned so red in the face! It was all Hannah could do not to burst out laughing!"

Widow Thomsen chuckled at the recollection.

'Tis good to see Mother smile so.

"How come I do not remember that?" Sarah wiped a splotch of gruel from her face.

"Because, little miss, you were only two." Daniel pointed his spoon at the girl. "If it makes you feel better, I do not remember the occasion either."

"Daniel and I do not remember it." Sarah giggled. "'Tis strange to call you by your Christian name."

"So may I call you by your Christian name?"

Sarah contemplated his question. "No, I think not. You may still call me 'little miss.' But no one else may do so. That is your special name for me." Her little sister seemed so serious, Mary could barely hold back laughter.

"Quite so, little miss. 'Twill be my privilege alone." Daniel's mock serious expression matched Sarah's.

Mary groaned at their declaration but grinned in amusement. She was grateful her husband blended so well with her family, as if he had been a part of them all along. And now that he was a part of her, she felt complete.

"Let us get the chores done before the heat sets in." Widow Thomsen fanned herself with a towel.

Daniel drank a large tankard of cider. "Time to head out for the flax field."

Mary touched his hand. "I hate how hard you've had to work these many days, Daniel. Flax is so difficult and I know this heat is taxing."

He pecked her on the cheek. "I'll drink plenty and rest when I must."

By noon, Mary saw her exhausted husband walking toward the farmhouse covered with dirt and sweat. She had just finished digging up turnips and sweet potatoes from the vegetable garden and carried a basketful. She thrilled at the sight of her husband.

Even covered in grime he is still the most handsome man.

They both stopped at the basin on the log near the front door. They used bayberry soap and water to wash their faces and hands. The water still dripped off Daniel's chin when he leaned over and kissed her wet face.

"May I kiss you twenty times today in honor of your twentieth birthday?" Daniel grinned like a naughty schoolboy.

"Why so few?" Mary asked in mock displeasure.

"Well then, I had best get started since you require so many."

They were still laughing when they went in to the farmhouse to eat their noon meal. Mary's mouth watered at the smell of cooked vegetables from the garden, cheese, salt pork, and more cider. They all ate heartily, then rested in their chairs around the table.

Daniel leaned back in his chair and stretched. "So, Mother Thomsen, tell me about when Mary was born."

Widow Thomsen got a faraway look on her face.

"'Twas a wonderful day and a sad one as well," her mother began.

"Sad?" Mary was surprised. "You never told me that."

"Well, it was mostly happy because you were born, Mary. A strong and beautiful child — you made my heart melt when I laid eyes on you. But the sad part was your father was not there to see you, and he could not come for several days."

"Why have you never told me this before?" Mary's jaw opened in amazement.

"I suppose because I always just dwelt on the happier side of the memory." She smiled but her eyes moistened. "It all started when family came to visit from Bridgewater. We had a lovely time seeing them, of course, but one of the young ones was not feeling too well. After they left we received a letter from a postrider that said the ill child had smallpox and we should take measures to contain the contagion. 'Twas not four days later that your brother James came down with the illness. He was but two years old."

This news stunned Mary. "What happened?"

"Your father had to send me away because I was with child — I was carrying you, Mary. Your father took care of little James and made arrangements hastily for some friends to take me to stay with Widow Baxter, the midwife in Williamston. I stayed with her for two weeks before you were born." The widow wiped at a tear as she recalled the difficult separation. "I had to write your father a letter to tell him he had a beautiful daughter."

Everyone was silent, then the widow continued. "But little James recovered well and no one else came down with the dreaded pox. When your father was finally able to come to Williamston, he looked at you, Mary, with his handsome green eyes and said, 'Welcome, my sweet daughter.'"

Mary's eyes brimmed with tears. "I miss Father." She wiped the wetness from her cheeks.

Daniel took her hand. "So that is where you got those beautiful eyes." Mary gazed with affection at her husband.

"Well, then." Widow Thomsen spoke quickly as she wiped away her own tears. "This day is not getting any longer." She stood up from her chair and began to pick up the bowls.

Daniel and Mary began to clean up from the meal and then retired for some rest from the heat and work. The young couple lay down in their bed and fell in to a deep slumber with Mary nestled against Daniel.

When Mary awoke hours later, she was by herself in the bed. She arose sleepily from the quilts and came in to the main room.

"Where is Daniel?" She looked at her mother who was preparing the cake for the evening's birthday celebration.

"He is in the barn working on something. I think 'tis a surprise for you."

"I wonder what it could be?" She tried to imagine what Daniel was up to.

"Hannah is here." Sarah ran for the door to let her in.

Hannah carried a large basket with fresh cherries and green apples from her orchard, but the young woman bore something far more valuable than produce. She toted letters from James — one for the whole family and one just for Mary, for her birthday.

"James asked me to hold on to these until Mary's birthday, Widow Thomsen," Hannah explained. "I hope you do not mind waiting these extra few days for word from him?"

Widow Thomsen trembled as she held the pages. "No, of course not. I'm just so relieved he is well."

They all sat down to hear the news from James, gone to war now for over two years. The widow began to read aloud:

My dearest Mother and Sisters,
Words cannot convey how much I miss you. I pray for you every

day as I know that I am in your prayers as well. I trust that the Lord is watching over you, as He has been so faithful in doing for me.

This war seems as if it goes on forever. We have been fighting southward from you. I cannot disclose the location, but I can tell you that our troops continue on with great fervor and excellence of endeavor.

General Washington continues as always to be an inspiring leader, even rallying our troops when others (that is Major General Lee) had our men in complete disarray. I must confess to our troops giving a hearty cheer when, due to Lee's inept leadership, Gen. Washington was inspired to set off a volley of oaths at the man. (I know you will think this offensive, Mother—please forgive me this small pleasure).

The heat has been unbearable causing the loss of nearly one hundred of our soldiers. It seems that if it is not agonizingly cold in our battles, then it is insufferably hot. Disease continues to plague us in the camps.

But I will not belabor these difficulties. I am certain that you are bearing your own arduous endeavors just trying to survive.

I hope to obtain leave to see all of you within the next year. I have enclosed a separate letter for Mary since I know it is soon time for her twentieth birthday. And of course, a private correspondence for Hannah.

With my earnest hope and prayers for seeing you all soon.

Your loving son and brother, James.

Widow Thomsen set the letter down in her lap and wept. Hannah, Mary, and Sarah all gathered round her in an embrace, fresh tears on their faces. Daniel walked in from the barn and saw the distraught group.

"What has happened?" His brows furrowed in concern.

Mary looked up at her husband. "We finally received news from James. He is well, but we have been so fearful for his safety that we are crying with relief."

He looked visibly relieved. "I am grateful he is well."

"Let us get the cake ready." Her mother rose from her chair and busied herself with food preparations. "There is comfort for me in staying occupied." She set out plates for the dessert.

They were soon in a festive mood, celebrating Mary's twenty years. This was an especially memorable birthday for Mary, as it was her first as a married woman. She was unable to keep her eyes off her new husband, the main source of her joy on this happy occasion. She still had to pinch herself at times to be sure she was not dreaming.

After the birthday song was sung and the cake served, Daniel presented Mary with the surprise he'd been working on. It was a wooden deer to decorate the base of Mary's distaff on her spinning wheel. On the deer were inscribed the initials "DL" and "ML" with a carved heart in between.

Mary held the gift in her hand as if it were the most precious possession in the world, worth far more than gold. She didn't know how to express her gratitude.

"Mr. Eaton taught me how to whittle the wood." He shifted his feet, looking embarrassed.

"Thank you, Daniel," she whispered. Her heart overflowed with love for this man. "Thank you, so much." She put her arms around him and held him tight.

Hannah smiled but then became somber. "Well," she said, "'tis time I went back home. Father will be looking for me before dark." Her friend stood up and everyone bid her farewell.

Mary thanked her for coming and the two long-time friends hugged warmly.

It was after Mary and Daniel had retired to their room for the night when Mary finally had a chance to read the letter James had written just for her.

Dear Mary,

So you are now a young woman of twenty. 'Tis difficult to believe my little sister is so grown up. I wish so that I could be there to make sure that you are well and that only young men of good character are pursuing you.

Ever since I was little, I have felt a strong urge to protect you. If there was danger involved, I wanted to be the one to stand between you and whatever the threat was. Unfortunately, my desire to protect you and the rest of the family necessitates me being so far away, as the threat is far wider and greater than a mere mean-spirited bully from a village.

The danger is our Mother country, who has abandoned her infant colonies and denied them her maternal sustenance. I will be eternally grateful when this new country of ours has left the birth nest and flown to freedom. Then we can rest in the loving arms of liberty. Be well, my dear sister, and know that I am fighting for you on this your birthday.

Your loving brother, James

Then there was a postscript added. "Be assured of the necessity of staying away from Josiah Grant."

I already surmised the need for that. She sighed. *And now, dear brother, I am a married woman. But you would not know that.*

Mary looked up and saw her husband gazing at her, waiting for her to finish reading.

"Please come to bed with me." His voice whispered as he held out his arms to her.

She happily complied with his request.

26

Expectations

M ary walked on unsteady legs as she entered the farmhouse. "I don't feel well." As she spoke to her mother, she could hear her voice shake. A rush of panic caused her to hurry into her bedroom just in time to vomit in the basin.

It was late September and Mary had picked through her gruel at breakfast, her usual hearty appetite now dulled.

She lay on the bed breathing in spurts, waves of nausea roiling inside. She tried to open her eyes, but the room kept spinning so she closed them tight. Her mother placed a cool cloth on her forehead.

After several moments the tumultuous sensation in her stomach began to ebb and Mary opened her eyes.

"I don't know what happened. I was just bending to get the sweet potatoes from the ground and my head started to spin. I thought I would vomit right there, but after a few seconds the feeling stopped — for a moment anyway. When I did not feel much better, I decided I had best come inside out of the sun."

Sarah came into the room, a concerned look on her face. "Are you ill, Mary?"

"I'll be fine, Sarah. I'm just so very tired today."

"Sarah, please go in and stir the vegetables. Then set the tableboard for our supper, dear." Their mother shooed Sarah out of the room.

Sarah still had a furrowed brow. "Please get well, Mary." The child dutifully left the room.

Mary attempted a smile, then closed her eyes again. "I don't think I can eat anything. I'm still feeling queasy."

"'Twill not hurt you to miss a meal or two. Just try to eat a few bites every day, several times a day."

Mary looked at her mother quizzically. "I don't understand what you are saying, Mother. Every day? I'm certain I just ate something disagreeable to my digestion, or perhaps 'tis the heat. I shall recover by tomorrow."

"You will certainly recover." Widow Thomsen gave a mischievous look. "In about nine months or so."

Mary opened her eyes as wide as she could. She sat up too quickly, bringing on the nausea again, which forced her to lie back down.

"Nine months?" *How can this be?* "But we've only just been married two months. What will Daniel think? What if he's disappointed?"

Fear gripped her thoughts as she mused over Daniel's reaction. Her mother sat down on the bed and patted her arm.

"I'm quite sure Daniel is aware this can happen. Why would he be so surprised — or even disappointed? Give the man a chance. Most fathers get used to the idea, whether they thought it would happen or not."

"But… are you sure that I am with child?" Mary's mind whirled.

"Have you been in the manner of a woman recently?"

"Well, no… I suppose I was not even paying attention to that. I have not been in that manner since Daniel and I were married."

Mary's lips trembled and tears welled in her eyes as the reality of the situation became clear. "It is not that I do not wish for a child. I just do not know how Daniel will respond."

"You will both be capable parents." Her mother kissed her on top of the head and gave her a hug. She turned toward the doorway of the room when she heard the front door unlatch. "There's the young father, now," she whispered. "Do not wait too long before you tell him."

The widow stood up just as Daniel appeared in the doorway. His face fell with concern when he saw his wife lying on the bed.

"What's wrong, Mary?" He sat on the edge of the bed, took her hand and kissed it, looking anxious. "You're so pale."

"I'm faring better now," Mary responded in her bravest voice. "I think I was in the sun too long, that's all."

"May I get you something that will bring relief?" He smoothed her damp hair back from her face.

"No, I think I shall just rest for a bit." Mary's eyelids grew so heavy she was forced to close them. She fell into a deep slumber.

Daniel reluctantly left Mary's side and went to eat his dinner. He checked on his wife again after he was finished with his meal but found her still sleeping peacefully. He brushed his lips across her forehead and resumed the afternoon fieldwork.

When he returned, he immediately checked on her and found her stirring awake.

"I cannot believe I slept all afternoon." Mary sat up gingerly in their bed and took several slow breaths. "I'm so grateful my stomach has finally settled."

Daniel sat down and took her hand. "I've been thinking, Mary. I must be keeping you awake too much at night." Guilt flooded his conscience. "I am so very sorry. Please forgive me. You work so hard all day and then —"

"Daniel." She gently touched his lips with one finger and then stroked his cheek. "I love being with you. I love loving you."

"I do not want you to be ill because of me."

"I am not ill because of you. In fact, I am quite hungry now. Let's see what my mother has fixed for evening meal."

Mary's appetite seemed revived as she ate a hearty portion of gruel as well as sausage and vegetables. Now that everything appeared normal once again, Daniel relaxed and put his fears about her health to rest.

Mary, however, could not close her eyes after the candles were extinguished that night.

How will I tell Daniel? She fought back tears.

The next day was Sunday and everyone was in a hurry at the Thomsen house. Chores needed to be done early so they could attend service at the meetinghouse.

Once again, Mary picked away at her morning gruel, only managing to swallow a few bites. But she did not want to miss this day of worship and visiting with her friends, especially Hannah. There was much she wanted to share with her good friend today.

The family began the mile-long trek to the center of town. The walk was far easier on the way to the village, since it was downhill. Mary bravely marched next to her husband making every effort to keep up with his longer strides. His war injury caused him to limp but he still managed to outpace her.

They strode past the blacksmith, who worked on some new horseshoes for a mount belonging to a soldier who waited nearby.

I wonder if the sheriff will chide the smithy for working on Sabbath? She hoped the magistrate would understand the needs of a soldier during war.

Mary managed to maintain her composure until she and Daniel rounded the bend to the meetinghouse. There, affixed to the outside wall of the structure were three wolf heads. They had been recently hung following a bounty-induced hunt. The horrific sight startled Mary. The long fangs jutted out from the open jaws and dried blood covered the fur. The worst part of the macabre scene was the stench.

That familiar sick feeling gripped Mary. She was terrified she was going to vomit right in front of Daniel as well as the entire inhabitants of Deer Run. Releasing Daniel's arm, she scurried behind the meetinghouse building just as the waves of nausea overtook her.

Hannah had been standing just a few feet away and ran to help. Mary gasped for air as the retching slowly ebbed. As Mary took a kerchief from her to wipe her mouth, a smile spread across Hannah's face.

"When will your child be birthed?"

Mary looked at her friend who knew her so well. "Early May, I think." She plopped down on a log lest her shaking legs give out.

Daniel hurried around the edge of the building with fear in his eyes.

"Mary!" His voice was frantic with concern.

"I shall leave you two alone." Hannah rejoined her father, who was entering the meetinghouse.

Daniel sat next to Mary on the log and put his arm around her. "Does not your mother have any medicinals that can help you?" Anxiety filled his demeanor.

Mary fought back a smile and tried to appear serious. "She says that there is no medicine that can cure my condition."

Her husband appeared distraught.

The church congregation began singing a hymn. The plaintive melody coming through the open window seemed to add to Daniel's emotions as he bowed in silent prayer.

Mary saw the look of fear on his face and knew she could no longer leave him in misery. She drew his strong jaw to face her.

"Daniel, I am with child." She smoothed her fingers across the cheek of the man who held her heart.

The look on Daniel's face went from fear to confusion to relief and then joy all in a single moment. He hugged her tight and then released her.

"How long have you known?"

She looked down and bit her lip. "I must confess I have wondered for several days now, but I knew it in my heart yesterday when I became so ill." Her eyes narrowed as concern gripped her words. "Are you disappointed?"

Daniel seemed confused. "Disappointed? Why would you think I would be?"

She turned away from his intent gaze. "We've been married such a short time... I didn't know how you would feel."

It was Daniel's turn to bring her face toward his. "Mary, our love has made this child. God has sent him... or her to us because we became one. This child is a gift. You are a gift to me." He held her in a tender embrace and she clung to him for a long while.

Return

aniel had much weighing on his heart with this news of Mary's pregnancy.

He could not have been happier about the baby, but apprehension about the birthing that Mary would endure months from now instilled great anxiety. It was during his own mother's last childbirth that he had lost the first woman in his life. He was terrified of now losing the most important woman in his life, his beloved wife.

To add to his worries, Widow Thomsen seemed to expect Mary to work outside far too much. His growing impatience with his mother-in-law threatened to undo the normally peaceful household.

"Mother Thomsen, Mary needs to rest. She should not labor so hard outdoors."

The widow put her hands on her hips. "Daniel, women have been birthing babies since the beginning of time — AND working outdoors while carrying them. You mustn't coddle her so."

Daniel's anger nearly poured out until Mary interrupted the discussion.

"Mother. And Daniel. As long as I am not vomiting or completely exhausted, working in the garden will do me good. There is nothing worrisome about pulling a few weeds, Daniel. I have been doing such work since I was able to walk."

"She's got a point there, young man." Mr. Eaton, who was visiting on a late September evening, shared some baked pumpkin and milk with the family. "She'll know if she's doin' too much, lad. Mrs. Eaton always did."

Widow Thomsen had a pensive look on her face. "I do see your point though, Daniel. Perhaps if I had worked a bit less strenuously on the farm, I would have more children that survived."

Mary looked with sympathy at her mother. "I'm certain your losses still pain your heart, Mother."

"Perhaps you were right, Daniel, in wanting to allow Mary more rest."

Daniel's anger receded. "Thank you, Mother Thomsen."

As the days progressed, Mary's fatigue grew. Daniel assumed it was to be expected but his mother-in-law seemed surprised by her daughter's exhaustion.

When Mary awoke one morning in late September, her pale face with circles under her eyes prompted Daniel to send her back to bed. She returned to her quilts and mattress without arguing.

"Poor dear." Mother Thomsen shook her head.

"I'll be back at the flax field today, Mother Thomsen. Please call me if you or Mary need anything." Daniel drank a final gulp from his tankard of cider. "Just one more day should finish the job."

Daniel headed for the barn to retrieve the hetchel, a three-foot long wooden plank that had sixty sharp iron teeth affixed to the center of the board. These five-inch-long metal combs separated the strands of flax into fibers suitable for spinning. Once he was finished with the hetcheling today, the flax would be ready to hand over to the women. It had been difficult and tedious work, but he was satisfied with his nearly completed labors.

There was just a hint of autumn in the air. He welcomed the relief from the heat, as he was able to move more quickly at his task. These warm summers in America were an adjustment for him. Living most of his years in England, he was more accustomed to less sunshine and more rain. Still, he was beginning to adapt to this new land and home, and he looked forward to felling the trees on the land deeded to the young couple on their wedding day.

Daniel envisioned him and Mary in their own log cabin raising their family. His heart stirred with emotion as he thought about their expected child. He recalled the description he had read in the Psalms: Fearfully and wonderfully made. The realization caused him to pause in his labors and thank the Lord who had instilled life into this child, now forming in his wife.

Just thinking about Mary caused his heart to warm. His initial assessment from when he met her nearly a year ago still held true — she had completely disarmed his emotions. Long before he had met this young colonial woman and before the many months of disillusionment and defeat, Daniel Lowe had been a dedicated lieutenant in the King's army. He'd been loyal to the Crown, an expert marksman and fighter.

Settling down with a British wife had been somewhere in his future, he thought, but war was his skill and conquering opposing armies his goal.

That is, until Mary Thomsen conquered his heart. He knew when he met her that he would never be the same. And he knew when he met the Shepherd of his soul that he would be refined into the man God wanted him to be. He had surrendered to them both and he had no regrets.

As he contemplated these changes in his life, a lone figure coming down the dirt road caught his attention. He did not recognize the man, but he recognized the familiar deerskin uniform of the Continental forces. When the soldier came closer, Daniel greeted the man.

"May I help you, sir?" Daniel viewed the stranger with caution.

"Just lookin' to see Miss Mary Thomsen, not that it's your concern, sir."

He may not have recognized the face, but Daniel would never forget that voice. He had heard it from the bed where he had been recovering from his wound nearly a year ago. That voice belonged to Josiah Grant.

"I do believe you are referring to Missus Daniel Lowe, sir." Daniel glared at the man. "She is my wife."

The words struck the Continental soldier like a physical blow. He stopped short in his brisk walk toward the farmhouse.

"Your wife? That cannot be. She was waitin' for me." Josiah's eyes widened in anger and disbelief.

"That is obviously not true, sir."

"Everyone in town knows that's true." Josiah's voice rose with rage, his face turning a bright shade of red.

"Then why is it that no one in Deer Run objected to our marriage? The announcement was posted at the meetinghouse for three Sundays, sir."

Daniel kept seeing in his mind the bruises that this man had inflicted upon his wife's arms so very long ago. The thought still enraged him.

Josiah's attempt at speaking failed as his words caught in his throat.

"Good day, sir," Daniel snapped.

Fighting back the fury, he knew he was finished working the flax today. He needed to return to the farmhouse and cool off from his anger. Daniel picked up the long hetchel and turned to walk back to the house.

An ugly laugh erupted from Josiah.

"Well, Mr. Lowe. You were not the first with her you know."

Daniel stopped in his tracks, his back to the man. His heart raced with fury. From the corner of his eye, he viewed the sharp metal prongs pointing upward on the hetchel sitting on his shoulder.

It would be so easy to impale this liar on those spikes and be done with the man. In the same moment he repented of this murderous thought.

But the object of Daniel's hatred was not finished with his lies just yet.

"So tell me, Mr. Lowe, is her skin still so soft under the quilts?"

The soldier could get no further in his slander. In a swift and studied maneuver, Daniel spun the hetchel over his arm and forcefully plied the wooden end of the tool into Josiah's jaw. The spurned suitor landed with a thud on the ground. The stunned soldier could only stare at Daniel in disbelief and moan from the severe impact.

"Get your lying tongue out of here. And do not ever set foot near my wife or I shall kill you." Daniel's breathing felt out of control.

He watched Josiah slowly get up and walk back down the road from where he'd come. Daniel waited until the unwelcome guest was out of sight before stomping back to the farmhouse.

⌒◯

Josiah held his jaw as he walked home in defeat. Then a realization struck. "That lying swine is no patriot," he muttered to himself. "I've seen those moves a time or two in battle."

A smile grew on Josiah's swollen face as he surmised the obvious.

"Miss Mary Thomsen has married a Redcoat." The jilted suitor smirked with satisfaction. "We'll just see how soon we can make her a widow."

Josiah hurried down the road to his father's house. His pace quickened as he began to hatch his plot.

Daniel felt the heat of anger boiling in his face as he returned the hetchel to the barn. He started to throw the wooden tool at the wall but something stopped him — an inner voice that urged him to plead for God's help in overcoming this fury. He submitted to the silent appeal in his heart and sat down on the hay. He held his head and prayed for God to forgive him for this hatred toward Josiah, and for his desire to kill the man.

Then he began to pray for protection for his wife. He sensed a danger here that he could not put words to. He did not know what else to do but give this fear to God. When he finished, he slowly got up from sitting on the hay and walked somberly back to the farmhouse.

Widow Thomsen was starting to spin flax on her wheel in preparation for weaving the fine threads into linen. She paused in her work and placed a finger to her lips, pointing to the couple's bedroom, indicating Mary was still asleep.

"Has something happened, Daniel? I see on your face something weighs on your heart."

Daniel leaned against the warm hearth that burned steadily and looked at the flames. He turned toward the widow and gave a hushed reply.

"Josiah Grant has returned."

The widow's mouth opened in surprise and anger.

"What did he want?" Her words spit with indignation.

"He was looking for 'Miss Thomsen.'" Daniel shook his head at the gall of the man. "After what he did... I cannot believe he has the unmitigated nerve to return here."

"What did you tell him?"

"I told him that Mary and I were married. He said that was impossible, that Mary was waiting for him. He said… some other words… and I hit him."

For a brief moment, Widow Thomsen looked pleased that Daniel had injured the man, but her smile just as quickly disappeared.

"Do you think he'll come back?"

Daniel stared at the fire again. "I don't know." Weariness flooded his limbs. He turned to sit on the chair by the hearth and rubbed his head slowly.

"Why do you not take the remainder of the day to rest, Daniel. You can finish the hetcheling tomorrow."

"I thank you, but no. I must complete the task. I'm much calmer now and the work will consume my energies so my thoughts do not overwhelm me." He stood up and swallowed a drink of cider. "I am well," he said, trying to put the widow's mind at ease.

Daniel went out the front door and headed back to the barn to retrieve the tool.

28

Revenge

J onathan Grant stared at his son in disbelief.

"You must be mad, Josiah. Mary Thomsen's husband is no Redcoat. I've seen the man about the village myself."

Jonathan took a long gulp of rum, poured to celebrate his son's return but now a means to dull his growing anxiety.

"It's true, Father." Josiah raged as he took another hearty swallow of the spirits. Some of the brew dripped down the side of his mouth and he wiped it off with the sleeve of his deerskin coat. "I saw the man fightin' like a King's soldier myself. No one in our regiment can fight like that. He spun that hetchel so fast over his arm I did not even see it comin'. And you can see what he did with it." Josiah pointed to his swollen and reddened jaw.

"The man could have done far worse damage to you than he did. A hetchel can be deadly." Jonathan eyed his son. "I don't suppose you did anything to set him off?"

"I did nothin'!" Josiah yelled, averting his eyes. He paced across the room, spilling some of his rum as he went. "And his fine, mannerly speech — it's a dead giveaway. He's a Lobster, to be sure!"

"This wouldn't have anything to do with your feelings for Missus Lowe?" Jonathan stood up slowly and gripped the edge of the table. "Please tell me this is not about revenge."

Josiah's back was to him, but Jonathan saw Josiah's shoulders stiffen. Josiah spun around and faced him.

"I am a soldier of the Continental Army. Do not accuse me of having a personal vendetta against a soldier of the King!" He set his empty tankard of rum down on the wooden table with force and glared at his father. "So are you a true patriot, Father? Are you going to defend our town from this spy?"

Jonathan scrutinized his only son, who had become such a disappointment to him. "I regret that I was gone too long fighting in the French War. You did not even know me when I returned." Jonathan's mind reeled with the memory.

Josiah stared at his father in confusion. "What are you saying, Father. What does this have to do with a British spy in our midst? Have you taken leave of your senses?" His words blazed with anger.

"Your mother… your mother coddled you so while I was away. She thought you could do no wrong, but I could see your lying ways. If the war taught me one thing, Josiah, it taught me to recognize a liar and a cheat when I saw one." He stared at his handsome son. "Your fine features cannot hide your evil heart. And what you are proposing has the stench of evil through and through. I will not bring such charges against the man. And I will not be a part of this hanging." He finished his rum, sat down, and placed his head in both hands as he stared at the table.

Josiah glared with hatred at his father and wiped the sweat off his reddened face.

"Then I shall find others who will." He stomped out of the house and slammed the door. He headed for the home of another of the town's leaders. On the way there, he stopped walking for a moment and held his head.

This wretched sunlight. I need some ale for this pain. Or a few camp women to ease my discomfort. He stood for a moment under the shade of a maple tree and rubbed his temples. *But those females can never satisfy like Mary. I'll feel like a new man when her bloody Redcoat is dead and in the ground. Then my pain will turn to pleasure.*

He resumed his walk down the road, more determined than ever to get rid of Daniel Lowe.

Hannah answered the knock on the door and was startled to see Josiah. "Josiah, how good to see you."

He pushed past her into the house. "Your father here?" He looked around for Selectman White, then sneezed and wiped his nose off with his sleeve.

"He's outside, working on muskets. I must say, I'm surprised to see you." Hannah wanted to engage him in conversation to learn how James fared, but Josiah pushed past her once again to find her father. She went to the doorway and saw the soldier approach him. She heard Josiah begin to rage about the presence of a British spy right in their own village. When she heard the name Daniel Lowe, she gasped and went to the window. She was able to hear their conversation without being seen by the two men.

"I tell you that man is a Redcoat, a spy." Josiah shouted with such anger, his spittle flew in her father's face. She noticed the soldier's reddened countenance and the sweat pouring from his brow despite the cool September weather.

Her father listened to Josiah's every word.

"Do not believe him, Father." Hannah spoke under her breath, her heart pounding.

"All right," her father said. "We shall gather as many men with muskets as we can. We'll assemble at the meetinghouse tonight at midnight. We can take him from the Thomsen farm and bring him back to the village. We'll not allow a bloody Redcoat to remain in our midst. The big oak tree will serve for the hanging."

Josiah tipped his tricorne hat at Mr. White and strutted off with a look of satisfaction. When her father came in, Hannah stared at him in horror.

"Please, do not do this terrible thing, Father."

Her eyes overflowed with tears.

"Do not interfere, daughter. If Mary's husband is a British spy then he deserves to die." Her father's words chilled the air. "And do not attempt to warn your friend."

"But, Father. Mary… Mary is with child."

"That cannot be helped. Justice must be done and I am responsible for the safekeeping of the citizens here. I shall begin to gather the townsfolk. And you… you are confined to this house."

He walked out the door and locked it from the outside. Hannah covered her mouth as hot tears flowed down her cheeks. She knew if she tried to escape from her home to warn Mary, she would pay the price with a beating from her father. But she knew she had to do something.

"Gracious Father in heaven," Hannah prayed. "Show me what to do. Please protect Daniel from this evil."

Once her tears subsided, she pieced together a plan. Standing up, she found an empty basket used to collect fruit in their orchard. She packed the basket with red apples and one green one. Hannah grabbed a piece of paper and wrote a short note that she attached with a hairpin to the bottom of the green apple. Then she went to an open window that faced the road and waited. She knew the boys would soon be getting out of school and she peered down the path looking for a student. It seemed an interminable wait, but her patience was soon rewarded. It was red-haired Richard Beal, Sarah Thomsen's friend.

"I say, Richard." Hannah called out to the boy from the window. The confused child looked around and Hannah called his name again. He finally saw the source of the greeting and waved.

"Hello, Miss White."

"Richard, can you take something to Missus Lowe for me over at the Thomsen farm?" She struggled to keep her voice calm.

The child's face brightened.

"Certainly, Miss White." The child walked over to the window and Hannah handed him the basket.

"I want my friend Missus Lowe to have some fresh apples from my orchard." In spite of her tranquil manner, her heart was in her throat. "You may eat one of the red ones, if you like."

"Thank you, Miss White." Richard grabbed the piece of fruit and eagerly took a huge bite.

"And Richard — this is most important — please tell Missus Lowe that the green one is especially tasty. She will want to eat that one before the others." Hannah tried to control the trembling in her voice.

"All right, Miss White. I shall tell her." He started to walk away but then turned back toward the window. "The green one, right?" He seemed perplexed.

"Yes, Richard, the green one." She nearly broke down in tears.

The preoccupied child did not seem to notice her distress, and he walked down the road happily. Hannah watched the innocent dispatcher head for the Thomsen farm. Only then did she allow herself to weep.

Dear Lord above, please protect my friends from harm.

29

Terror

When Mary awoke from her afternoon rest, she thrilled at the unexpected discovery. A small bump on her belly was distinctly making its presence felt beneath her fingers.

She sat up, then stood, placing her fingers on top of the new life within. *I did not imagine it!*

Walking out into the late afternoon sunshine, the invigorating cool air refreshed her. The woods in the distance displayed the fall hues of red and gold, which only added to her bliss. Mary always loved this time of year, but this season seemed especially glorious for another reason. She carried Daniel's child.

She heard him in the barn and headed for the open door. She knew her husband would likely be finished with the flax today and was relieved he'd soon be finished with this tedious task. Although he did not complain, Mary knew the strain this chore was on her husband's war injury. She often noticed him rubbing the muscles on his left leg after a long day in the field and worried about the stress this placed on his already-injured limb.

As she strode into the barn, Daniel looked up in surprise.

"I thought you were resting." He set down the tools and walked toward her, placing his arms around her waist. "Are you feeling well?" He smoothed a wayward lock of hair from her forehead.

"I am well. I want to show you something." She took Daniel's large hand and placed it on her belly. "There. Has the baby not grown?"

Daniel looked at her in amazement.

"Already? I did not think we would notice him — or her — just yet."

"Neither did I. But when I awoke, I placed my hand over him and there he was. Our baby."

Daniel held her close. "This child becomes more real to me each day."

Sarah's shouting out from the garden interrupted their embrace.

"Richard! Richard Beal!" The excited seven-year-old jumped up and down, waving.

"Richard? I wonder why he is here?" She pulled away from Daniel's arms.

"He probably could not wait for Sabbath day to visit with her. Richard's flirtation with Sarah is quite amusing." Daniel smirked.

"I'd best go see if his mother needs anything. Perhaps someone in their home is ill." Mary walked toward the farmhouse where the two youngsters were.

"Good day, Miss… I mean Missus Lowe," Richard bowed from the waist. "Miss White has asked me to bring you these apples to eat."

"Hannah? How thoughtful of her. This is an unexpected gift."

Why did she not bring them herself?

"Thank you, Richard. And how was school today?"

"It was quite exhilarating, Missus Lowe." Richard stood taller.

Mary smothered a smile. Richard always loved to try out new words from his spelling lessons at every opportunity. "Exhilarating" must have been one of his recent assignments.

"I wish I could go to school." Sarah folded her arms and pouted. "Williamston has a summer school for girls. Why cannot Deer Run have a girls' school?"

"We hope to have one soon, Sarah. In the meantime, keep up your lessons at home. I'm certain you will find Mother's teaching exhilarating as well."

"Well, I'd best get home before my mother wonders where I have been." Richard remained standing there, clearly having no desire to leave.

"We're very grateful to you for this special gift you've delivered, Richard. Do come again soon. By the way, would you like one of these apples? I'm sure you must be hungry."

"Miss White has already offered me one, but thank you kindly."

With gentlemanly grace, he bowed to Mary, then to Sarah. Sarah giggled at the gesture.

The boy turned to go back home, then spun around so fast he nearly lost his balance.

"Missus Lowe, Miss White says that the green one is especially tasty. She says you should eat it first."

"All right, Richard." As she watched him go back down the road, confusion crossed her thoughts.

Hannah knows the red ones are my favorite. And why did she only put one green one in the basket?

Mary walked inside the farmhouse and Sarah returned to weeding the garden and gathering vegetables. Her mother was still at work spinning the flax from the abundant crop.

"That is odd."

"What is odd, Mary?" Her mother stopped spinning.

"These apples from Hannah. She sent them with Richard instead of bringing them herself. And then she said I should eat the green one first."

Mary picked up the green apple and only then noticed there was a note attached to the bottom.

"What's this?"

"What is it?" Mother Thomsen got up from her spinning wheel and walked toward Mary.

Mary's words choked in her throat as she read the note from Hannah. The message sent terror through her heart.

"No!" Mary covered her mouth with her hands and dropped the note to the floor.

Widow Thomsen picked it up and read the frightening message: "They are coming for Daniel tonight. He must hide."

Mary slumped to the floor and shook uncontrollably. Her throat tightened with fear. "Get Daniel," she whispered. Widow Thomsen rushed out the door and returned moments later with her husband.

"Mary, what is it?" Alarm filled his voice.

Mary couldn't speak but handed him the note from Hannah. The color drained from Daniel's face as he read the ominous message. Mary shook with fear and she sobbed uncontrollably. Daniel held her in his arms, shaking nearly as much as she was.

Their joy was suddenly threatened by an unseen enemy. Mary was at a loss to understand this horrible turn of events.

Daniel knew exactly who the source of this terror was. He had encountered the man earlier today, and Josiah Grant was bent on revenge.

Daniel tried to gather his wits about him. He needed to be brave for his wife. "Mary, listen." He cupped her chin in his hands. His expression struggled to be stalwart when he saw the pain on her face. "You must be strong. I shall hide in the wigwam until dawn. Then I will go through the woods back toward New York. I shall send for you when it is safe."

"Daniel, take my horse," Widow Thomsen offered. Daniel noticed the fear on her face as well.

"I cannot ride that well, and they would likely overtake me. My safest course is to go on foot. I know the way."

"Please take me with you, Daniel." Mary sobbed pitifully.

"I cannot." Daniel's voice whispered. "If they catch me then you will be endangered as well. And so will our child."

They clung to each other again. This time he feared letting go, afraid this could be their last embrace.

"Daniel, you must hasten." Widow Thomsen's voice trembled. "Evening draws nigh. I shall pack you food and drink." She was already gathering supplies and putting them in a leather pouch.

He helped Mary to her feet.

"Please, take care of our child." His emotions clamored for release but he held them back.

Mary threw her arms around his neck and would not let go. Daniel finally freed himself from her desperate grip. He kissed her with heartbreaking passion, then turned away from his wife before walking toward the door.

"Daniel." Mary called to him, sobbing, her hand over her chest. "You are the song in my heart."

Daniel looked at his wife with so much pain in his eyes, Ruth Thomsen looked away.

"Why Lord?" She prayed under her breath but her pleas to heaven went unanswered. When she turned back around, Daniel was gone.

Mary seemed inconsolable. Widow Thomsen held her daughter as if she were a small child. But it had been far easier to soothe away the pains of childhood heartache then it was to alleviate the deep despair her daughter suffered from today.

Sarah walked into the house looking confused. When she saw how upset Mary was, she started to cry as well. "What is happening, Mother?"

Ruth drew her younger daughter toward herself and the three of them held each other and wept. It was not long before they heard someone on horseback approach the farmhouse. They all looked up in fear.

"Stay here, daughters." She took down her late husband's musket from the wall and made sure the powder and ball were at the ready. Cracking the door open, she breathed a sigh of relief when she saw a friendly face.

"Mr. Eaton!" Widow Thomsen broke down in tears and rested the weapon at her side.

"Caught wind of the village rumor." Mr. Eaton dismounted his horse with a grave expression upon his face. "Thought you could use a friend — and a firearm." He held up his musket.

"Yes." Widow Thomsen spoke through her tears. "We could use both."

30

Intervention

The sun dropped below the horizon when Daniel reached the wigwam.

Even though he knew where it was located, he still had difficulty finding the entrance. Abundant vines clustered over the structure, serving as camouflage. It took several frantic attempts on Daniel's part to locate the door in the midst of the entwined reddened leaves. He opened the precariously hinged door — barely hanging together with a stiff leather strap — and stepped into the dim interior.

The scent of lavender consumed his senses. Mary had left this private hideaway intact since their wedding day, and it had often served as an oasis for their love. Today, however, he felt desperately alone. The reminders of the encounters he had shared here with his wife, now filled him with despair.

Will we ever be together again?

Daniel sat down on one of the quilts, remembering their wedding day. He'd never forget Mary smoothing her hands across the wretched scar on his thigh. She had looked at him with tenderness and spoken words that he treasured: "This shall always remind me of how we were brought together."

Daniel's eyes stung with tears at the memory of their passion that day. He closed his eyes and held his head.

"Dear God," he whispered in prayer, "please bring us back together again."

He did not have a Bible with him but he remembered the words he'd recently read in Psalms. They consumed his present thoughts: *In thee, O LORD, do I put my trust: let me never be put to confusion. Deliver me in thy righteousness, and cause me to escape: incline thine ear unto me, and save me.*

These words had been written so long ago by the young King David while fleeing from a man bent on killing him. The verses took on an aura of reality for Daniel.

And then he began to wonder.

How many others in Deer Run will follow Josiah's urging? How many other townspeople will turn on me?

Then an unbearable fear consumed him.

What if they turn on Mary?

Daniel had forgotten to remind his wife that she should deny any knowledge about his past. But even if she did, would they believe her?

Surely they must.

Terror still gripped at his heart. He'd seen too many mobs get out of control with misplaced fervor.

Oh, God — please protect my wife.

Myles Eaton stood guard outside the front door of the Thomsen farmhouse, his eyes fixed to the road where the men intent upon hanging Daniel Lowe would soon come. He glanced over at the musket sticking out of the side-room window, the room where Mary and Daniel usually slept. Widow Thomsen had her firearm at the ready.

It had been nearly two hours since everyone's lives were upended by the ominous note. Few words had been spoken since, but tension was written on everyone's faces.

Mr. Eaton finally broke the silence. "How's Missus Lowe doin'?"

"She's lying on Daniel's pillow in my bed, hugging her sister. Sarah finally went to sleep but Mary is still crying." Mr. Eaton could hear the widow's trembling pitch. "Mary says the scent of Daniel on his pillow brings her comfort."

"Aye, I understand." Myles Eaton recalled his own memories of despair after his wife died. "I remember takin' my wife's shawl to bed with me after she passed on." He looked over at Ruth, feeling vulnerable. "I never shared that with no one before."

Widow Thomsen stared at him with a look of compassion.

"I feel pleased that you would entrust me with your sad memories, Mr. Eaton."

Myles Eaton nodded in acknowledgment. No words were spoken for several moments.

"So when do you suppose Josiah and the others will come?" Widow Thomsen broke the silence.

"Hard tellin', Widow Thomsen."

They both startled at the sound of a wolf howling in the distance. He tried to relax when they realized the source of the plaintive noise, but the tension never fully abated, lingering in the air as surely as the early fall breeze.

"Have I told you how grateful I am for your help, Myles?" Widow Thomsen appeared to be holding back fresh tears.

"Aye, Ruth Thomsen, you've told me you were grateful. But you don't need to thank me. 'Tis just what I do for my friends."

Mr. Eaton smiled. It was the first time they'd called each other by their Christian names.

Several of the armed men who gathered on horseback at the meetinghouse carried torches. Selectman White and a mob awaited their leader, Josiah Grant, but he'd yet to show and impatience rippled through the group.

"So where is Josiah?" One gray-haired man glared at Caleb White. "The man spreads the word about this Redcoat and now we're all waitin' on the instigator. I thought he was leadin' the group?"

Most of the dozen men gathered for the lynching were over the age of fifty. Many had sons serving in the war of Revolution, but most in the village were too old or infirm to carry their own muskets on the battlefront. They were forced to defend their new nation on the home front, and they were more than willing participants in carrying out justice. But Caleb White knew none of them wanted to lead this particular crusade, especially since Josiah seemed to have enough youthful fighting spirit to carry out that task himself. The men were ready to follow him at this midnight hour — if only he were here.

"Let's ride over to the Grant place. Maybe something has delayed the man." Caleb wanted to get this hanging done as soon as possible; no sense in delaying the inevitable.

They rode slowly over the half-mile distance to the home of Josiah and his father. There was a new moon that evening that shed little light and Caleb feared injuring one of their horses on the rough terrain.

I wish Josiah had chosen a night with a full moon. I wish this night were over.

When the group arrived at the Grant home, it was strangely quiet. Caleb thought Josiah's horse would be at the ready.

Wouldn't he be preparing to rouse our patriotic fervor? To bring justice to our village and our new country?

The mob sat in their leather saddles looking at each other with confusion.

"I'll go see where he is." Dismounting from his large brown mare, he walked up to the door and knocked.

Instead of Josiah answering, Jonathan Grant opened the door. He had a look in his eyes reflecting fear and anger. The distraught father held a wet cloth in his hand and a basin of water.

"Lookin' for your captain, are you? Well, there he is, gentleman." He pointed to the bed where his son lay.

Caleb White walked over to the young man lying on the drenched sheets and gasped. The selectman drew back from the bed, for the sight of the stricken soldier imbued him with horror and dread. Even in the dim candlelight, he could see the hundreds of raised, red marks all over Josiah's face, arms, and legs. These pustules revealed a frightening truth.

Smallpox.

"You'd best be on your way, Mr. White." Jonathan Grant pointed toward the door.

The terrified man did not need convinced. He exited the front door as fast as his legs could run. Caleb looked up at the men on horseback, his voice strained with apprehension.

"There's smallpox here. Everyone who was with Josiah Grant needs to be confined to their homes lest we have an epidemic."

The blood drained from the men's faces. The subdued mob rapidly made their way back to their separate homes. There would be no further talk of a hanging this night. Caleb knew the men were aware of the terror of smallpox. And all of them knew this deadly plague could decimate the entire town of Deer Run.

31

Enemies

The pounding of a solitary set of hooves stirred Ruth Thomsen and Myles Eaton to alarm.

They readied their muskets to fire at whatever danger was approaching. Their moist fingers gripped the triggers, their nerves on edge in this dark of night just before dawn.

They each breathed a sigh of relief when they realized the rider was not Josiah Grant. It was his father, Jonathan.

"Widow Thomsen." Jonathan shifted in his saddle. "Please help me. My son is dreadfully ill. It's the smallpox."

Ruth and Mr. Eaton gasped at the news.

"Are you certain?" This news was horror upon horror.

"As sure as I've been of anything." Jonathan nervously fingered the horse's reins. "I've seen it plenty in the last war. The whole town is in quarantine."

Ruth put down her musket. She went to the main room to get some medicine for the man's son, moving silently so as to not awaken her two daughters. Mary and Sarah were finally asleep in the large bed. Ruth gathered hyssop leaves to make a tea for Josiah's fever. She also gathered a large portion of the inner bark of several trees, including sumac, pine, and Spanish oak. These would induce vomiting, which was recommended in the physician's guide. He'd also require clean linens to soothe his sores.

Moving automatically in response to the request for help, it was a moment before a realization dawned on her.

I cannot go to help Josiah. I could bring back this dreaded disease to my whole family. I cannot risk this. I will not risk it.

But she knew someone who could do this — if he was willing to go.

After writing out directions for the use of the powders and leaves, she walked outside with the supplies. She handed them in a pouch to Jonathan Grant, who was waiting anxiously on his horse.

"Mr. Grant, 'tis impossible for me to attend to your son. My daughter is with child and I cannot take the chance on bringing this contagion into my home. However, there is someone I know who has survived the pox. With your permission — and his — I shall send him to attend your son, and to you in the event that you become ill."

Jonathan Grant looked at the widow and swallowed visibly. "And who would that be, ma'am?"

Ruth took a deep breath.

"'Tis my daughter's husband, Daniel Lowe."

The father paused only a moment before giving the only sensible answer he could.

"Yes, of course, Widow Thomsen. If he is willing, I would be grateful for his help. I thank you, ma'am, for your gracious spirit." He tipped his tricorne hat to the woman and rode back to his home and his stricken son.

Myles Eaton turned to Ruth with a questioning look.

"Are you sure you want to ask Daniel to do this? After what Josiah has been up to?"

"'Tis Daniel's decision to help the man or not. But if Daniel shows himself to be a loyal help to the people of Deer Run at such a critical time, how can they deny his allegiance to the citizens of America?"

Mr. Eaton appeared ready to object, then he changed his mind. "There's a truth in what you say, Ruth. But are you sure Daniel will be willin' to help his enemy?"

"That will be between him and God."

Ruth went into the house and picked up her Bible before heading off to the wigwam.

"I shall return forthwith, Myles. Please guard my family while they sleep."

"I shall."

Ruth walked down the long path toward the old structure in the woods. She wondered how the aged wigwam had lasted through the years despite so many storms. The leaves of fall were just beginning their annual descent from the branches. There was a thin carpet of gold and red on the path leading through the dense trees.

She arrived just before dawn.

Daniel threw his food-filled haversack over his shoulder. When he heard someone's footsteps, he hid behind the crude hinge of the door and stood prepared to fight. When he saw it was his mother-in-law, he sighed with relief.

"Is Mary well?"

"She was sleeping when I left, Daniel. Mr. Eaton is guarding the house, musket in hand."

A feeling of gratitude overtook Daniel. Then he wondered what had transpired during the night.

"What about the people from the town? Did they come? Did Josiah come?"

"The only one who came was Josiah's father. Jonathan Grant brought some news. An unexpected report." She paused. "Josiah has the smallpox."

Baffled by the news, Daniel took in a deep breath for the first time since seeing the note from Hannah.

"So he's not coming? Thank God."

The widow continued. "I understand your relief, Daniel, but this will be short lived. Once he is well — if he recovers — and once the rest of the town is deemed clear of infection, the mob will come again."

He regarded her somberly.

"You are right of course. I must think this through." He sat on the dirt floor of the wigwam and put his hands on his temples.

"I have an idea that might change the town's belief in your loyalty to the colonies once and for all." Daniel looked up at her. She continued. "I know that you have survived the pox and will likely never get it again. If you go and take care of the victims in the village, starting with Josiah, it will make them see you for who you really are — a loyal and caring American."

"Nurse Josiah Grant through this illness?" Daniel sputtered in disbelief. "Do you honestly think I could tend to his needs? He is my sworn enemy! Do you know what he has done? Do you know what he said?" Rage engulfed Daniel as he leapt to his feet and paced angrily.

"I can well imagine." Widow Thomsen paused until Daniel calmed down, then she resumed speaking. "You know, Daniel, when Mary first came and told me about you, I felt the same way. I was so infested with hatred toward you, toward all the King's soldiers, I could not imagine helping my enemy."

Daniel's anger sobered at her words. He remembered the unexpected turn the widow had taken, even helping to bring him back to her own home.

"Why did you help me, Mother Thomsen? I… I never really understood your explanation."

"It was God speaking to my heart, Daniel — through His words in the Bible. I read about tending to the needs of my enemy and helping those being led away to death." Tears brimmed in her eyes. "There are many words about loving your enemy, doing good to them that hate you, blessing them that curse you, and praying for them which despitefully use you."

He placed hands on hips and looked away.

"I don't think I can do that, Mother Thomsen."

"None of us can do that, without the power of God to help us." She placed her hand on his bent arm. "Would you like me to leave you alone to think about it?"

He covered his eyes tightly with his soil-encrusted hands.

"Yes. I need to contemplate this. And I need to pray." He stared at the dirt floor of the wigwam.

"And I shall pray for wisdom for you, Daniel." She placed her Bible on the quilts. "Here is my book of wisdom, if you care to consult it."

Widow Thomsen walked out the door and left him alone.

Daniel sat down on the makeshift bed once again and struggled in his spirit. He did not want to do this thing, but he wanted to do the right thing, the honorable thing in God's eyes. He resisted the image in his mind of the bruises Josiah had left on Mary's arms and the memory of the horrible things the man had said to her and about her.

Then Daniel thought about the ramifications of Widow Thomsen's forgiveness. While the woman had struggled with her feelings to make the right decision, her ultimate choice had a profound impact. It had brought health to his body, healing to his soul, and, ultimately, love to his life. He could not deny the powerful changes her resolve had birthed.

Can I make the same choice to smother my hatred and forgive?

"Oh, God," he prayed in anguish. "Help me to do the right thing. Help me to do Your will."

He sat there for several moments before he heard the familiar creak of the dry hinge on the wigwam door. He looked up and saw the face of the woman he loved. Mary's eyes were swollen from crying and her long hair disheveled. She'd just awakened and still wore her night shift. She'd covered herself with a shawl for warmth but neglected to put shoes on over her bare feet. Despite her unkempt appearance, she was the most beautiful sight to Daniel.

"Mother told me what she said to you." Mary's mouth trembled. "Are you really going over to Josiah Grant's to tend to his illness?"

"Yes." Daniel reached his arm up toward his wife.

Mary sat next to him, putting her arms around his waist.

"But what if you get the smallpox from him." Tears slipped down her cheeks.

"That will not happen. I've been around many in the camps who had smallpox and I've never become ill. You know that I had it as a child." He laid her head on his shoulder and stroked her hair.

"I know, but, Daniel… you'll be gone for so long. 'Twill be weeks before 'tis safe to come back and not carry the contagion. I cannot bear the thought of being without you. Especially now." She placed one hand on her growing belly.

Daniel touched her cheek with his fingers, wiping away her tears. "Mary, this is my only chance to show everyone I am one of you — a loyal American. They will not believe me otherwise. Besides…" He kissed her moist face. "This is what I feel I must do. Deep in my spirit, I know this is right."

He gazed at her, remembering when they had met nearly a year ago.

"I need to do good to my enemy," he whispered near her ear. "Just as you did for me."

His lips met hers and he drew her down onto the quilts. They both clung to one another in a desperate passion. The couple shared their love once more before the separation they both dreaded.

32

Smallpox

aniel and Mr. Eaton sat on their horses looking down the hill at the Grant home.

"Are you sure you want to do this thing?" Myles Eaton's voice brimmed with worry.

"Want to?" Daniel gave a wry smile. "I do not think that is quite the word for it. Feel compelled to, yes, but my desire is to turn Dash around, right here and now, and return to my wife."

He stared with trepidation at the house that harbored not only disease but hatred — hatred that was directed right at him. He fought the urge to escape this confrontation and prayed for a firm resolve to complete this mission of mercy. He slid off the bare back of Dash and handed the reins to Mr. Eaton. With no saddle for a man's use at the Thomsen farm, Daniel had been forced to ride bareback.

Myles Eaton looked at him one last time and tipped his hat. "You're a far better Christian than I."

"I think not, sir." Daniel threw a sack over his shoulder. "Just a Christian who is hopeful for peace in my heart. And desperate for safe-keeping for my family. Not better than you, sir."

He started to walk away to the Grant house when he remembered something important.

"Mr. Eaton, can you please watch out for Mary whilst I'm gone?"

"I shall check in on her every day, lad. Do not worry about your wife — she's in good hands."

Daniel bowed to his friend gratefully and walked with determination toward the log house with the wood smoke drifting skyward from the chimney.

That warm hearth is probably the only inviting thing I'll experience here. He limped toward the front door and knocked twice. After what seemed like an interminable wait, an older man answered. He held a vomit-filled basin.

"Good day, lad. I'm Jonathan Grant. I've been giving my son the elixir of tree roots Widow Thomsen sent over. They seem to work quick and without mercy."

Daniel nearly lost all resolve to stay when the stench of the basin's contents reached his nostrils.

"Come in, lad." Mr. Grant held the door wide. Daniel took a deep breath and walked inside the cabin. He fought away the urge to spew the gruel that Mary had served him that morning.

The smells of a single man's world engulfed the cabin. "I've not had much time to keep the place clean since my wife died. Guess I lost the will to keep it up."

Daniel stared at the piles of filthy clothes and linens, while food-encrusted utensils and bowls were stacked on the tableboard. The stench of disease only added to the foul aroma. The only welcoming smell was the smoke from the heavy oak log burning in the long fireplace.

Jonathan looked down at the basin in his hand and then seemed to notice the look on Daniel's face. "Let me dump this outside."

The father walked out the door and threw the contents on the ground. Daniel watched him grab a bucket of water from the well and pour some into the bowl. Weariness etched the man's face as he swished it around a bit before throwing that on the ground as well.

"There, that's done." The father walked back inside and saw Josiah glaring at Daniel.

"You will make Mr. Lowe welcome here, Josiah." Jonathan's terse voice left no room for discussion. "He has come to help."

Josiah lay on his bed, moving little. The only energy apparent in his entire being was in his eyes, which were intense with hatred for Daniel.

Daniel looked at the weakened man and was moved with pity. The pox were everywhere, making the man almost unrecognizable. One sore blended into another on his face, distorting his features and making it difficult for the man to move his lips or open his eyes. He was pathetic in his illness, yet still consumed with loathing for the man who had come to bring mercy. Josiah seemed even more suffused with rancor now that Daniel could observe him in such an unsightly state.

The waves of nausea from the emetic began to take hold of Josiah again. Jonathan had gone outside to stir the linens in the large washing kettle. This prompted Daniel to grab the basin and hold it under Josiah's mouth while the patient expelled the contents of his stomach.

When he finished puking, Josiah looked up with fresh rage in his eyes. He grabbed the basin and flung the putrid contents all over Daniel's clothing. Josiah gave a self-satisfied smirk as he weakly settled back onto his bed.

Repulsion filled Daniel's every pore. He wanted to grab the ungrateful pox-covered man by the throat, but something stopped him from carrying out his vengeful thoughts. Instead, he turned around and walked toward the front door, praying for self-control.

Jonathan was in the doorway and must have witnessed his son's disgraceful behavior. He glared at the patient in the bed.

"I'm certain my son has some clean clothes for you, Mr. Lowe." Jonathan continued to frown at his grown child while taking out fresh clothing from the chest of drawers. "Let's take those clothes of yours out to the lye soap."

The two men walked out toward the large laundry kettle in the yard. Jonathan also brought over a bucket of fresh water and bar soap for Daniel to wash the vomit off of his skin. Feeling a fresh wave of fury at the disgusting assault on the piece of clothing Mary had so skillfully wrought, Daniel unbuttoned the linen shirt she had stitched for him last winter.

How dare Josiah dump something so foul and odious on her work. As Daniel seethed with regret that he'd ever decided to come here, Jonathan interrupted his thoughts.

"My son's actions are unforgivable, Mr. Lowe. I hardly know what to say."

Jonathan placed each piece of soiled clothing into the large steaming kettle as Daniel undressed.

Daniel paused in his angry musings long enough to look with compassion upon this saddened veteran. He remembered that Jonathan Grant had been the inspiring reader of the Declaration of Independence at the Fourth of July celebration. He was astonished at the difference in demeanor between this father and son.

"I'm certain this illness is adding to Josiah's difficult behavior." Daniel tried to reassure the man. "His fever appears to be affecting his judgment."

"That is kind of you to say, sir. I think we both know that it is more than smallpox that influences Josiah's disposition."

Daniel picked up the bar of soap and washed with haste. He was shirtless and wet, and the chill of the late September air caused him to shiver. Despite his discomfort, he was pleased to wash away all evidence of Josiah's insult. After Daniel had removed all the soiled clothing, he dressed himself in Josiah's simple attire. The sleeves were not quite long enough, but they would do. They were clean.

"Thank you for the clothing, sir."

The older man stirred the contents of the kettle that almost overflowed with lye soap and water. It was obvious he had other things than cleaning on his mind.

"I should have been a better father to Josiah." Jonathan's regrets seemed to fill his demeanor with despair. "I was so happy to see him and his mother when I returned from war. I didn't want to appear too harsh about his behavior, but I should have been more diligent. He was so spoiled…" The man's voice drifted off.

"I… I'm certain none of us gets through life without regrets, sir."

"That is true enough, young man. But you do not want to have too many regrets about your children. You want to know that you raised them up proper-like." He looked toward his house.

"Not undisciplined or ungrateful." He pointed his chin toward the structure. Jonathan looked back at the kettle for a moment then looked at Daniel. "Lowe, is it?"

"Yes, sir."

"I served under a Major William Lowe in the French War." Jonathan stared into the distance as though reliving those days long ago.

"That was my uncle, sir."

"He was a good man. One of the King's faithful officers. Very brave on the battlefield." He paused for a moment. "Sorry loss for our troops when he was killed. A sad loss for your family as well, I am sure."

"Yes, sir. I do not remember him myself but I do remember my father's sorrow when we heard of his demise."

"I see that you have a limp and a nasty scar from the war as well, Mr. Lowe." His eyes settled on Daniel's face. "I am sure you were very brave and honorable in war, just like your uncle was."

Daniel looked down at the ground and then met the man's eyes. "I hope so, sir."

"Well then, Mr. Lowe, I've not even asked you how your wife is doing."

"She is quite well. Thank you." Daniel brightened at the mention of Mary.

"I am certain you'll have a fine family to be proud of one day."

"Well, as a matter of fact, we expect a child come next spring." Daniel stood tall with pride.

"That is wonderful news, sir, indeed." He pat Daniel on the shoulder.

Josiah Grant lay in bed inside the house, but he could hear the conversation between the two men outdoors. He'd heard every word.

And when he heard that Mary was expecting Daniel Lowe's child, salty tears burned like fire on the open sores around his eyes.

The scourge of the pox continued for several days. Daniel tried to assist Josiah with cold cloths for his fever, but the angry patient just grabbed the linens out of Daniel's hands.

"I can do it myself." Even in his weakened state, Josiah's hatred energized him.

Daniel refused to respond to this unruly behavior. He just continued making soups for the patient and cleaning the soiled linens and clothing.

He made the hyssop tea that Widow Thomsen had sent over and placed the tankard by Josiah's bedside. Daniel knew that the resentful patient would only drink the brew after he walked away. Josiah's pride would not allow him to appear grateful in any manner. The pox-ridden patient did his best to provoke Daniel with his vindictive behavior. But no matter how hateful his actions were, Josiah could not arouse the response he seemed to hope for.

On the fifth day of Josiah's illness, the situation took an ominous turn when Jonathan began to complain of a throbbing headache.

Daniel noted the flaming redness in the man's cheeks and was forced to acknowledge the obvious — Josiah's father was the next victim of this dreaded illness.

"Of all the times there was pox in the camps, I never became ill." Sweat covered Jonathan's face. He fell with weakness onto his bed. "Why now?"

"I know not, sir. But I shall take care of you as well." Daniel had grown fond of this older gentleman in the last few days and prayed the man had the strength to recover. But dread filled Daniel's heart at the thought of giving the older man the strong elixir.

The emetic concoction that would bring on violent vomiting was difficult enough for a younger man to endure. It could be devastating for an older man like Jonathan Grant.

The drink brought about the desired result, but it did not alleviate the symptoms of disease. Instead, the fevers became worse. Each day, Daniel attempted to cool down the man with fresh water from the well, but the illness continued to rage.

In the middle of the night on the fifth day of Jonathan's illness, the older man's breathing began to change. A strange rattling emerged from Jonathan's chest and he was unable to speak. Daniel had heard this sound before and he knew the end was near. He walked slowly over to Josiah's bedside and looked down at the recovering soldier.

Josiah's pox were just beginning to dry out. Several of the scabs clung to his beard as they slowly fell away from his face, leaving behind their telltale craters in his skin.

"Your father is not doing well, Josiah." Daniel wiped sweat off his own forehead with the back of his hand.

"I have brought this illness upon my father." Josiah's lips trembled. He rose with unsteady legs from his bed and walked to his parent's bedside. Daniel watched Josiah's face contort with indescribable pain as he looked at his dying parent.

Whatever Josiah wishes to say to his father is best left between the two.

Daniel walked outside and closed the door. He moved away from the house and looked up at the stars on this clear and cool October evening. He breathed in deeply, grateful for the refreshing it brought to his body and spirit.

As he stood there in the quiet, homesickness overwhelmed him. But it was not desire for his family in England. He longed to be home with Mary, to hold her in his arms and feel her vitality. Tears stung at his eyes as he wondered how his wife fared. With the village quarantine, it was impossible to send letters to her for fear that even the paper he touched might transmit the illness to Mary. His feelings of emptiness were soon interrupted by the sobs of Josiah at his father's bedside.

Daniel knew that Jonathan Grant would never again recite the Declaration of Independence at a Fourth of July celebration. That thought steeped his spirit with immeasurable sadness.

⁓

Daniel had just completed burying Jonathan Grant when he heard someone shout at him from a distance.

"Daniel!" It was the voice of Mother Thomsen, standing up on the hillside, the same bluff that he and Myles Eaton had stood upon nearly two weeks prior.

"Mother Thomsen! How is Mary?"

"She is well, Daniel. But the White family has come down with the smallpox. Can you take the medicinals over there?" The widow cupped her mouth so Daniel could hear her.

Daniel's heart sank. He'd hoped to wait another week for Josiah to completely recover before he would feel secure in not bringing the smallpox back home. But this news would mean delaying his return even longer. Fatigue and anxiety instilled a craving to see his wife. But he knew there was an even greater concern. Smallpox at the White home had great significance for his family. Hannah White was Mary's best friend. This young victim of the pox had also promised to wait for Mary's brother James, who was away at war.

Mary must be beside herself with worry. "Yes, of course, Mother Thomsen."

The widow pointed at the freshly mounded grave that Daniel stood near as he held a shovel.

"Who has died, Daniel?"

"Jonathan Grant."

"And Josiah?"

"He is recovering."

He watched Widow Thomsen place her hands over her mouth. After a moment she spoke.

"I see. How are you, Daniel? Mary wanted to ask you herself but I would not let her come. I knew she would not be able to keep herself from running to you."

Daniel had to smile at the woman's words. He knew he'd not be able to resist holding Mary in his arms either.

"Tell her I am well. And tell her," he stopped and swallowed, "tell her how much I miss her."

"I shall, Daniel. And thank you for what you are doing. You've never been braver on the battlefield."

The widow turned and disappeared into the woods leading to the Thomsen farm.

Battlefield, indeed. He had never been in such a fight before that did not involve muskets and bayonets. He felt wounded and weary but definitely not defeated. The most effective weapon, he had come to realize, can often be the "sword of the Spirit, which is the word of God."

As Daniel followed the directions given by Josiah Grant to the White's home, he thought about the last few weeks with both sadness and satisfaction. Sadness at the passing of Jonathan Grant and satisfaction at the parting words Josiah had said to him before Daniel left the Grant home.

"Please tell your wife I'm sorry." Josiah refused to meet Daniel in the eye. "And, I'm sorry to you, as well. I see now what my father tried to teach me. That 'love that is self-seeking is without honor.' Too bad I came to see that far too late."

Daniel had stared at the broken man covered with unsightly pock marks and felt pity for one who had lost so much.

"I shall relay your apologies to Mary." He shook the man's hand but Josiah quickly withdrew his unsightly hand covered with scars. The look of sadness in Josiah's eyes was palpable.

As the home of Selectman White appeared in the distance, Daniel experienced renewed apprehension. He now had to prepare to face the village leader who was ready to send him to the gallows. Daniel steeled himself for this next skirmish and prayed for victory.

No one answered his knock at the door. Unsure of what to do, Daniel opened the front door.

"I say, Mr. White? Miss White?"

No one answered. Perplexed, Daniel grew anxious to find them.

When he did, it was a most disturbing sight. Mr. White's fever caused delirium. Barely able to recognize Daniel, his words were unintelligible. Hannah fared not much better, although she recognized Daniel and tried to smile.

"Thank you for coming, Daniel." Her labored breathing unnerved him, reminding him of Jonathan Grant's condition. Her reddened face testified of a high fever.

Hannah and her father required Daniel's prompt intervention. He immediately prepared the tree root concoction that encouraged the dreadful vomiting. Although the patients were barely able to swallow, the little they consumed produced the desired result. Daniel would just finish assisting with one patient before the one in the next room needed his assistance. By the time the emesis treatments were complete, exhaustion permeated Daniel.

The dreaded pustules had already broken out all over their faces and limbs. Daniel hoped the delay in his arrival had not cost them their health. All he could do now was apply cool water for their fever, bring them hyssop tea to drink, and pray.

⁓

Three days later, Daniel made a fresh batch of chicken broth in the large hearth when he heard Hannah's voice calling his name. Relief flooded his spirit when he appeared in her doorway. Her fever seemed to abate.

"You are looking much better, Miss White."

"I'm feeling better. I cannot thank you enough for helping us, Mr. Lowe. I...I heard how you helped out at the Grant home. You're very brave."

"Not so brave, really."

"Mary thinks you are the bravest man she's ever met. Not to mention the handsomest." Hannah gave a weak smile.

"I'm afraid my wife must suffer from an affliction of her sight."

"May I tell you something, Mr. Lowe?" Hannah's voice sounded weak.

"Yes, of course."

"I've known your wife since we were children. She was always the one who attracted the glances of the village lads intent upon winning her heart. But none of them ever won her affections the way you have. Mary looked for a very special partner in life — and she has found her perfect consort in you. I've never seen her love another as she loves you."

Daniel's face contorted in pain, his emotions fragile from exhaustion.

"I'm sorry. I did not mean to upset you."

"It's not your fault, Miss White. It's just that ... I miss Mary so, and your words remind me just how much I long for her. And I am so very tired."

"I hope that you can be with her soon."

"As do I."

Nearly three weeks passed with no further outbreaks of the disease. Daniel heard the residents of Deer Run were cautiously beginning to venture out of doors. He prayed it was safe to return home.

After thoroughly cleaning his clothing with lye soap and laying them out in the sun to dry, he carefully scrubbed himself with soap and water, paying special attention to cleaning the beard that had grown in the last few weeks. He wanted to remove any possible remnant of the illness.

He was outside the White's house preparing to finally return home when Hannah's father came out the front door. Still weakened from the devastating disease, Selectman White had multiple scars from the pox, which made him appear much older.

"I hear that you are going home, sir." Caleb White leaned against the house for support.

"Yes, sir, I am."

Mr. White focused on the ground near his feet, avoiding Daniel's gaze. "Our lives were in your hands, Mr. Lowe, and I do not know how to thank you. My daughter and I are beholden to you."

"I administered the medicinals, Mr. White, but it was God Who healed you." Daniel squinted in the sunshine. "I'm grateful I was able to assist you and your daughter."

"I hear you and the Missus are expecting a child in spring. Perhaps you and she would like to have dinner with Hannah and myself sometime before winter sets in."

"I'd like that, sir. When you are feeling recovered, of course."

"Of course."

Hannah came out of the house. She had fewer pock marks on her face and arms than her father did, but the evidence of the illness was there nevertheless. She was already shy, Daniel knew, and he hoped that these scars would not increase her withdrawn demeanor, especially with James.

"It should not be long before James comes home for a visit." He tried to sound encouraging. Hannah touched her cheeks and felt the marks beneath her fingers. A shadow of concern crossed her eyes.

"I know he'll be most anxious to see his beloved Miss White." Daniel smiled and she returned the grin.

"Thank you for everything, Mr. Lowe." She and her father waved good-bye.

Daniel would have run the entire way home except for the leg wound that prevented such a gait for more than a short distance. Instead, he limped along as quickly as he was able. He could barely contain his joy at finally returning to his wife.

He saw an unfamiliar child walking along the road.

"I say there, lad. Do you know the way to the Thomsen farm?"

"Everyone knows the way to the Thomsen farm, sir. That's where the midwife lives."

"Yes, of course." Daniel grinned so wide his mouth began to hurt. "Can you take a message for me to Missus Lowe who lives there?"

"Why yes, sir."

"Please tell Missus Lowe that her husband is coming home and to please meet him in their special place."

"Their special place?" He scratched his head.

"Yes, lad. She'll know what that means." Daniel hurried down the road. "And tell her I said you can have an apple," he called back to the boy.

The child looked at him and shrugged his shoulders before heading to the Thomsen farm to deliver the message.

33

Reunion

As Mary knit stockings for the baby, she sat in a chair by the fire that early November morning. Clouds started to gather outdoors, dimming the light inside the farmhouse. The grayness in the room mirrored her mood.

Daniel had been gone from home nearly six weeks now and she wrestled with thoughts of despair. *When will he return? What if he has come down with the pox? What if Mr. White has decided to arrest Daniel despite being a Good Samaritan?*

What if I never see my husband again?

She fought back tears as she struggled to hide her turmoil from her mother and sister. They were only a few feet away doing a reading lesson.

Mary looked down at the yarn that draped over her rapidly growing belly. Although she was not overly large for a pregnant woman, she was far more swollen than she or her mother thought she should be at this point. There had been a questioning look on her mother's face containing the suggestion that Mary and Daniel had given in to their passions before they married. This profoundly annoyed Mary. Although she and Daniel had both been anxious to share their affections, they had managed to delay that fulfillment until after their marriage.

Yet, despite their commitment to save their love for the wedding day, this child was growing so fast, and Mary wondered why.

Dear Lord, please do not let this child be so large I cannot deliver him. She shuddered when she heard stories from her mother about difficult deliveries when the child was far too big. Mary tried on a daily basis to push these fears aside.

A small knock at the door interrupted her anxious thoughts. Widow Thomsen was in the middle of the lesson with Sarah, so Mary carefully arose from her chair and set the knitting upon it.

When she opened the door, she was surprised to see young Benjamin Putney. The sweet-faced boy with the impish grin had a larger-than-usual smile on his face.

"Good day, Missus Lowe." Benjamin gave a formal bow.

They must be teaching more on manners at school these days, Mary thought with amusement.

"Yes, Benjamin, how may I help you?" She'd not heard that the boy's mother should be near childbirth just yet, and he seemed far too light-hearted to be reporting an illness.

"I have a message for you, Missus Lowe. From Mr. Lowe." The boy grinned wider than ever.

Mary's heart leaped and her throat dried. "Yes?"

Benjamin seemed to enjoy being the courier of happy news. The whole town was aware of the sacrifice Daniel Lowe had made for the desperately ill in their community, and everyone was in a grateful and celebratory mood. Despite the tragic loss of Jonathan Grant, the townsfolk of Deer Run knew they had been spared a far worse outcome. And they had Daniel to thank for his efforts.

"Mr. Lowe says you should meet him in your special place."

No sooner had the words proceeded from the boy's mouth than Mary grabbed her shawl and began to race for the wigwam.

"Do not run," her mother yelled after Mary.

"I shall not run. I shall just walk extremely quickly." Mary spoke to no one in particular as she slowed down her pace.

In the distance, she could faintly hear Benjamin Putney asking for an apple.

Mary hurried as fast as her rapid walk could carry her.

Was the wigwam really this far? It seemed as if she would never close the distance to the hideaway that secluded her husband.

As she neared the bark structure, fear assaulted her mind. Daniel had not seen her in six weeks and she knew that her appearance had changed. Would he be dismayed at her growing belly? Would he still desire her?

Mary carefully opened the door to the wigwam and walked inside. Daniel turned to face her and she gasped at the appearance of the bearded man standing in front of her. Once she realized it was her husband, she smiled shyly, her heart racing.

Daniel self-consciously rubbed the bristly hair on his face.

"I did not have a razor. I apologize for my unkempt appearance. I didn't mean to frighten you."

Her eyes moistened as she walked closer to this man she loved and stroked the hair on his cheek.

"It reminds me of when we met — just over a year ago." Her voice shivered with excitement.

"When you touched my face with your hand when I was so ill, I wanted it to stay there always." He kissed her palm gently.

Daniel reached over to her linen cap and carefully removed it from her head. He slowly undid the pins that held her long curls in place and watched as her locks fell around her shoulders.

"When your hair stroked against my cheek, I was mesmerized by your beauty. I wanted you to tarry longer. I never wanted you to go away. But when you did, you came back again to me. You saved my life." The passion in his voice thrilled her.

Mary touched the scar on his cheek above his beard. "As you saved mine."

"You risked everything for me." Daniel placed his hand upon her firmly growing belly. "You even hid my coat as though you were with child. And now…" His voice trailed off as he gazed upon the evidence of their baby beneath her wool gown.

He looked at her face with moist eyes. "You are so beautiful, Mary."

He moved his hands around her lower back and drew her close to himself. He kissed her with such deep fervor, she melted in to his embrace. He began to caress her neck with kisses that craved.

"Daniel, I missed you so much." Her whispered voice quivered.

Daniel looked down at Mary, picked her up in his arms and gently laid her down on the quilts covering the hay. He tenderly embraced her, as their desire for each other obliterated all the fears and sadness of the last several weeks.

34

Recollections

aniel and Mary spent most of the afternoon in the wigwam. They knew it would likely be their last visit to this hideaway before the severe cold of winter set in, and Daniel was not anxious to leave.

"I shall miss coming out here to be alone with you." He stroked her hair as they lay next to one another on the quilt.

"I shall as well." Mary snuggled closer to him. "But as long as you are by my side, it does not matter where we are." She looked up at him and nuzzled his neck. "And someday we shall have our own home where we can be quite alone."

"We will not be alone. We will have our little one." Daniel grinned and kissed her slowly. "Have I told you how happy I am to be home?"

"About ten times now. But you can tell me as often as you want and I will not tire of the words. Speaking of our own home, would you like to go see our land?" She looked up at him, excitement edging her voice.

"If you'd like. Are you sure that would not be too long a walk for you? It is getting quite cold by the sound of the wind."

"We can put the quilts around our shoulders to keep warm. We need to take them home for the winter anyway."

They reluctantly got up from the bed of hay and Daniel wrapped one of the blankets around his wife. He used it to draw her close and give her one last kiss before leaving their haven.

"We must remember to come back here next year." He stroked her hair from the top of her head to her waist. "And every year after."

They held each other for a long moment before leaving the warmth of the enclosure to face the cold outdoors. The clouds that had been slowly building through the day started to release small flakes of snow, and the wind stirred the frozen particles into a gentle dance.

"At least 'tis not so freezing as when I brought you here, year last." Mary clung to his waist.

Daniel had his arm around his wife to keep her warm as they walked toward their property. It seemed ironic to him that the land he now owned encompassed the very path he had used as his escape from the Continental guards. When their home was built, he would be able to view the road to Deer Run he had trod upon as a prisoner of war. He hoped his yearlong pilgrimage since that time would help remind him to never despair again. That there was always hope if he would trust in the God Who spared his life and Who had blessed him with his wife and unborn child.

He looked down and squeezed his wife's shoulders.

Mary looked up at him. "What?" Snowflakes started to land upon her hair and he brushed them away.

"I was just thinking about the first time I came along this path. I was running for my life. I thought I was running away, but now I realize I was hastening toward something... toward someone." He kissed the top of her head as they continued their stroll.

Mary rested her head against Daniel's shoulder and hugged his waist more tightly. "I so missed your tender touch."

They walked a short distance farther when Daniel stopped. "What...?" He could not believe his eyes. Where thick rows of birch and maple trees had once stood, now lay several dozen fallen timbers, leaving a large opening in the woods.

Mary looked up at him, her eyes dancing with excitement. "Several of the men from the village came by last week and offered to clear our land for us. They asked me where you and I wanted our home built and I showed them. They've not quite finished felling the trees, but they said they would come back in early spring."

Daniel stood there in silent disbelief.

"'Twas all right for them to start, was it not?" Mary bit her lower lip.

"It is more than all right." Overwhelmed with gratitude, he knew by this neighborly act of kindness that he was accepted into this community. And he knew his past would no longer need to haunt him or cause either of them to fear.

Daniel wrapped his arms around Mary. A great weight had been lifted off his shoulders. They held each other and Daniel dreamed of a peaceful future.

The wind started to pick up in intensity and Mary shivered.

"Let's sally to the farmhouse." Daniel wrapped the quilt more snugly around his wife.

"You missed seeing Jubo and Gibb while you were gone. And Aunt Prudence, of course." She grinned.

Daniel had to smile remembering the previous visit. The great aunt had assumed that Mary had become engaged to Daniel solely due to the older woman's encouragement. She'd been adamant that it was Mary's patriotic duty to bear children to replenish the colonies.

"Aunt Prudence must have been beside herself with joy that you were with child."

"I think she was ready to sign up our son for the Continental Army."

He stopped and looked at Mary more seriously. "I hope that our sons never have to face a war."

Mary touched Daniel's bearded cheeks. "I pray that as well, Daniel."

They resumed their walk in a more sober demeanor. War was still on everyone's mind as the colonial forces continued to clash with the King's army. They both wondered when this conflict would finally be over.

Daniel broke the silence.

"I've been wondering how Sarah took the news — about my past?"

He was concerned about his young sister-in-law and the friendship they had developed. He feared the truth might jeopardize her trust in him. Mary paused before answering.

"At first, she did not believe it, but then, when she realized you actually had been a British soldier, she was quite angry. She cried much over it." Mary paused in their walk. "You seem distressed, Daniel."

"It grieves me she feels I betrayed her."

She put her arms around his waist.

"And then one day she woke up and said, 'I do not care who my brother used to fight for. He is now an American and he is my brother.'"

Mary held Daniel close and he returned the embrace. "Thank you, Mary."

"For what?"

"For believing in me when no one else would."

"Well that was easy," she teased. "You quite swept me off my feet with your passionate glances. I could not resist you."

"So you could not resist my filthy clothing, wretched wound, and scraggly beard?"

She kissed him.

"'Twas your eyes that won my heart, Daniel Lowe."

She shivered again from the wind, and Daniel encouraged her to quicken the pace.

Mary's teeth chattered as she spoke. "I forgot to tell you that Mr. Eaton brought over some fresh lamb's wool for the baby. I spun it into the softest yarn and I'm making him little stockings." Daniel noticed Mary always referred to their unborn child as a boy.

"Mr. Eaton is a true friend." Daniel remembered how the man had helped the family so many times in the last months.

"Do you know that he came over every day whilst you were gone?"

"I am not surprised." He grinned, recalling the man's promise back at the Grant house.

As they neared the Thomsen home, Mary tried to tidy her appearance some before entering the house. Daniel looked at her and couldn't keep from laughing. Bits of hay completely covered her clothes and unkempt hair.

As Daniel picked a piece of straw out of Mary's tresses, he grinned mischievously. "Do you suppose your mother will know where we've been?"

35

Meetings

The deep cold of winter set in with ferocity, forcing Mary and most of the residents of Deer Run to stay indoors as much as possible.

A brief thaw in mid-December, however, allowed the Thomsens and Lowes to attend Sabbath services at the village meetinghouse.

As Mary dressed in her woolen gown for the occasion, she slowly smoothed the soft fabric tightly over her large belly. Her baby now grew at an alarming rate, and the young mother knew that eager tongues would likely wag concerning the timing of the conception.

Tears stung at her eyes as she anticipated the unfair gossip.

Daniel walked over to her, still buttoning his waistcoat.

"What is troubling you, Mary?" He embraced her waist — what was left of it.

"You know what everyone will think, Daniel." Her voice quivered. "I am far too large to be ready to give birth in May. At least, that is what they will intimate with their glances."

"Mary, look at me." Daniel pulled her chin up. "You and I know that this child started after we said our vows. Do not fear their glances. It does not matter what the townspeople say. We know the truth." He tenderly placed his large hands across her belly.

"You and I know the truth. But even Mother looks at me in wonder as she sees how much this child has grown. I confess, I am at a loss to explain it." Her tears started — again. Mary's fragile emotions were a source of consternation for her. Likely for Daniel as well.

"If you do not want to go today, I shall stay home with you."

"Why? Are you ashamed of how I look?" She cried even more.

"No! Of course not." He gave a deep sigh and held her while she wept uncontrollably. When she finished crying, she stood back from him.

"I shall go to the meetinghouse and sit proudly, knowing I have done nothing wrong." She nodded her head with resolve.

"There's my strong Mary."

She washed the tears from her face and set her cap over her pinned up hair. "There. I am ready."

Mary and Daniel walked out of their bedroom and saw that Widow Thomsen and Sarah were already waiting for them.

"Would you like to ride on Dash to the meetinghouse, Mary?" Her mother looked at her with concern.

"No, I think the walk will do me good."

Sarah openly stared at Mary's belly with wide eyes. The thin wool garment seemed to accentuate the size of the growing baby. Widow Thomsen must have noticed for she placed her hands on the girl's shoulders.

"Let's be off then, Sarah. We will discuss these long gazes at an appropriate time later." Mary's cheeks burned with embarrassment when she heard her mother's whispers to the curious girl.

The women all donned their woolen capes and Daniel put on the deerskin coat over his waistcoat. Mary was still in the midst of sewing him a woolen coat, but it was not yet complete.

The chilly air refreshed and revived Mary's spirits, and the family soon chatted the entire length of the walk to the village. It would be Daniel's initial visit to the meetinghouse since the outbreak of smallpox and Mary worried about the reception he would receive. But her fears abated rather quickly. It seemed the townsfolk of Deer Run awaited his return with open hearts.

"Welcome back, Mr. Lowe." A gray-haired gent shook his hand with fervor.

"Thank you, sir." Daniel's smile appeared cautious. Myles Eaton approached the family with a wide grin.

"Good to see you back in town, Daniel." He wrapped his arm around the young man's shoulders.

As the group walked toward the wooden building, Selectman White turned toward the family to greet them.

"Hello, Mr. Lowe." The man gripped Daniel's hand.

Mary took note of the deep scars on the man's hands and face from the disease that had nearly taken his life. Daniel smiled as though he did not notice them.

"Hello to you, sir. I am glad to see you are well." Daniel's smile was open and relaxed.

"Thanks to you, I am." Mr. White's voice seemed more humble than his usual. "I am indebted to you, sir."

Daniel bowed to the selectman.

Mary saw Hannah a few feet away and waddled slightly to close the distance. "Hannah, 'tis splendid to see you well. You look wonderful." They embraced for a long moment. "'Tis God's gift to our family that you are recovered."

Although Hannah still had several visible scars, she'd been spared from serious disfigurement. Unfortunately for Josiah Grant, the same could not be said. The numerous pox had left insidious craters over his face and hands. The previously handsome young soldier had lost his prideful swagger, now replaced by the slumped shoulders of a broken man.

Mary startled at the appearance of Josiah. Although she knew he'd been ill, nothing could have prepared her for this metamorphosis.

"Good day, Josiah." Mary attempted to swallow although her dry throat resisted.

Josiah's gaze was drawn automatically to Mary's large belly, and it was with obvious pain that he looked at her face. Daniel put his arm around her waist and drew her close to him protectively. The move did not go unnoticed by the unsuccessful suitor.

"Good day, Daniel. Mary." Josiah seemed nervous as he tipped his tricorne hat far too quickly.

"Good day, Josiah." Daniel still held her closely. "I am glad you are recovered from your illness." His words were sincere, but Daniel still seemed guarded.

"Yes, thanks to you, sir." Josiah cast his eyes downward.

"So what are your plans, sir?" Daniel words were formal yet friendly.

"I leave tomorrow to return to camp." Josiah wiped the hair off his forehead with shaking hands. "I've closed the house up in the meantime. Don't know when I'll return." He glanced for a brief moment at Mary with a pained look. "There's nothin' for me here."

Mary paused nervously. She was grateful for Daniel's firm grip, as her knees weakened. This was her initial encounter with Josiah since the incident so long ago and she trembled with the memory.

"I shall pray for your safety, Josiah." Mary words sounded more calm than she felt.

"Thank you, Mary." Tears brimmed his eyes, as he tipped his hat again and hurried inside the building.

"Let's go sit down." Daniel guided her toward the meetinghouse steps. She nodded in assent and the two made their way to the pew.

No sooner had Mary taken her seat than she noticed the Howard sisters looking at her and whispering to one another. They counted on their fingers, apparently trying to determine the number of months that Mary and Daniel had been man and wife.

They probably cannot count without using their fingers.

Mary noticed Daniel glaring at the Howard sisters' obvious insult. He took Mary's hand and squeezed it, giving her a reassuring smile.

The singing was soon underway, and the soothing lyrics from the Psalms were a comforting respite for Mary. They helped her focus on God's encouragement amidst the many storms in her life.

Mary felt ill after the morning service, and Widow Thomsen hurried over to Mr. Eaton. "Myles," she said in earnest, "would you be so kind as to drive Mary home in your wagon?"

A shadow of concern etched across Mr. Eaton's countenance. "Be pleased to help, Widow Thomsen. I'll get my wagon ready with haste and take you both home." Mary watched Mr. Eaton discreetly give her mother's hand a reassuring squeeze.

"Thank you, Myles."

For the first time, Mary realized she was pleased at the friendship forming between her mother and Mr. Eaton. He was a good man of integrity, who treated all of them with care and concern.

Mary noticed Sarah's look of disappointment.

"May I stay for the afternoon service, Mother?" Sarah's eyes pleaded with their mother.

Mary hated to be the cause of disrupting her younger sister's day.

This would perhaps be Sarah's last time at the meetinghouse through the long winter ahead. And yet Mary knew she needed her mother more than anyone else right now.

"Daniel, would you be willing to stay with Sarah for the afternoon? My mother can look after me."

"Of course I can stay with her. We shall have a grand picnic together."

"Thank you, Daniel." Sarah seemed grateful although a bit subdued.

In one respect, Daniel was thankful for this opportunity to spend time with the seven-year-old child. He'd noted a slight change in her demeanor toward him since he'd returned from the White's home. He suspected that, although she loved him as her brother, she still struggled in her mind with his past. He hoped Sarah could resolve in her mind that he'd once been an enemy soldier. The opportunity to speak about the situation finally afforded itself on their walk home later that afternoon.

They sauntered mostly in silence, and Daniel noted Sarah was not her usually talkative self.

"So how did you enjoy the afternoon service, little miss?" Daniel made an effort to begin communication.

"Fine." She looked straight ahead with little enthusiasm on her face.

"Fine? That is all you have to say to me?" Daniel tried to appear lighthearted. "We used to have such jolly conversations, little miss."

"That was before…" She stopped herself and frowned.

"Before you knew I was a King's soldier?" He dared to put words to her unspoken thoughts.

"You lied to me, Daniel." Her unexpected outburst of rage caught him by surprise. "You said you were injured in the war!"

"That was not a lie. I was injured in the war." They paused on the road home.

"But you did not tell me you were a Redcoat!"

"And what would you have done if I had told you I was?"

"I do not know, but it was not right that you made me think you were one of us."

Her childish words stung at his heart. He looked off into the distance at the clouds that threatened to bring measurable snow. He was not certain if the air or her words chilled him the most.

Sarah seemed to realize her speech had been cruel.

"I'm sorry, Daniel." Her voice edged with sadness. "I do not wish to hurt you. I just felt — betrayed. I know you are an American now." She paused. "Why did you become a King's soldier?"

Daniel looked at his young sister-in-law. "Where I come from, that is what second sons do."

"Second sons? So you have an older brother?" She tilted her head inquisitively.

"Yes. His name is William and he inherited the family home."

"I see. And… why did you have to come here to fight our people?"

"I was told to, little miss." He remembered the day he received his orders. "I did not have a choice."

Sarah seemed to ponder all these revelations, then took his hand. "I'm sorry I was so angry with you, Daniel. I did not understand." She looked up at him.

"It's all right, little miss. Many things in life are difficult to understand."

"I'm glad you were told to come here, because… now you are my brother."

"I am grateful as well."

He squeezed her small hand in his and the two walked hand-in-hand up the hill toward home.

When Daniel and Sarah arrived home, he inquired about his wife's health.

"She is well, Daniel. 'Twas a very difficult time for her at the meetinghouse, what with seeing Josiah Grant and all."

Daniel resisted the urge to bristle at the name. "Yes, I know." His jaw worked to restrain his emotions. "Is Mary asleep?"

"I know she's resting, but I do not think she's asleep." The widow resumed stirring a large kettle of beans.

"I will see how she fares." He went to their bedroom and closed the door.

"Daniel?" Mary sat up in bed.

"Please do not get up, Mary. How are you?" He kissed her cheek and sat next to her on the bed.

"Better, thank you." She lay back down on her pillow. "I'm very tired, that's all."

Daniel lay down next to her and wrapped his arms around her.

Mary gasped and grabbed at her belly.

"What is it?" Daniel asked in alarm.

"He's moving." She laughed. "A great deal."

She placed Daniel's hand on her belly so he could feel their child. He waited but felt nothing. "Every time I put my hand on you, the child stops moving."

"Well, he is an active little one. He must be a boy." Mary started to laugh. "That's exactly what I said to that soldier last year when I was hiding your coat."

"What soldier?" His curiosity piqued.

"I never told you? 'Twas when I wrapped your red coat in my petticoat and pretended to be with child. A soldier came by on horseback and I said I was out walking for my health."

Daniel looked at her in complete surprise and concern.

"You never told me this. I did not realize you were so endangered."

"I was safe, Daniel." She squeezed his hand. "But my bundle in the petticoat slipped at one point and I nearly gave birth to your coat right in front of the soldier."

She seemed amused by the incident. Daniel was not.

"You could have been arrested." He held her close, horrified at the possible outcome.

"Daniel, I did not mean to cause you distress. I was just remembering what I had said to the soldier: 'Active little one. Must be a boy.' I'm sorry this distressed you."

He kissed the back of her neck. "You continue to amaze me, Mary Thomsen."

"Excuse me, sir." Her voice held mock disdain. "That is Mary Lowe, if you please. I am a married woman."

He placed his hand upon her belly. "Well that is a fortunate thing considering your condition, Missus Lowe."

When he said these words in jest, he felt a forceful kick against his hand. Mary burst out laughing when she turned and saw the shocked look on his face.

"Mr. Lowe, please meet your son. He's trying to shake your hand."

36

Patriot

James pressed forward with resolve, walking down the spring-dampened dirt road.

Mud and the powdery residue of musket fire covered his blue uniform. The facing on his coat, which used to be white, was now a dingy gray. He attempted to wipe it off but it was useless. An occasional stain of old blood added more color than was intended for this Continental uniform. The only purposeful scarlet was the single epaulette on his right shoulder, signifying a rank of sergeant. He straightened out the entwined strands.

Drawing closer to his destination, his gait quickened, as did his anticipation. He'd been away at war the better part of three years, but James Thomsen was finally home. As he approached the family farm that late-March afternoon, he wondered how much had changed since his last visit. His previous journey had been the most painful of his life. His mission that sweltering summer day was to return the lifeless body of his younger brother Asa, who was then buried in the family plot next to their father. James shivered at the memory. He hoped this short respite from war would prove a far happier visit.

In the distance he noticed his mother. She walked out of the barn carrying a bucket when she stopped abruptly and scanned his way.

He saw her running toward him with tears streaming down her cheeks. He grinned wide, his green eyes dancing. They embraced silently in a mutual grip of relief and joy.

She released him and touched his face with shaking hands.

"You are well?" Tears flowed freely down her face.

"I am, Mother."

"Your youth is still alive in your eyes. But I see the scars of war revealing you've been in danger more than once." Her lips trembled.

"Let us not speak of war. I'm so elated to be home!"

She touched his graying lapel. "This uniform, is it new?"

James looked down at his apparel. "Not exactly new. 'Twas issued several months ago. I'm now a sergeant."

"Your father would be so proud." Her lips quivered again. "Come to the house. There is much news to tell you."

As they headed down the road, the door of the house opened and a stranger walked outside.

"Who is that?" James asked his mother. He stared at the man with suspicion.

"That is part of the news, James —"

"That man is not from Deer Run." James eyed the stranger. Something about the man's features sparked an ominous recognition in his mind. At first he could not place the familiar face, but it only took a moment for him to recall that moment in battle he would never forget.

From a distance, the smiling man appeared to welcome his appearance. But as he approached him more closely, the stranger's smile began to fade. James noticed a look of surprise, then hesitation before the man stopped altogether. Uncertainty flashed across the stranger's face. James could feel the heat of anger boil in his blood.

"You bloody Redcoat." James drew his sword. "Did I spare your life so you could prey upon my family? I've never stayed my bayonet in battle before. I should not have done so in Saratoga!"

James stalked toward Daniel.

"James, stop! You do not understand," Widow Thomsen yelled frantically at her son.

But it was the voice of his sister, screaming and crying from the open door that prompted him to stop in his tracks.

"James, no! He is my husband!" Mary cried hysterically.

Startled, he halted his advance and looked at his sister in disbelief. He had to stare long and hard to comprehend the unexpected sight — Mary, who appeared ready to give birth at any moment. The very pregnant Mary slowly made her way to him with tears streaming down her face.

"He is my husband, James," she whispered as she wiped her wet face with her apron.

Carefully placing his arms around Mary, his fury stopped cold, but his heart still pounded in his chest. James looked over her shoulder at Daniel.

"You are her husband?" This was too difficult to believe.

Daniel swallowed visibly and wiped the sweat from his brow.

"Yes." The man's eyes widened at the near attack.

James held his sister a moment longer as her tears subsided. Widow Thomsen touched James' arm.

"Son, we must speak with one another. Please come with me."

She drew him aside, and he released his embrace on his sister, still glaring at Daniel. James followed his mother reluctantly. He was upset and baffled by this situation.

<hr />

Daniel put his arm around his wife as Widow Thomsen and James walked toward the barn.

"Mary, let us go back inside." Daniel feared this stress could bring on the birth of their child too early.

Although labor appeared to be imminent, the expected arrival was not for another month. However, the size of Mary's belly seemed to indicate otherwise.

They walked back into the farmhouse. Daniel helped his wife up the step that led to the main room and led her to the chair by the fire. Although spring was on its way, the air still held a damp chill.

"Daniel, I am so sorry about James." Mary shuddered and Daniel placed a woolen shawl around her shoulders. "How did he know you were a King's soldier?"

He sat in a chair next to hers and took her hand.

"Do you remember when I told you about Oliver? How I held him as he died? A Continental soldier came with his bayonet uplifted, and I thought it was my demise?"

Mary nodded. "You closed your eyes for a moment and when you opened them, he was gone."

Daniel took a deep breath. He still tried to comprehend this strange turn of events but he finally spoke the words that were difficult even for him to believe.

"That soldier who spared my life was your brother James."

Mary's eyes opened wide. "James?" She sat back in the wooden chair and was silent for a moment. "Did you recognize him as well?"

"Yes. As soon as I saw him I knew he was familiar. It only took a few moments to realize who he was. I envisioned his green eyes staring at me with his bayonet held high. I was just getting ready to thank him when he made the same connection between us. I realized then that he sorely regretted his mercy back in Saratoga."

Mary squeezed his hand. "Thank God he did spare you."

"I hope he begins to feel that way as well."

His wife shifted restlessly in the chair as she placed her hands over her enormous belly.

"This child seems far too active." She winced. "He moves so much — 'tis exhausting."

He looked at her with sympathy. "I'm sorry you're suffering so." He rubbed her arm, wishing this simple motion could relieve her discomfort. And no wonder she was uncomfortable. Though he would never say this to his wife, he'd never before seen a pregnant woman so large. And on her slender frame, the contrast with her enlarged belly was startling.

He kissed his wife and served her some warm cider in a pewter tankard. Mary had finished most of the cider when her mother, James, and Sarah all came in to the house. Sarah had been collecting eggs in the barn and had missed the initial encounter between Daniel and James. The young girl brimmed with enthusiasm over the return of her brother.

"Did you see who is home?" Sarah danced around the room.

The couple smiled at Sarah's joyful demeanor.

"Sarah, please put the basket of eggs down before you break them," Widow Thomsen chided. The young girl giggled and set the container down before hugging her brother once again. James embraced Sarah in return before removing his tricorne hat.

He meekly approached Daniel with an apologetic attitude. He cast his eyes downward for a moment and fidgeted with his hat.

"Mother has spoken with me at length, Mr. Lowe. I am greatly humbled by the enlightening reports regarding your help to my family." James continued to fidget with his hat. "I beg your forgiveness for my aggression toward you upon my arrival."

"Please call me Daniel. And your response was certainly understandable." Daniel held his hand out to Mary's sibling. "Let us be friends — as well as brothers."

James' green eyes looked intently at Daniel. The Continental soldier still bore the hyper-vigilant edge of someone fresh off the field of battle. His demeanor was now more subdued, however, and his eyes glistened with gratitude.

After a long pause he spoke. "It appears the Lord had me spare you for a reason. And I thank you for saving my sisters whilst I was gone."

James took his hand and the two men shook. Daniel noticed the strong familial resemblance between Mary and her brother. It somehow made him feel an immediate kinship with the man.

Turning his attention to Mary, James bent down near her chair and looked at her belly.

"It appears you've been occupying your time well whilst I've been gone, little sister." He smirked playfully.

She pushed him on his shoulder. "You're always the jester, James."

"So when is the little one due to arrive? It looks to be any moment." Mary's face grew serious.

"Not for another month or more." She rubbed her swollen belly. James' expression showed his surprise.

"Really? I hoped the little one might arrive while I'm home on leave." Mary's demeanor saddened.

"You have to go back soon? You've only just arrived. Please tarry as long as possible."

Her brother touched her arm. "I'll be here for a short while — long enough to ask Hannah to be my wife. If she'll have me, of course."

Mary grinned. "I don't know, James. She may have decided you were not worth waiting for."

Daniel saw the look of consternation on James' face.

"My wife can be cruel, can she not?" Daniel laughed. "Of course, Hannah has been waiting for you. She'll be beside herself with joy that you're home."

James smiled in relief and pinched his sister's cheek. "Some things never change between brothers and sisters." He laughed, then stood up and hugged his sister awkwardly, trying to avoid her belly.

"I'm going to see Hannah immediately, before she decides that I am not worth the wait." He looked back at his very pregnant sister and pointed at her belly. "Do not birth that baby before I get back."

He grinned at her, put his hat back on, and walked out the front door.

"'Tis such relief to have my brother home, even for only a short while."

Daniel breathed in relief, as well. He finally relaxed from the tension of James' arrival.

Widow Thomsen began setting out the evening meal. Daniel helped Mary out of her chair so she could go over to the table. She would not be able to eat a great deal, but the small amount she could manage would sustain her for a few hours — until the middle of the night, when she would awaken Daniel to get her some bread and milk, which had become their nighttime ritual.

When they retired to their room that evening, Daniel lay awake in bed, reflecting on the events of the day.

He watched in awe at the movements of his child in Mary's belly as she lay on her back, propped up on several pillows. It was amazing to him just how active their little one truly was.

"So what should we name our child, Mary?" He stroked her belly, enjoying the small feet kicking at his touch.

"I think we should call him Daniel."

"Daniel?" The young father furrowed his brow. "How about James, after your father?"

"We shall see." Mary nestled next to her husband.

"We've not discussed lasses' names. I think we should call her Mary."
He kissed her, then Mary placed her hand on his cheek.

"I think a daughter should be named Polly — after your sister."
Mary caressed his face.

Daniel nuzzled his wife's forehead and held her close. "Thank you, Mary."

⁓

They held each other in a comforting embrace. Soon she could hear
the quiet snore of her husband and feel his arms relaxed in sleep.

Mary, however, was wide-awake. She removed his arm from around
her and, after trying to find a more comfortable position in the bed,
she realized her mind was far too active to rest. She picked up the Bible
on her bedside table.

*Perhaps reading about new mothers in God's word will soothe my
anxious thoughts.*

She opened the pages to the book of Genesis and read about the
birth of Isaac to his mother Sarah in her old age.

Poor woman. I'm grateful I am not so old as Sarah.

Mary continued to peruse the pages until she found the passages
about the delivery of Rebekah, wife of Isaac. She read about the woman's difficult pregnancy and how she'd entreated God for an answer as
to why there was such an uproar in her belly.

"And when her days to be delivered were fulfilled, behold, there were
twins in her womb." Mary read in a whisper. She paused in her reading and
looked down at her enormous belly of activity. She thought for a moment.

"No, 'tis not possible."

She placed the Bible back on the table and blew out the candle.

Travail

It had stormed heavily in Deer Run during the night, but it was sunny and clear that early April morning. The earth started to awaken from its long winter hibernation, and the new life in her surroundings filled Mary with energy.

She paused for a moment as she did every day to check the progress of her favorite lavender plants. The gray leaves were just starting to come back as they did each spring, the gradual greening of the dormant spikes promising another year of fragrant purple flowers. Mary stared at the cornfield ready for planting. The rows of dirt mounds were meant to simulate the belly of a pregnant woman, according to Indian lore. Mary looked down and draped her linen gown tightly over her growing child. She had always thought the piles of soil were similar to the dimensions of an actual pregnancy. Somehow, the hills in the field seemed inadequate to any comparison to her belly. She furrowed her brow.

"I think we need to add more dirt to the mounds." Mary continued her waddling walk to the barn, milk bucket in hand. She entered the barn and smiled at Daniel, who cleaned tools for the upcoming planting. Aunt Prudence would be here any day now and everything needed to be ready for Jubo and Gibb.

"And how do you fare this morning?" Daniel noticed the bucket she carried. "You're not going to milk Susannah, are you?"

"My mother says sitting on the milking stool will help prepare me for the birth. Besides, I am feeling so energetic this morning — I could probably start planting, I feel so good."

"Well that is not going to happen." Daniel stopped long enough to kiss her. "I'm certain that milking Susannah is quite enough. But once you've filled the bucket, let me carry it back inside. I know your back has been feeling the strain."

Her husband resumed his task of cleaning the tools when Mary stopped him.

"Daniel, I've been thinking. Have you thought about writing to your father to tell him about the baby? He does not even know we are married. I know you greatly miss him." Her heart overflowed with sympathy.

Daniel eyes filled with sadness. "That would cause me great joy, Mary… but with the war still going on, I cannot risk communicating with him just yet." He looked at his wife with tenderness. "Thank you for thinking of him. I hope that someday he'll be able to meet both you and our child."

He kissed his wife and returned to his labors. Daniel had a somber look on his face.

To lighten the mood, Mary began to sing a lyric she'd composed for him. She knew he loved to hear her sing. She would occasionally write down words and then put them to music in her mind. It was a pastime she and her brother Asa had enjoyed before he went off to war — before the war had silenced his music on the fife forever.

She walked toward Susannah's stall and started to sing. "There was a lad named Daniel Lowe, Across the sea come sailin'. He met a girl, set his heart atwirl…"

Before Mary could get out the next line, a tightness seized her belly with such force she could not speak. She gripped the wooden post in the stall, her knuckles turning white. The intensity of the contraction brought her down onto her knees and she felt a warm liquid coming out from between her legs. She knew now this child was going to be born — and soon.

Daniel looked down at the tools he oiled, smiling at the song.

"What is the next line, Mary?" When she did not answer, he looked up in surprise and saw his wife's hand clutching the post above the wooden barrier of the stall.

His heart skipped a beat. "Mary!" Running toward her, he crouched beside her, his wounded leg jutting out awkwardly.

"Daniel." Her breathing came in gasps. "The baby — it's too early." Fear filled her voice.

"This child has decided otherwise." He tried not to panic. Standing, he picked her up to carry her to the house.

"I can walk, Daniel. The pain has lessened." He reluctantly set her back on the ground. "My mother will keep me walking through much of my travail."

He kept his arm around her as they walked cautiously back to the house. Before they reached the front door, Mary grasped her belly again, her knees bending with the force. Daniel held her up and noticed her cheeks turning a bright red with the effort of the contraction. It seemed to go on forever, stretching the time before she was able to breathe with ease. She headed back toward the farmhouse, as he supported her with both arms.

Entering the house Daniel saw Widow Thomsen and James speaking together. When they noticed Daniel assisting Mary indoors, a look of distress appeared on both of their faces.

"'Tis time?" Widow Thomsen looked concerned but not surprised. Mary nodded in assent as yet another intense pain clenched at her belly. "Bring her to the bedroom, Daniel," she instructed. "And please get the birthing stool from the barn, James."

⌒‿⊙

James ran to the barn followed by Sarah.

"The baby is coming, James? So soon?" Sarah breathed in gasps from the excitement. "I thought 'twas coming month next?"

He reached up to grab the birthing stool from a hook on the wall. He also grabbed an old rag and dusted it off.

"Sometimes babies come sooner than we thought." James and his mother had previously discussed their mutual belief that the baby had been conceived prior to the wedding.

James looked at the old wooden birthing stool and was impressed with its design. The slender edge of the chair allowed the woman to sit while providing an opening for the baby to be delivered.

"I remember getting this down for our mother when you were born, Sarah." James pinched her cheek.

"But that was a very long time ago, James. I'm quite grown up now." Sarah stood as tall as her short height would allow.

James tousled her hair with one hand. "Then you'd best get that hair pinned up under a cap if you are such a lady." He smiled then grew more serious. "But do not grow up too quickly. Having one sister marry and start a family is sufficient for now."

They both walked back to the farmhouse, one on each side of the birthing stool. Together they transported the chair that would soon witness the birth of their nephew or niece.

Sitting in the chair by the fire, Daniel nervously rubbed his head. His child was birthing sooner than expected and this concerned him greatly.

James and Sarah arrived with the birthing chair; when Daniel saw it, he took it gratefully and brought it to the door of the bedroom. He knocked. Widow Thomsen opened the door, grabbed the stool, and shut the door quickly. Daniel caught a brief glimpse of his wife bending over in yet another bout of gut wrenching pain. Breathing far too quickly, he turned his back to the door.

James looked at his brother-in-law with concern. "Perhaps you should sit back down, Daniel. You look a bit done in."

Daniel accepted his advice. Sarah approached him, her brows furrowed.

"'Twill be all right, Daniel." She touched his large hand with her small one. "Would you like to pray — like we did when Mary was ill?"

Daniel looked at Sarah with gratitude. "Yes, little miss. That is what we should do."

James joined the group in a prayer for Mary and her unborn baby. Daniel tried to put to rest the never-ending fear that arose in him at the memory of his mother dying in childbirth.

Dear God, please take this fear away from me.

When the prayer finished, James looked up. "I must go and get Hannah. Mary wanted her to come at this time."

"You'll have to ride bareback, James. There's only a side saddle here."

"Ah, well…" He shook his head and left.

Daniel continued to sit in the chair near the hearth. He tried not to flinch every time he heard his wife's moans from the bedroom. Sarah brought him some apple cider to drink.

"Thank you, little miss." The liquid soothed his dry throat.

His young sister-in-law then brought over *Aesop's Fables* so she could read to him. Daniel tried to pay attention to the stories, but his mind constantly returned to the events taking place in the side room.

Although it seemed like hours, James soon returned with Hannah astride Dash. The young woman hurried into the house, her eyes wide with concern. Daniel nodded toward the bedroom and Hannah hurried inside. She shut the door behind her, but for a few seconds, they were able to hear Mary's groans more audibly.

"You look a bit strained, Daniel. Let us go work, rather than worry." James patted him on his shoulder.

Reluctantly, Daniel got up and looked at Sarah.

"You will call me if Mary needs me?"

"Yes, Daniel. But… I think she just needs the women right now."

The two men went outdoors and Daniel breathed in deeply of the fresh air. He looked out toward the distant woods. The emerging buds promised lush greenery before long.

"This child is coming too soon." Daniel's anxiety grew.

James stared at him for a long while.

"You mean, this truly 'tis not expected?"

Daniel stared at Mary's brother.

"No, it is not — although I understand why you ask that. I have never seen a woman so large with child before. Mary and I have both been concerned all along. But no, this baby began its life right after our wedding day." Daniel exhaled in exasperation, tired from the assumptions of others.

After a long pause James said, "I believe you. But now I'm concerned as well."

A rider came down the road toward the farmhouse and the two brothers looked over and saw Mr. Eaton approaching.

"Heard there were big goings on at the Thomsen farm." Mr. Eaton paused as he noted their expressions. "Why so somber, gentlemen? This is a happy occasion." He dismounted, then slapped the soon-to-be father on the back.

Daniel and James told the visitor about the baby arriving ahead of schedule and the three of them stood in deep thought. Daniel's fears worsened when Widow Thomsen came to the door, yelling for the men to come quickly.

"Daniel, something is wrong." The midwife tried to appear calm but her trembling lips betrayed her apprehension. "I need someone to get Widow Baxter, the midwife in Williamston."

James stared blankly at his mother.

"Widow Baxter?" James' mouth gaped in surprise. "Is she not dead?"

Widow Thomsen glared at her son. "Of course she's not dead, James!"

"No, really, I thought she was. Is she not nigh a hundred?"

"She's in her eighties, but she is still able to help with a birthing. And I need her experience right now, so please hasten!"

"Right."

James ran to get Dash from the barn once again. He rode away as quickly as he could to fetch the elderly midwife, who lived three miles down the road in Williamston.

While the widow argued with James, Daniel had slipped into the house and went to the door of the bedroom. He opened it cautiously and saw Mary in bed crying.

"Daniel, I need to speak with you alone." Mary sobbed and appeared in great distress.

Hannah exited the room quickly and Daniel shut the door. He hurried over to Mary and grabbed her hand.

"Daniel," Mary gasped. "You must promise me something." She spoke in between labored breaths, her red face dripping with sweat.

"Yes, anything." He battled tears.

"If I do not survive this birth, I want you to tell our son that I want him to grow up to be a good man, just like his father."

Daniel shook his head, unable to speak for fear the tears would begin to flow along with his words.

"And tell him that I love him." Mary blurted out these words just before another grinding pain assaulted her swollen abdomen.

Daniel watched as his wife put every ounce of her being into delivering their child. He suddenly felt an overpowering surge of hope and conviction, and he was determined to be stalwart for Mary. When her pain abated, Daniel looked at her with tears but with strength.

"You will survive this birth." He spoke with firm but gentle resolve. "And you will tell him you love him yourself."

He kissed her with a brief but passionate kiss and released her back to the care of her mother, who had hurried back to the birthing.

Daniel limped back to the main room, wiping the tears away from his face. Myles Eaton looked at him with sympathy.

"Come on, lad." Myles put his arm around Daniel's shoulders. "Let us take a walk and clear our heads."

38

Midwife

It took James only twenty minutes to ride from the Thomsen's farm to Williamston. With the strain of the situation, however, it felt much longer. As he arrived at the edge of the town square, he slowed the mare to a canter. He scanned the somewhat familiar surroundings, yet could not locate the home of Widow Baxter. Seven years earlier he had come here to fetch the midwife for Sarah's birthing. But the town had grown and changed since then, and he could not discern which cabin it was. His anxiety made the effort even more difficult.

He spotted two boys of perhaps thirteen years of age. "Good day, lads. Can you tell me where the midwife lives?"

"Yes, sir." They saluted him. "Follow us, sir."

They ran down the road a short way and pointed to the log cabin, which James now recognized instantly.

"Thank you, lads. You are worthy young soldiers."

James knew these boys were likely anxious to be at war, helping the cause for freedom. So many colonial youths expressed frustration at the age restriction of sixteen years.

"Thank you, sir." They spoke in unison, looking at James' uniform with admiration. The taller lad asked him about the need for Widow Baxter.

"Is it your wife needing the midwife, sir?"

"No — my sister." James jumped off of Dash's back. "Can one of you lads hold the reins for me whilst I get the widow?"

The boys' eyes danced at the request and gave their hearty consent.

They stroked Dash's nose and forehead as though she were the steed of General Washington himself. James raced to the front door and knocked loudly. He waited a moment with no response and knocked even harder.

"Maybe she did die." He desperately hoped he was wrong. At length, the slow-moving woman finally opened the door. She looked at James with her head tilted back to allow her to see him through her spectacles.

"Yes, young man, may I help you?" Her voice crackled.

James fought the despair that rose in his spirit. Her ancient appearance seemed to support the jests of local children that Widow Baxter had likely birthed those born aboard the Mayflower over a hundred years before. James attempted to smother any signs of his growing panic.

"I am Sergeant Thomsen from Deer Run, ma'am. You are still the midwife, Widow Baxter?" James swallowed with difficulty.

"I still do some birthings, sir, that is correct." She flashed a nearly toothless grin, then examined him more carefully. "Do I know you, sir? Your face looks familiar."

"Yes, ma'am, I fetched you seven years ago for the birth of my younger sister in Deer Run. But I am here today to ask you to assist in the birthing of my other sister's child. She is in some distress and my mother needs your help."

The light of recognition appeared in Widow Baxter's pale eyes.

"Ah yes. Your mother is midwife in Deer Run — Widow Thomsen. I taught your mother the art of birthing babes." She paused and James fidgeted. "So 'tis your sister in distress." She put her finger to her lips. "She must be the lass that was born here in my own home whilst you were home ill with the smallpox, as I recall."

"Yes, Widow Baxter, that is correct." Sweat began to form on James' brow. "If you please, ma'am, my mother is most anxious for your help. I can take you to Deer Run on horseback, but we must hasten."

The widow reached up to touch James' cheek and pat it gently. "Do not fear, young man. I shall get my things."

Slowly, she walked over toward a cabinet and pulled down a bottle of spirits. "Does your mother have enough wine for the new mother?"

James scratched his head. "I suppose she does, Widow Baxter. She is always quite prepared for these events."

"Good."

The elderly woman took the lid off the flask of spirits and took a hearty guzzle. She replaced the bottle in the cupboard.

James helped the midwife get her shawl over her shoulders and practically carried the thin woman out the door.

The two boys faithfully guarded Dash. The horse seemed content with all the attention being lavished upon her. As James approached the mare with Widow Baxter, he paused to determine the safest way to get her aboard the horse's back. He came up with a plan.

"If we can get cannon up a hill, surely you men can help me get the midwife up onto this steed." He chose words to inspire the boys' patriotic spirit.

"Yes, sir."

James brought Dash over to a sturdy maple tree with large overhanging limbs.

"Men, climb up onto these branches and I shall hand you Widow Baxter. You can then assist her in getting mounted safely onto the horse."

"Aye, sir," the lads answered in unison. The limber youths immediately clambered up the tree. Once they were in proper position on the branches, James lifted the midwife up into their waiting arms. They carefully placed the frail woman onto the horse's back as securely as they could.

"Hold on to the horse's mane whilst I climb up there to secure you further," he instructed Widow Baxter.

Widow Baxter laughed heartily at all this activity.

"Why, I have not had that many hands of young men upon me since my courting days." She chuckled.

The two boys in the tree looked at each other with raised eyebrows.

"Someone courted this shriveled woman?" one whispered to the other. The boys shared a look of amazement.

James looked at them and squelched a laugh. The elderly woman's poor hearing prevented her from catching their words, and she sat happily awaiting the ride to help the new mother.

"Good job, men." James climbed behind Widow Baxter onto the

horse's back. "I'm grateful for your help. You've assisted in the safe delivery of what will be the newest patriot in the colonies. Well done!"

James saluted the boys and they returned the gesture, beaming with pride.

Holding the reins tightly, he wrapped his arms protectively around the elderly widow. To ensure safe passage for Widow Baxter, he trotted Dash at a somewhat slower pace than he had on the ride out.

It seemed so long since he had left his distressed sister. He prayed their arrival would not be too late.

39

Birth

Back at the farm, James' arrival was met with both relief and consternation. Daniel experienced comfort that a second midwife was now on the premises, but alarm at how frail the woman appeared. Daniel and Mr. Eaton carefully assisted the woman off the mare as James handed her down.

"Thank you for coming, Widow Baxter." Daniel tried not to appear as frightened as he felt.

"You must be the young father." The toothless woman grinned. "Let's see what we can do for your wife, sir. Show me the way."

Daniel assisted the woman inside and led her to the bedroom. He heard Mary's wails of discomfort and rubbed the sweat off his brow. Widow Baxter turned toward the group of men who stood there looking helpless.

"Why don't you gents take a walk." All three men followed her advice.

Daniel watched Sarah a moment. She kept occupied fetching small buckets of water from the well and tending the hot water over the fire. Whenever the women inside the birthing room requested warm cloths to soothe Mary's abdomen, the young girl had them at the ready.

He turned and walked outside to join the other men. He only wished there was something he could do to help.

When Ruth Thomsen saw the midwife from Williamston enter the birthing room, relief filled her with hope. Help had finally arrived.

"Thank you for coming, Widow Baxter." Near exhaustion from trying to assist Mary, Ruth had first tried one position for her laboring daughter, then another. It seemed this child could not present itself to the world and Ruth was near despair.

The older woman greeted her, than assessed the situation closely but spoke few words. She went over to Mary. "I see you're much fatigued from this travail, child." Widow Baxter gave her a comforting pat on the shoulder. "Haven't seen you in some time, lass. Now, let me put my hands on your belly here to see what is where."

The elderly woman deftly felt each portion of the huge abdomen. Although she appeared frail, the older midwife worked with a strength that came only with experience. She moved her hands all around Mary's belly.

"I see." She wiped her hands on her apron. "It appears that they are both trying to be birthed at the same time."

The women all stared at Widow Baxter. Words caught in Ruth's throat. Finally Hannah White broke the silence.

"Both?" Hannah's voice sounded small and weak.

"You did not know there were twins?" The midwife seemed perplexed.

Ruth's face burned with embarrassment. "No... I thought... that is... I should have known." She stammered.

The older woman patted her shoulder.

"Do not fret, Widow Thomsen. It can be easy to miss, especially when it's your own daughter. We midwives can be fooled."

A severe pain gripped at Mary's belly. "I need to push."

Widow Baxter suddenly became commander of the delivery.

"All right then. We're going to figure out just which babe is ready to come out first. They seem to be jammed like logs in a river. We need to hold one back to let the other downstream."

Mary was in the midst of a bearing down pain when the older midwife ascertained which twin should be firstborn and which was the log-jammer. When the urge to push ceased, Widow Baxter encouraged her troops.

"All right, ladies, let's get this brave mother onto the birthing stool."

Widow Baxter helped Mary as much as she was able. Ruth and

Hannah did most of the lifting. Mary's exhaustion from hours of labor grieved Ruth.

How could I have missed this? But there was no time for guilt as there was work to be done. Her grandchildren needed to be birthed.

"Let us lean her forward some. And you, young miss, put your hands like this." Widow Baxter directed Hannah.

The old woman showed Hannah how to put upward pressure that would slightly lift the second baby off its twin. This would allow an easier exit for the firstborn. It was a difficult maneuver to carry out, especially once the muscle contracted so tightly.

Ruth joined in the effort to lift the baby in front upward. This would allow the baby in the back — the one struggling to be born first — to finally make its way into the world. Bent down almost to the floor, the older midwife encouraged Mary to bear down with all her might. Mary drew upon inner resources of strength she likely didn't know she possessed. As she grimaced and groaned deeply, Widow Baxter said triumphantly, "Here is the head!"

Encouraged by the woman's words, Ruth nevertheless lamented her daughter's great fatigue. As the pain temporarily ceased, Mary rested her head upon her mother's shoulders and breathed in deeply, sweat dripping from her brow. Ruth was overwhelmed with guilt that she'd failed to notice the presence of the second child. The thought of two children in her daughter's womb had never crossed her mind. And with the one child tucked behind the other, it would not always be obvious even for an experienced midwife's hands.

"Mary, I'm sorry. I did not realize there were twins. I should have known —"

But there was no more time for conversation as one twin was now intent upon arriving. The laboring mother gathered her strength once again and bore down with all her might.

"It's a boy!" Widow Baxter shouted.

~

"It's a boy!" Sarah shouted to the group of men huddling outside. "I heard them say it through the door!" She jumped up and down before returning to the house.

Daniel's mouth opened in amazement at the realization he'd become a father. A smile slowly emerged on his face. Both James and Myles Eaton slapped the new parent on his back, congratulating him.

"I have seven daughters and you get a son on your first go round." Mr. Eaton shook his head and grinned. "Well done, lad."

Mary realized Daniel had no idea a second birth was about to occur. She soon put that thought aside as the urge to push gripped her again.

While Widow Thomsen held her firstborn grandchild, Hannah took on the role of encouraging Mary to bear down once again.

Mary followed Hannah's instructions. Within a moment, Mary felt her second child arrive into the awaiting hands of Widow Baxter.

"It's another boy!"

Daniel saw Sarah run out the door again — nearly tripping on the bucket this time.

"'Tis another boy," she shouted. "'Tis twins!"

All three men stood silently. Words caught in Daniel's throat.

"Twins?" James grinned in astonishment. "No wonder Mary's travail came early."

"Well done, Daniel!" Myles Eaton slapped him jovially on the back.

Disbelief encompassed Daniel. Then profound joy. Then he thought about all this labor Mary had been through and his heart broke for her pain.

"Is Mary well?" His trembling hands gripped Sarah's shoulders.

"I think so, Daniel, but I'm not certain. They would not let me in."

He did not wait for her answer as he raced toward the house to his new family. Daniel stopped short of bursting through the door. He managed to knock gently despite his racing heart.

Hannah answered the knock, her face grinning.

"You must be patient, Daniel." She closed the door in his face.

Daniel shut his eyes and put his back to the door as he slid into a sitting position on the floor. He was able to relax as gratitude and relief enveloped him. God had blessed him and Mary with not one but two sons. And he was so grateful Mary had survived.

"Thank you," he whispered as he looked up toward heaven.

Inside the birthing room, Widows Baxter and Thomsen were assisting each infant to nurse. When the eager infants latched on to their mother, Mary winced with pain.

"Will that always feel like that? Like my toes are curling from the discomfort?" Mary squeezed her eyes shut.

"It will get easier," both midwives said simultaneously. They looked at each other and laughed at their identical words of encouragement.

As the infants settled into their eager but gentler suckle, Mary became desperate to see her husband.

"Where is Daniel?" She looked in earnest at her mother. "I want him to meet his sons."

Her mother seemed uncomfortable with the idea. "Why do you not wait until they are finished eating?"

Mary grinned. "Do you think Daniel has never seen his wife before?"

Widow Baxter smiled and looked at the new mother. "Most grandmothers prefer to assume their grandchildren were conceived miraculously." The older woman bore a mischievous glint in her pale eyes. "In my time, I have delivered many a miracle that began its life beneath the quilts on a cold winter's night."

Widow Baxter winked at Mary. She smiled appreciatively at the older midwife. She was grateful for her humor and for her help. Widow Thomsen rolled her eyes in defeat.

"All right then. I shall get your husband." The new grandmother gave an exasperated sigh at this breach in proper protocol.

When Mother Thomsen opened the door, Daniel still leaned against it and nearly fell inside.

"I'm sorry, Daniel." She helped him to his feet. "I did not realize you were there."

He approached his new family, and the three women quickly exited as a group. Daniel stood at the end of the bed and viewed the incredible sight of his wife feeding his two new sons. Transfixed by the beauty of the scene, it brought tears to his eyes and a smile to his countenance.

"Mary." He was finally able to speak. "Two sons?" He whispered the words in disbelief.

His wife appeared exhausted but elated.

"Come meet them, Daniel."

One of the boys had finished eating and contentedly closed his eyes with his mouth still open.

"Here is our older son. This is Daniel." Then she nodded at her second born. "This is James." She laughed at the smaller twin vigorously suckling. "He has quite an appetite."

Daniel just stared at his sons. Although he spoke no words, his eyes reflected a depth of gratitude to Mary — an overwhelming love that was deeper than any he could have imagined. He finally was able to speak.

"You are amazing." He stroked her face as his mouth began to tremble.

"I love you, Daniel." Her eyes welled with tears.

Daniel leaned over her and kissed her moist lips, tinged with the sweet flavor of wine.

"Thank you, Mary. Thank you for our sons," he whispered.

Mary's heart was so full of love for her husband and now for their children. The blessings of this day were only now beginning to be felt as an indescribable joy within her heart. This was a moment in her life she would always treasure — and never forget.

"Would you like to hold young Daniel?"

The new father looked uncomfortable and more than a little worried. "I do not want to injure him."

"Just hold him behind his head. He'll be safe in your arms."

With great care, he lifted up the bundle in the linen blanket and held his firstborn in his strong hands. He looked down upon his sleeping child and tenderly kissed his face.

"Welcome, my son," he said. "Welcome to America."

40

Peace

Four years to the day after General Burgoyne's surrender at Saratoga in 1777, British General Cornwallis began to work out his own terms of surrender at Yorktown with General George Washington. It was four years to the day since the start of Daniel's new journey in America.

The hostilities between England and the colonies continued until February of 1783. There had been nearly eight years of war between the mother country and her colonial offspring, and with the end of the fighting came Daniel's opportunity to finally write to his father. This long-awaited attempt occurred nearly five years after Daniel and Mary had become husband and wife.

"I only hope he is still alive." Daniel spoke to his wife as he sent the message off with the postrider that spring.

Fortunately, Daniel — now the father of three children, with another imminent arrival — did not have to wait long for an answer. It was mid-summer that year of 1783 when he saw Mary slowly make her way to the field. The four-year-old twins were helping Daniel weed. He grinned at the sight of Mary holding onto the hand of two-year-old Polly. Then he noticed his wife held a folded parchment in her other hand.

"Daniel!" Her voice rippled with excitement.

"Is it time?"

"No." Mary seemed out of breath from climbing up the slight embankment. Her brows furrowed with irritation. "Look at them."

Young Daniel and James had taken advantage of this moment when their father's back was turned to them. Instead of using their hoes to weed, they were pointing them at each other, pretending the tools were muskets.

"Daniel! James!" She scolded the boys.

Her husband turned around toward the mischievous children.

"Cease fire, gentleman." His voice shouted in military-like fashion. The boys hung their heads submissively and resumed their work. "It helps to have experience in the army." He smiled at her, then looked down at his daughter.

"And what have you been doing today, Polly?" He picked up the young girl. "Helping your mother?" He gave her a kiss on the cheek.

"Not exactly." Mary had her hands on her hips and spoke with exasperation.

Polly laid her head, flowing with soft blond hair, onto her father's shoulder and pouted.

"Now Polly, you know you must mind your mother," Daniel chided the girl. "I'm sure you'll do better now, yes?" Polly smiled at her father and gave him a peck on his cheek. "There's my lassie. Now, what's this in your hand, Mary?"

Mary grinned with excitement as she handed him the parchment.

"A letter… from your father." She covered her mouth with both hands.

Daniel stared at the folded piece for a moment, his hand shaking.

"Open it, Daniel, please!" Mary pleaded with him. "I am as anxious as you are."

He set Polly down next to Mary and opened the letter, turning away from his wife so she could not see the emotional struggle playing across his face. He had not spoken to his father or heard from him since the day Daniel and Oliver had set sail for the colonies — and war. Daniel had had to write the excruciating news to his father about Oliver's death and then about his own disgrace as a prisoner of war.

But he was also able to tell his parent about Mary — how she had saved his life, how they had fallen in love and married, and how they had made him a grandfather.

He heard Mary sigh. "Well?"

At length, he slowly turned around and she could see he'd been weeping. Mary appeared crestfallen, assuming his tears meant a distressing report.

Then Daniel's face brightened. "He is coming to see us, Mary." He wiped his tears away. "My father thought I was dead." He sobbed.

Mary put her arms around his waist and Polly hugged his legs.

"Do not cry, Papa." His daughter clung to him.

Daniel picked her up and hugged her in one arm as he held Mary with his other. "These are happy tears, Polly." He turned to look at the twins. "Lads! Your grandsire is coming to visit you in America. Let us celebrate!"

The twins threw their tools down in excitement and ran ahead of their parents and Polly, as they went down the small embankment toward their home — the log cabin Daniel had built on the road to Deer Run.

Across the Sea

There was a lad named Daniel Lowe
Across the sea come sailin'.
He met a girl, set his heart atwirl,
Now his love is never failin'.

"O love, now come away with me
Our love's beyond all measure.
Please be my wife and share my life,
Your love's my greatest treasure."

"I'll be your bride, dear Daniel Lowe,
My heart with yours is one.
We'll kiss until our love's fulfilled,
I'll gladly bear your son."

There was a lad named Daniel Lowe
Across the sea come sailin'.
He met a girl, set his heart atwirl,
Now his love is never failin'.

From the diary of Mary Lowe

Author's Note

The story of British solder-turned-American Daniel Lowe was inspired by my real-life great-great-great-great grandfather Daniel Prince.

Here is part of his true story:

It was likely a chilly day on that eighth of December 1775, when twenty-year-old Daniel Prince was recruited into the British Army. Little did he know the long and treacherous journey he was about to embark upon.

He signed up with the Twenty-first Regiment of Foot, also known as the Royal North British Fusiliers. That regiment had been scouting all over Great Britain to increase their ranks. After all, it was going to take thousands of soldiers to put down the rebellion going on in those upstart American colonies.

The Twenty-first Regiment of Foot was placed under General John Burgoyne. Private Daniel Prince was one of the 658 soldiers that set sail for America from Plymouth Dock, England, on April 7, 1776.

The journey across the Atlantic Ocean took nearly two months. While crossing the ocean on his way to war, Daniel turned twenty-one years of age on the first of May.

These long voyages were fraught with dangers, and recruits often died of disease along the way. The weary company arrived in the Americas on May 31.

Daniel Prince's regiment was involved in the British campaign along Lake Champlain in New York. They wintered in Canada that year before resuming the long and bitter British struggle against the colonists.

These soldiers of the King's army were quite successful for a time, even intimidating the small numbers of Americans at Ticonderoga to abandon that fort in the summer of 1777. But another enemy began to make its presence known in the Americas against the British regiments — disease.

Beset by scurvy, dysentery, malaria, and other maladies, a sizeable percentage of the troops were too ill to fight at any given time. The official British Army muster rolls for the Twenty-first Regiment in July of 1777 indicate that Daniel and at least a dozen of his fellow soldiers were "sick."

Their troubles continued. Hoped-for support from British forces, commanded by General William Howe and Colonel Barry St. Leger, did not arrive. Hunger also became a huge problem, weakening the already disease-ridden soldiers.

And then the Battle of Freeman's Farm near Saratoga occurred. The colonists had rallied many thousands of troops to hold back the British — and the King's army paid dearly. The Twenty-first Regiment was one of three British regiments hit hard at this turning point in the Revolution. Many were wounded and many killed. It is not documented that Daniel received any injuries at this time but it is certainly a possibility.

After the British surrender at Saratoga, all the surviving soldiers were marched away as prisoners of war. They were sent to Rutland, Massachusetts, more than 150 miles from Saratoga, and ordered to build a fortress of wood. This would be their prison camp for nearly a year.

Following his unexpected defeat, Burgoyne had tried to have his defeated army moved to Boston for eventual return to England. But General George Washington would have none of that plan.

The American general feared that a British attack on Boston — some sixty miles to the east of Rutland — could result in a siege that would free the imprisoned soldiers. If so, they would again turn against the colonists. In order to lessen the chances of rescue by the British, Washington decided to send Burgoyne's troops to Virginia.

One can only imagine the despair of Private Prince and his fellow soldiers at this prospect. It was now autumn of 1778. They had been gone from home for over two years and had already survived diseases, battles, and a prison camp. Now they were to move even farther from their homeland.

So as the regiments were marched down another road southward, hundreds of the troops escaped into the Massachusetts countryside. This is likely when Daniel Prince escaped.

While his exact journey is not known, we do know that by the following year he had met and married my fourth great-grandmother, Mary "Polly" Packard of the small town of Goshen, Massachusetts.

The new family settled in Williamsburg, Massachusetts, where Daniel built a log cabin. Their first child, a girl, was born in 1780. Twins Daniel Jr. and James were from Mary's third pregnancy.

I am descended from Daniel Prince Jr. The site of the log cabin where they were born is marked with a chiseled rock called the Prince Monument that is still in existence today. I have visited this site where my ancestors trod.

Daniel Prince never did return to the British Army. But he did become an American.

When I was young and first heard that one of my grandfathers had been a Redcoat during the Revolutionary War, I was somewhat embarrassed. Growing up in Massachusetts had made me proud of our country's heritage. But instead of finding zealous patriots in my bloodline, my DNA was from an enemy soldier! Calmer reasoning prevailed, however, as I thought about the reality of Daniel and Mary's tale. Living conditions in Colonial times were difficult, to say the least. It was a frightening period in our history for both Americans and the British. And in the midst of our nation struggling to be birthed, two people on opposing sides in a bloody war met and fell in love.

This story from my family's history was transformed in my thinking into an inspiring one of romance, unhindered by the politics of the day. It became, purely and simply, a love story.

And so was birthed the idea to create a fictional account of actual events. Since the story is from my imagination, I opted to change last names, the names of the communities, and many other details of the time.

However, many of the historical events such as the Thanksgiving Proclamation of the Continental Congress, Mary's background genealogy, and descriptions of the Battle at Monmouth, New Jersey, as described in James' letter, are documented facts.

The particular information on Daniel Prince's military background was discovered thanks to the diligent work of Betty Thomson, independent researcher at the National Archives, Kew, in England. Well done, Betty!

My visit to the Prince Monument was arranged courtesy of Ralmon Black, historian at Williamsburg, Massachusetts. He trekked up into the woods with my husband, nephew, two cousins, and myself on a chilly October morning to show us the actual site where the cabin was built. I cannot express how moving a moment this was for me.

In *Road to Deer Run*, I made every effort to stay true to the times. Descriptions of food, homes, clothing, farming, and worship practices are the result of extensive research. And, yes, even the wolf heads mounted on the outside of meeting houses occurred in the 1700s to encourage hunting the animals. I am grateful we do not see that today.

And I am even more relieved that our medical practices have improved. As a registered nurse, I shudder to read how some diseases were treated, often making the patient worse off than when they started.

It has been a personally inspiring experience to write this novel. While the times have changed since the eighteenth century, the same struggles of their day are our own. Forgiveness, fear, pain, illness, despair, the worry of having a family member at war, the death of a loved one — these are all the battles we contend with in the twenty-first century.

But we also share faith, laughter, love, the excitement of that first kiss, and the wonder of looking at a newborn. These are the same joys that we share with our ancestors who are so much a part of who we are.

Their journeys are interwoven with our own.

Book Club
Discussion Questions

1. Discuss the ethics of Mary helping the enemy and then lying to her mother. How might you have reacted to finding an enemy soldier? Think of other times in history when civil disobedience was utilized.

2. In what ways was Daniel a stranger in a strange land during his first few months after escaping from the POW line?

3. What have you learned about daily life in the 1700s for those living on farms carved out of New England's woodlands?

4. Go online and find the text for the Congressional Thanksgiving Proclamation of 1777. Read it. What does this document say about what was important to Americans in the 1700s? Do these beliefs and sentiments have anything to teach Americans today?

5. Aunt Prudence was a businesswoman. Widow Thompson was a midwife. Mary Thompson was brave enough to help a stranger. What kind of character did a woman need to live through those times? How can the lives and choices of these characters speak to women today?

6. In Chapter 22, Daniel, Mary, and the Thompson women go to church. Based on their experiences among others who lived in Deer Run, how was the community of that day different from the community we share today with others? How is it the same?

7. Who was your favorite character and why? Which character could you relate to the most?

8. The character of James is away from home for nearly three years before he comes home on furlough. Compare that to military deployments today.

9. The character of Daniel goes through numerous trials before turning to God for help. In your own life, was there ever a time when the difficulties of your life made you pause to consider turning to God in prayer and faith for His help?

10. The ravages of smallpox turned the handsome face of Josiah Grant into a scarred and disfigured image. Talk about the implications of sinful living in people's lives. Does it always produce such stark ramifications and, if not, how does it play out in other ways?

ELAINE MARIE COOPER

Novelist Elaine Marie Cooper is the author of the Deer Run saga (*Road to Deer Run, Promise of Deer Run* and *Legacy of Deer Run*) as well as *Bethany's Calendar* and *Fields of the Fatherless*. Her passions are her family, her faith in Christ, and the history of the American Revolution, a frequent subject of her historical fiction. She grew up in Massachusetts, the setting for many of her novels.

Elaine is a contributing writer to *Fighting Fear, Winning the War at Home* by Edie Melson, and *I Choose You*, a romance anthology. Her freelance work has appeared in both newspapers and magazines, and she blogs regularly at ColonialQuills.blogspot.com as well as her own blog on her website at ElaineMarieCooper.com.

www.ElaineMarieCooper.com
www.Facebook.com/ElaineMarieCooperAuthor
www.Twitter.com/ElaineMCooper

CROSSRIVER

If you enjoyed this book, will you
consider sharing it with others?

- Please mention the book on Facebook, Twitter,
  Pinterest, or your blog.

- Recommend this book to your small group,
  book club, and workplace.

- Head over to Facebook.com/CrossRiverMedia,
  'Like' the page and post a comment as to what
  you enjoyed the most.

- Pick up a copy for someone you know who
  would be challenged or encouraged by this
  message.

- Join CrossRiver's fan group on Facebook and
  discuss the book with other readers.

- Write a review on Amazon.com, BN.com, or
  Goodreads.com.

- To learn about our latest releases subscribe to
  our newsletter at www.CrossRiverMedia.com.

MORE GREAT BOOKS FROM CROSSRIVERMEDIA.COM

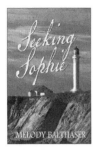

SEEKING SOPHIE

Melody Balthaser

Indentured servant Sophie Stalz stabs her master to protect herself from rape. Escaping through the Underground Railroad, she now finds herself stranded on an island in the hands of a stranger. Surrounded by the sea, Jackson Scott just wants to be left alone with his memories. His fortress crumbles when Sophie shows up on his doorstep. As her master is *Seeking Sophie*, can Sophie and Jackson build a life together free from their past?

WILTED DANDELIONS

Catherine Ulrich Brakefield

Rachael Rothburn just wants to be a missionary to the Native Americans out west, but the missionary alliance says she can't go unless she is married. When Dr. Jonathan Wheaton, another missionary hopeful, offers her a marriage of convenience, she quickly agrees. But she soon finds that his jealousy may be an even greater threat than the hostile Indians and raging rivers they face along the way.

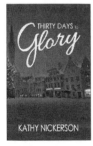

THIRTY DAYS TO GLORY

Kathy Nickerson

Catherine Benson longs to do one great thing before she dies, while Elmer Grigsby hopes to stay drunk until he slips out of the world unnoticed. Against a Christmas backdrop, Catherine searches for purpose while fighting the best intentions of her children. She gains the support of her faithful housekeeper and quirky friends. Elmer isn't supported by anyone, except maybe his cat. When their destinies intersect one Tuesday in December, they both discover it is only *Thirty Days to Glory*.

POSTMARK FROM THE PAST

Vickie Phelps

In November 1989, Emily Patterson is enjoying a quiet life in west Texas, but emptiness nips at her heart. Then a red envelope appears in her mailbox with no return address and a postmark from 1968. It's a letter from Mark who declares his love for her, but who is Mark? Is someone playing a cruel joke? As Emily seeks to solve the mystery, can she risk her heart to find a miracle in the *Postmark from the Past*?

25699732R00168

Made in the USA
San Bernardino, CA
09 November 2015